Down Among the Women

One of the most successful advertising copywriters of her generation, Fay Weldon's credits as a writer include classic novels like *The Life and Loves of a She-Devil* and *Growing Rich*. In 2001 she was awarded a CBE for services to literature.

PRAISE FOR FAY WELDON

'If you want to know about the man–woman thing, read Fay Weldon.'
New York Times

'The best woman writer in Britain. Sharp, funny, very modern.'
Woman

'Weldon is a gifted tease of a writer.'
Sunday Times

'Readable, articulate and fascinating.'
Scotsman

'There is simply no touching Weldon as a writer.'
Observer

ALSO BY FAY WELDON

Down Among the Women

Fay Weldon

HEAD of ZEUS

First published by William Heinemann Ltd in 1971

This paperback edition first published in the UK in 2014 by Head of Zeus Ltd

9 7 5 3 1 2 4 6 8

A catalogue record for this book is available from the British Library.

Paperback ISBN: 9781784080747
eBook ISBN: 9781781857984

Printed by Clays Ltd, St Ives Plc

Head of Zeus Ltd
Clerkenwell House
45-47 Clerkenwell Green
London EC1R 0HT

WWW.HEADOFZEUS.COM

Wanda, Scarlet and Byzantia

Down among the women. What a place to be! Yet here we all are by accident of birth, sprouted breasts and bellies, as cyclical of nature as our timekeeper the moon – and down here among the women we have no option but to stay. So says Scarlet's mother Wanda, aged sixty-four, gritting her teeth.

On good afternoons I take the children to the park. I sit on a wooden bench while they play on the swings, or roll over and over down the hill, or mob their yet more infant victims – disporting in dog mess and inhaling the swirling vapours that compose our city air.

The children look healthy enough, says Scarlet, Wanda's brutal daughter, my friend, when I complain.

The park is a woman's place, that's Scarlet's complaint. Only when the weather gets better do the men come out. They lie semi-nude in the grass, and add the flavour of unknown possibilities to the blandness of our lives. Then sometimes Scarlet joins me on my bench.

Today the vapours are swirling pretty chill. It's just us

women today. I have nothing to read. I fold the edges of my cloak around my body and consider my friends.

One can't take a step without treading on an ant, says Audrey, who abandoned her children on moral grounds, and now lives with a married man in more comfort and happiness than she has ever known before. She, once imprisoned on a poultry farm, now runs a women's magazine, bullies her lover and teases her chauffeur. How's that for the wages of sin? With her children, his children, her husband, his wife, that makes eight. Eight down and two to play, as Audrey boasts. With the chauffeur's wife creeping up on the outside to make nine.

Sylvia, of course, got into the habit of being the ant; she kept running into pathways and waiting for the boot to fall. Sylvia too ran off with a married man. The day his divorce came through he left with her best friend, and her typewriter, leaving Sylvia pregnant, penniless, and stone deaf because he'd clouted her.

How's that for a best friend? You've got to be careful, down here among the women. So says Jocelyn, respectable Jocelyn, who not so long ago pitched her middle-class voice to its maternal coo and lowered her baby into a bath of scalding water. Seven years later the scars still show; not that Jocelyn seems to notice. In any case, the boy's away at prep school most of the time.

'Better not to be here at all,' says Helen to me from the grave, poor wandering wicked Helen, rootless and uprooted, who decided in the end that death was a more natural state than life; that anything was better than ending up like the rest of us, down here among the women.

It is true that others of my women friends live quiet and happy married lives, or would claim to do so. I watch them curl up and wither gently, and without drama, like cabbages in early March which have managed to survive the rigours of winter only to succumb to the passage of time. 'We are perfectly happy,' they say. Then why do they look so sad? Is it a temporary depression scurrying in from the North Sea, a passing desolation drifting over from Russia? No, I think not. There is no escape even for them. There is nothing more glorious than to be a young girl, and there is nothing worse than to have been one.

Down here among the women: it's what we all come to.

Or, as I heard a clergyman say on television the other night, bravely facing the challenge of the times; 'There's more to life,' he said, 'more to life than a good poke.'

Wanda's flat, at the present time, is two rooms and a kitchen in Belsize Park. It won't be for long. Wanda has moved twenty-five times in the last forty years. She is sixty-four now. Rents go up and up. Not for Wanda the cheap security of a long-standing tenancy. Wanda turns her naked soul to the face of every chilly blast that's going: competes in the accommodation market with every long-haired arse-licking mother-fucking (quoting Wanda) lout that ever wanted a cheap pad.

Wanda's flat then, twenty years ago, when we begin Byzantia's story, was two rooms and a kitchen in another part of Belsize Park. Some women have music wherever they go,

3

Wanda has green and yellow lino. Scarlet, who at this time is twenty, has been sleepwalking on this lino since she was five and last felt the tickle of wall-to-wall Axminster between her toes. That was before Wanda left her husband Kim in search of a nobler truth than comfort.

The lino used to be lifted, rolled, strung, tucked under some male arm and heaved into the removal van. Presently it cracked and folded instead of curling itself gracefully, and the male arms became impatient and scarcer, so Wanda hacked it into square tiles with a kitchen knife, and now when it's moved it goes piled, and Wanda carries it herself. Amazing how good things last. The lino belonged in the first place to Wanda's lover's wife. This lady, whose name was Millie, bravely threw it out along with the past when she discovered about Wanda and her husband Peter – Peter for short, Peterkin for affection – but depression returned, sneaking under the shiny doors (three coats best gloss, think of that, in wartime!), slithering over the purple Wilton (pre-war stock), grasping poor Millie by the neck and squeezing until she died of an asthmatic attack.

Wanda and Scarlet are preparing for the Thursday meeting of Divorcées Anonymous. The year being 1950, a group such as this is a rarity, and its lady members the more amazed at their fate. Scarlet, in the arrogance of youth, thinks they deserve their pain – how they complain, how grey their skin, how vile and orange their lipstick. How should any man wish to remain with such miseries; why should such miseries wish to remain with any man? Scarlet is nine and a quarter months pregnant: she is heavy, but she glows, she is twenty; she has to reach out over her belly to butter the water biscuits and arrange the wedges of basic cheddar with which each is topped.

Listen, now. Wanda sings as she scours the coffee pot. This is before the days of instant coffee. She will use Lyons coffee and chicory mixture, which comes in a blue tin. Wanda is a large, heavy-boned, unpretty woman with a weathered skin, and eyes too deep and close together for their owner to be taken as anything other than troublesome. In an age when women still walk with toes pointed delicately outwards, Wanda strides ahead, and makes others nervous. Let her granddaughter Byzantia, now curled head-down inside Scarlet, be grateful. Oh fuck! cries Wanda hopefully; oh bugger! she complains, in the days when words could still be wicked, and so she helps bring about a new world.

No wonder she has no husband; no wonder the Divorcées Anonymous munch her hideous water biscuit offerings with such helpless disdain.

Listen, now. Wanda sings as she scours the coffee pot. Wanda would have looked good in uniform, but they never let her have one. When Wanda walked into this headquarters or that, and demanded her right to help her country, there would be so much shifting of weights and pressures behind closed doors that even Wanda could not persevere. Why? Because she carried a Party Card and named her child after the blood of martyrs? How could that be? Was not Russia our ally? Nevertheless, there it was. She, who would have looked so good in Air Force glory, or Wren gloss, or even A.T.S. norm,

5

had to do without. Wanda is always having to do without. If it's not her own necessity, it's Scarlet's.

Listen, now. Wanda sings as she scours the coffee pot. Thinks herself lucky to have coffee. Millions in Europe still do not.

> *'Ta-ra-ra boom de-ay!*
> *Did you have yours today?*
> *I had mine yesterday,*
> *That's why I walk this way –'*

Scarlet is disconcerted. Scarlet is offended. Scarlet, impressed by the workings of her own body, is having a fit of sanctimonious motherhood. Scarlet believes – for this one suspended week – in love, life, mystery, meaning, sanctity. Byzantia lies very quiet and kindly allows her mother these few days of illusion. She is seven days late. Scarlet thinks she is a boy. So does Wanda.

'*I* know it's a boy,' said Scarlet, in the sixth month. 'But what can you possibly know about it?'

'It's a burden,' said Wanda, simpering, 'It's a boy.'

Scarlet gritted her teeth and folded herself metaphorically around her precious burden, which kindly went patter patter patter beneath her ribs. When the doctor asked her if the baby had quickened she said she didn't know. She felt something sometimes but thought it might be indigestion.

He looked at her as if she was a fool, reinforcing her own opinion of herself.

6

Wanda sings. The coffee pot is scoured. It shines in tinny splendour, worn thin by wire wool. This is before the days of detergents for the masses. The rivers of England still flow cool, clear and sweet. The towns are filthy; they have gone twelve years without paint, but in the country the hedgerows grow green and thick, still unperverted by insecticides, and the blackberries are glorious. Wanda and Scarlet would rather die than live in the country. Wanda tells horror stories of the fate of women who have done so.

'Don't sing that,' says Scarlet.

'Poor little Scarlet,' says Wanda, 'poor baby. Did it have a nasty rude Mummy then?'

'Yes.'

'Opportunity would be a fine thing,' says Wanda. 'Breathes there the man with soul so dead who would not kick your mother out of bed?' She is unkind to herself. At forty-four she is at her most handsome: little men like her. She does not like little men. She waits, and will wait for ever for a tall handsome bully who will penetrate her secret depths.

'Can't stand men with little cocks,' she cries, but what she means is, if only there was someone who would stay long enough to listen, go deep to touch my secret painful places, so I would feel again I was alive.

And how is Scarlet to know this? Scarlet sees a rude, crude mother. Scarlet scowls.

'What kind of mother are you anyway?' she asks.

'Bad,' replies Wanda, with satisfaction, and Scarlet moans in outrage. Wanda is egged on. She sings again.

> *'Ta-ra-ra boom de-ay,*
> *Have you had yours today?*
> *I had mine yesterday,*
> *That's why I walk this way.'*

'I feel sick,' says Scarlet. Her face has altogether lost its look of cosmic satisfaction; it nods mean and crabbed on top of her swollen body. She slices radishes stolidly in half, instead of bothering to carve them into the pretty flower shapes she normally makes.

'Good,' says Wanda.

Scarlet's eyelids droop lower. She's in a full-scale sulk. Nothing annoys her mother more. Scarlet has a round smooth face; her mother thinks she looks half-witted; certainly the more angry and miserable she becomes, the more stolid she appears.

'Pull yourself together,' says her mother sharply. 'Don't *look* like that.'

'Look like what?' Scarlet drawls.

'Like I'll have to support you for the rest of my life, let alone your bloody bastard.'

'Every harsh word you speak,' says Scarlet, 'goes flying off into infinity, to bear witness against you.'

Wanda can't bear such statements. Scarlet has become very good at making them. Wanda sings again.

'Please,' says Scarlet, 'Or you'll bring it on.'

'What else do you think I'm trying to do?' asks Wanda. 'Their brains get short of oxygen if they're overdue, don't you

8

even know that? Yours will need all the I.Q. points it can muster, I imagine. I am doing you a favour. Shall I tell you the story of the milkman, the lady, and the letter-box?'

'No,' says Scarlet.

Wanda tells the story.

'There was once a randy young milkman,' says Wanda, 'who was accustomed to calling on a certain lady at seven in the morning, when he was half-way through his delivery round. The lady's husband was on night duty.

For a time all went well, in fact so well that the milkman, reluctant to miss a second of his precious time, would unzip himself as he ran up the garden path. He would then thrust his you know what through the letter-box so that she wouldn't mistake him for another and open the door, all naked and waiting, to some stranger. One day, alas, the door was opened not by her, but by none other than her husband. Was the milkman taken aback? Only for a second. "If you don't pay your fucking bill," cried the milkman, "I'll piss all over you." '

Scarlet doesn't even smile. Wanda feels depressed. The coffee pot is boiling. She turns it upside down to filter it through; something inside goes wrong and boiling coffee bubbles over her hands. Wanda, stoical to the point of mania, does not scream or even complain, but holds her poor red hand under the tap.

'I wish you'd grow old gracefully,' says Scarlet presently.

'I wish you'd grow old,' says Wanda, with bitterness. 'I wish you'd grow old and see what it's like.'

'You're not old,' says Scarlet with unexpected kindness. Perhaps she is touched by her own good nature. At any rate she starts to cry.

'What's the matter with you?' asks Wanda, surprised. She can't bear to see Scarlet cry. She thinks it might start her off too, and Wanda hasn't cried since the day before she left Kim, Scarlet's father, back in 1935.

So Wanda sings, sweetly, as a benison, the mellifluous notes of Brahms' lullaby.

Hush, my little one, sleep,
Fond vigil I keep,
Lie warm in thy nest
By moonbeams caressed –'

Scarlet stops crying. She thinks perhaps Wanda means it. Something shifts in her universe. Cog wheels unlock, re-lock. The universe continues, but differently. What is happening? Her baby turning, unlocking? The waters shifting, slopping, heaving? No, it is the fact that Wanda is being sentimental.

Scarlet gapes.

'Shut you mouth, for God's sake,' says Wanda, and Scarlet obligingly closes it, for she has seen a tear in Wanda's eye and is frightened. Wanda, of course, has no mascara to run. Wanda wears brilliant lipstick, to give more shape and vehemence to her words, but otherwise has no time for make-up, which she sees as cowardice. It is a pure and leathery cheek which the tear runs down, and still only forty-odd years since she was born so tender, smooth and throbbing.

'I wish,' says Wanda hopelessly, 'I wish things didn't have to be the way they are. Why did you have to go and do it?'

It is as well the bell rings, because Scarlet is feeling quite sick from insecurity. She can bear her mother's anger, spite and indifference, and can return them in kind, but she cannot bear her mother to be unhappy.

It is the first of the ladies. A brave one this, in dirndl skirt and peasant blouse, with dangly ear-rings and bright eyes. Lottie. She ran off with a lover who ran off from her, and her husband wouldn't have her back. And why, as she herself says, the hell should he? Poor lady, poor brave Lottie, she died of cancer two years later, drifting painfully into nothingness in a hospital bed. She wrote to tell her husband she was ill, but he didn't come to visit her. Well, why the hell should he? Thrown-away spouses, says Wanda, lying, are like thrown-away trousers, soon forgotten. You have killed them in your mind: their real death is irrelevant.

This evening at any rate Lottie is happy, excited and animated. She puts on the gramophone; embraces Scarlet and tells her generously that she's a good brave girl and that she personally thinks unmarried mothers are to be pitied not blamed. She tells Wanda life begins at forty. She munches the water biscuits without noticeably wincing and drinks her coffee gratefully; tells Wanda about a good job in the Civil Service she has managed to land, untrained though she is, and announces that she is looking forward to a happy future without men.

Poor Lottie.

She has come early, she says, to get in her message of good

cheer before the others arrive and swamp her good spirits.

She is quite right. They swarm into the tiny room like a tide of despair. Scarlet goes to bed. They regard her, and she knows it, as Wanda's cross.

Down here among the girls.

How nice young girls are, especially when their own interests are not at stake, but even when they are.

Next morning a delegation of Scarlet's friends climb the stairs to the flat.

Scarlet is more embarrassed than grateful. She feels this morning she can't get up. She lies there on her back, her extremities flapping feebly, like a piece of crumpled paper held down in a draught by a paper-weight.

Jocelyn, Helen, Sylvia and Audrey crowd into Scarlet's tiny room. They have to pass through Wanda's room to reach her. They are frightened of Wanda. They think she is mad, bad and dangerous to know. They think she probably drinks. They think she is what is wrong with Scarlet. They may well be right.

'We thought if we all gave ten shillings a week,' says Jocelyn, 'that would be two pounds. That would help. It would pay the rent somewhere, anyway. And we could get up a collection as well.'

How full of confidence and kindness they are. Their eyes are misty with emotion. Scarlet is only conscious of Wanda pissing herself with laughter in the next room. It is one of Wanda's weaknesses, in fact. Too much excitement, sex or mirth and her

12

bladder tends to give up. It seems an alternative to weeping.

Scarlet could never tell her friends a fact like this. They have been too delicately reared – except for Audrey, who was brought up on cheerful fish and chips in a Liverpool slum, and Audrey cannot be relied upon to keep a secret.

The others have escaped their parents or believe they have.

Jocelyn, who was head girl of a good private school, writes home every week, visits once a month. She is, in these days, a rather plain, rather jolly, popular girl with legs made knobbly by hockey blows. She likes to drink gin and tonic with young rugger-blues in smart pubs; one will sometimes take her to bed and they will have a jolly, surprising, unemotional time. She will get up out of bed, bright and healthy, bathe, shave her legs, put on a white dress, and play a good game of tennis with her boyfriend if he's available and a girlfriend if he's not. She got one of her boyfriends in the eye once, with the edge of her racket, and eventually he lost the sight in it.

Jocelyn was at college with Scarlet. She took her degree in French. Now she is looking for a job.

Scarlet got sent down for failing all her exams, twice over. Now Scarlet is in trouble.

Sylvia, who did classics, and shares a flat with Jocelyn, has been in trouble already. She had an abortion when she was fifteen but can't really remember it. (Jocelyn, who was at school with Sylvia, and now more or less looks after her, seems to know more about it than Sylvia herself.) Sylvia is training to be a Personnel Officer at Marks and Spencer: she has a nice quiet boyfriend called Philip, and is, these days, a nice quiet girl. Sylvia is sorry to see Scarlet in this condition, but is frightened lest Scarlet suddenly bursts and spatters them all with blood and baby, which seems likely. Scarlet wears only a semi-transparent nightie; she is too far gone to consider decencies. Scarlet's nipples are brown and enlarged. Sylvia stares. Scarlet droops.

Even Helen, beautiful Helen, with her green witch eyes, her blood-red nails, her high white bosom, makes little impression on Scarlet today. Helen has been married and divorced already, in Australia. What a mysterious and magic creature this orphaned Helen seems, moving as she does in a grown-up world, where the others feel they still have no right to be.

Helen allows Audrey to share her flat, and pay the rent. Helen paints pictures, starves to buy paint, loves and is loved by men who have their names in the papers.

Audrey, who types in a solicitor's office, which is where her degree in English Literature has led her, not only pays the rent, but washes and irons Helen's clothes, and thinks herself privileged to do so.

These kind pretty girls, with their tightly belted waists and polished shoes, seem to Scarlet to come from an alien world. She can't think why they bother with her. There is, though Scarlet can't think why for the moment, something very wrong about their presence here.

Scarlet's stomach hardens and goes rigid. Scarlet frowns. The feeling is not so much unpleasant as an unwelcome reminder that her body now thinks it owns her.

'Is something the matter?' asks Sylvia, anxiously.

'Just getting into practice,' says Scarlet.

'Aren't you frightened?' whispers Sylvia.

'Don't put thoughts into her head,' says Jocelyn briskly. 'Scarlet is young and healthy. Think of native women. They just have their babies in a ditch, and then get up and go on harvesting or killing deer or whatever they're doing.'

'And then they go home and die,' says Audrey. 'I had two aunts died in childbirth within a week. Mind you they both had the flu, I'm not saying it's going to happen to Scarlet. And London hospitals are better, they say, than Liverpool. Though awful things do happen.'

'I'm not frightened,' says Scarlet, and it's true, she isn't.

Helen gives a little disbelieving laugh but says nothing. Sometimes she reminds Scarlet of Wanda.

'Anyway,' says Scarlet, hoping they will all go away, so she can ease herself out of her transfixed position, 'it's very kind of you, and I may take your offer up.'

She doesn't believe in any of it. She doesn't believe that Wanda is her mother; she doesn't believe she is pregnant; she doesn't believe she has no job and no money; she doesn't, if it comes to it, believe she's a day older than five. She has been sleepwalking for years and years. She has summoned up these four friends from some dim fantasy.

'I know what's wrong,' she says suddenly, looking round the startled girls, 'where are all the bloody men?'

She shuts her eyes and opens them again. They're still there. She can't understand it.

Down among the girls.

2

Ask Your Father

Contraceptives. It is the days before the pill. Babies are part of sex. Rumours abound. Diaphragms give you cancer. The Catholics have agents in the condom factories – they prick one in every fifty rubbers with a pin with the Pope's head on it. You don't get pregnant if you do it standing up. Or you can take your temperature every morning and when it rises that's ovulation and danger day. Other days are all right. Marie Stopes says soak a piece of sponge in vinegar and shove it up.

The moon, still untouched by human hand, rises, swells, diminishes, sets. Nights are warm; the wind blows: men are strange, powerful creatures, back from the wars: the future goes on for ever. Candles glitter in Chianti bottles; there are travel posters on the walls; the first whiffs of garlic are smelt in the land. To submit; how wonderful. It you don't anyway, little girl, someone else will. Rum and Merrydown cider makes sure you do, or so they say. Quite often it just makes you sick.

There is a birth control clinic down in the slums. You have to pretend to be married. They ask you how often you have intercourse – be prepared. They say it's for their statistics, but it's probably just to catch you out. They have men doctors there too. A friend knows one – he's a tiny little man who shows her dirty pictures and likes someone else to watch. Are they all like that? And how do you know, if you go to the clinic, that you won't get him?

Every month comes waiting time: searching for symptoms. How knowledgeable we are. Bleeding can be, often is, delayed by the anxiety itself. We know that. It's the fullness of the breasts, the spending of pennies in the night, the being sick in the mornings you have to watch out for. Though experience proves that these too can be hysterical symptoms. And what about parthenogenesis? Did you know a girl can get pregnant just by herself? Consider the Virgin Mary.

Try hot baths and gin. There's an abortionist down the Fulham Road does it for £50. But where is £50 going to come from? Who does one know with £50? No one. Could one go on the streets? And why not? Jocelyn once said, when drunk, it was her secret ambition. No, not to be a courtesan. Just a street-corner whore.

Down among the girls.

Helen has a diaphragm, and a gynaecologist. He fitted her privately, majestically, wearing a rubber finger stall; very nice. She keeps it in a very pretty white frilly bag. Where does she get the money? Audrey, who earns six pounds a week, degree and all, doesn't like to ask. In any case, Helen very often forgets the symbol of her common sense, and doesn't take it with her.

Audrey likes men to wear condoms. Helen says it's because she wishes to be protected not just from disease and babies, but from the man himself; Audrey, says Helen, prefers there to be no real contact. When Helen says things like this they all feel puzzled; 1950 London is not a motivation-conscious place. Audrey says no, she just likes rolling rubbers on, the same way she likes squeezing spots, plucking hens, and gutting fish.

Sylvia says, and possibly even believes, she doesn't go to bed with men, but every month there she used to be, worrying as much as anyone. Married men would take her out a lot; hard-drinking ones. Perhaps she simply didn't remember? At the moment, anyway, she is settling down with Philip. They hold hands: they love each other: they are happy. He is not married. It all seems lovely. She is not worried now, except for the possibility of parthenogenesis.

Jocelyn, surprisingly, takes no precautions at all. She doesn't believe she is a woman. In her mind, she still races round the hockey field, scoring goals, while the school cheers. Every month she doubts her own disbelief, is clenched and pale with anxiety, until her female flow once more underlines her female condition, and the cycle starts another round.

Now they stare at Scarlet, swollen and monstrous. There but for the grace of their hormones, the chancy consideration of men, go they. Yet they envy her. Something has actually happened to Scarlet. She has left the girls, and joined the women, and they know it.

'Why is it,' asks Audrey, for no apparent reason, 'when men expose themselves at you, it's all mottled and purple?'

It seems the wrong subject for the occasion. No one else wishes to discuss it. Only Scarlet rouses herself.

'Because it's cold,' she says.

The girls go. Scarlet gets up and dresses. During that afternoon, Wanda feels obliged to explain the incident of the Brahms lullaby.

'I'm teaching it to them at school,' she says. (Wanda is a primary school teacher – on supply. She roams from school to school and thus avoids the moral problem of having, under the Education Act, to teach religious knowledge.) 'All the little girls cradle their arms and lap it up and even the nasty little boys grow misty-eyed. If only mother love were like that.'

'If only,' says Scarlet sourly. She is conscious of a twinge which starts in the centre of her back and runs round to meet in the middle and then is pulled very gently tight, like a ribbon. She doesn't mention it to her mother. What, give her the pleasure? It is probably nothing, in any case. The ribbon is taken away. There, nothing.

'The snows of yesteryear,' says Wanda. 'How they do hang about, rotting us all. I have always wished for a torrent of truth to pour down and sweep the myths away; I thought this last war would have done it, but no. "Lie warm in thy nest, by moonbeams caressed,"' she sneers. 'Some man wrote that, and you needn't think he ever changed a nappy. And I am still required to teach it, plus other guff about my country right or wrong, and needlework for the girls, in this year of Our Lord 1950, or rather P.B.5, which means Post Belsen Five, if you want to know.'

'I think babies are rather sweet,' says Scarlet bravely, and watches for Wanda's nostrils to flare, as she has since she was a

19

tiny child. Tormenting Wanda was never without its pleasures.

'So do you,' Scarlet adds, 'because you cried.'

'It was the pickled onions,' says Wanda, cool as can be. 'I was watering them down for the lady divorcées, who are sour enough as it is. Lettice used to sing Brahms' lullaby, I do admit.'

Lettice was Wanda's mother, Scarlet's grandmother.

'What, to you?' enquires Scarlet, surprised. Lettice, who died under anaesthetic in 1925, while (according to Wanda) having a facelift, has hardly been presented as a maternal figure.

'No, of course not to me,' says Wanda harshly. 'If she wanted to keep me quiet she'd feed me opium. She would sing it to Harry; she would sit and tinkle at the grand piano on Sunday when he visited and hope he would be touched and leave his paramour and come home. It just irritated the piss out of him. He couldn't wait to get back and lay his hoary old bird.' Harry was Wanda's father, Scarlet's grandfather.

'All the same,' says Wanda, with a certain melancholy, 'it is a pretty tune, and she had a pretty voice, much good it did to her. When she moved into her bed-sitting room in Barons Court she took the grand piano with her. If one visited one had to sit under it, so one did not visit much. Not that that was the real reason. God, she was a useless woman.' Wanda is bitter.

'She must have given you something,' says Scarlet, who has always had a sneaking admiration for her unseen, long-past grandmother. Divorced, abandoned, disregarded, ageing, penniless – to forge her daughter's signature on an insurance policy, spend it on a facelift and *die* – or is Wanda just making it up? There is a photograph of Lettice taken in 1898; a young woman all hat, smiles and frills. Wanda can't bear to look at it. Scarlet has it on her wall, just to annoy.

'She gave me opium,' complains Wanda. 'There was a teething medicine on the market then, guaranteed to soothe any infant. She gave it to me by the bottleful. She gave me dreams I couldn't hope to keep up with in later life. She gave me lessons in how not to be, the useless bitch. But I won't hark back,' she says with a cold and dismal ferocity, and repeats, 'I won't hark back.'

'Something to be said for you as a mother,' says Scarlet. 'You've given me nothing to want to hark back to.'

'I have tried to be honest,' says Wanda, and adds, kindly for one so attacked, 'Do you feel all right?'

'Yes,' says Scarlet. She looks round the room, with its sparse furnishings, and it dissatisfies her. She thinks the green and yellow lino looks dirty.

'Going to start scrubbing?' enquires Wanda.

'No,' says Scarlet.

'But you want to, don't you? It's the nesting instinct. Down on your hands and knees. It means you're about to produce any minute now.'

'No, I am not. Actually, I think it's a phantom pregnancy,' says Scarlet hopefully. 'If it wasn't I'd have had it by now.'

Wanda snorts; puts water in a pail, produces a bar of green soap and a scrubbing brush and induces her daughter to scrub.

'When I was married to your father,' she says, 'we had a daily help to do the scrubbing.'

'How nice,' says Scarlet.

'It was revolting,' says Wanda. 'And so was she.'

'I wish I could remember her,' says Scarlet. 'I can't remember anything nice.'

'There was nothing nice about Mrs Richmond, the thieving old bag. She got killed in an air-raid, in the house of someone she was doing for. They'd gone away and she was having a bath. And why shouldn't she? Poor withered filthy old soul: at least she died happy, in green, hot, scented water. She didn't believe in doctors or medicine. She'd wave her deformed hands at me – she'd dislocated both thumbs at one time or another – and glare out of her rheumy eyes –she had a cataract in one of them, too – and thank God in her croaky voice for her perfect health. Silly old bitch.'

'You shouldn't speak so badly of the dead.' Scarlet swirls happily in soapy water. She loves to hear Wanda talk about the past. It makes her feel real.

'At least I remember her,' says Wanda. 'She used to water the whisky, too. Think of it, whisky in the 1930s, when the whole country was starving.'

'Perhaps you had a right to it,' says Scarlet. 'Perhaps you deserved a little treat. I mean people do, sometimes.'

'How like your father you are.' This is just about the worst thing Wanda can say to Scarlet, but Scarlet is in a kind of scrubbing trance. 'Your father had no guts, either. He could have been a good painter but he sold out. He painted what people wanted.'

'He had to live,' remarks Scarlet.

'Why?' enquires Wanda. 'He was no good to anyone. He woke up one morning and went all over his canvases painting the clothes out and all the genitalia back in.'

'Perhaps he thought it was better like that.'

'No, he thought it would sell and so it did. I thought it was piss-awful and told him so and he hit me. He got me on the side of the head, and shook my brains up good and proper; my ears sang me tunes for days. I fell on the floor. He poured water over me to revive me. He revived me all right. I got the side of his face with my nails, freshly cut with good thin edges. He hit me on the chest: he knew that would frighten me. Well, you know what happens to blows on the chest.'

'What?'

'You get cancer,' says Wanda.

'That's an old wives' tale,' says Scarlet.

'Of course it is,' says Wanda, 'but it doesn't half make you nervous. Other women's boobs were for selling to the bourgeoisie for wall decoration, mine were for turning rotten. That was what your father was like.'

'They were good paintings.'

'They were not. After he hit me I broke into his exhibition in the middle of the night and slashed them all, every one with the kitchen knife, which was what they deserved.'

Scarlet does not comment. She has heard the story often. It seems to worry Wanda – and certainly did her husband Kim at the time. The police prosecuted and he did nothing to stop them.

'Actually,' says Wanda, 'I was doing him a good turn because the publicity made him even richer. They said in Court I did it because I was jealous of his mistress, but I promise you that day in Court was the first time I ever knew she existed.'

'Was that when you cried?' asks Scarlet.

23

'Certainly not,' says Wanda, lying. 'Why should anything like that make me cry? He'd sold out his principles, that's why I did it.'

'He did good paintings,' says Scarlet obstinately. The ribbon tightens round her middle again, and presently loosens.

'He did not.'

'He did so.'

'What do you know about it?' asks Wanda.

'I've seen some.'

'Where?' Wanda is sharp.

'In the bloody Tate, so there,' says Scarlet.

There is silence from Wanda.

'I don't tell you everything, you see,' says Scarlet presently, smugly.

'Where were they? Down in the basement?' demands Wanda, clutching at straws.

'Yes,' admits Scarlet.

'I thought so,' says Wanda, relieved. 'They keep all their old rubbishy paintings down there, which they've bought in those fits of insanity and malice to which they appear to be prone. They ought to burn them and destroy the evidence, but they haven't got the guts in case later generations jeer.'

She points at her daughter's stomach.

'I can imagine that thing jeering, can't you?' she says.

'The thing about all those women he painted,' says Scarlet, 'is that they all look like you.'

'There is more to a woman,' says Wanda, 'than her tits, her arse and her cunt, although your father was never really

24

convinced. It's what turned him against Russia, in the end. All those women in boiler suits.'

Scarlet does not reply. She feels very cross.

'Tits, arse and cunt,' repeats Wanda, to annoy further. 'Why did you want to go and look at his paintings, anyway?'

'He is my father,' says Scarlet, plaintively.

'Now you're getting maudlin,' says Wanda.

'And there were good times, there must have been. I remember the feel of carpet between my toes. It's been this bloody lino ever since. It gets harder and harder to clean.'

'If you don't like living here,' says Wanda complacently, 'you can always leave.'

Scarlet – lumbering, helpless, trapped Scarlet – glares. Presently she says, 'You never used to wash the paint. I remember dried-up trickles running down the bedroom wall, where you'd thrown coffee at him. I dream about them sometimes. If I could paint it would be my motif, only I can't paint, I can't do anything.'

'I wasn't born to wash paint,' says Wanda. 'Nor was I born to bring men breakfast in bed either. Kim was perfectly healthy. Perhaps times have changed, I don't know. Did *your* young man expect you to bring him breakfast in bed? Wash his socks, iron his shirts? Come along now, Scarlet, give us your experience of men.'

She is being as disagreeable as she knows how, believing as she does that Scarlet has never had a steady boyfriend but merely sordid sexual encounters.

'Don't start,' says Scarlet, nervously.

'What me, start?' enquires Wanda in a voice shriller than

25

usual. She is starting, all right. 'Why should I start? I'm thrilled to bits about the baby. Such a surprise it's going to be. We don't know what we're going to get. Colour, shape or size, might be anything – except losing its I.Q. points daily, that we do know. Reminds me of the story of Royalty visiting the maternity hospital. Royalty inclines towards young mother. "What lovely red hair baby has, mother. Does he take after his father?" Answer: "Don't know, ma'am, he never took his hat off." '

'Do you think I wanted to get pregnant?' says Scarlet gritting her teeth.

'Yes, I do,' shrieks Wanda, 'or you wouldn't have.'

Scarlet snivels. Wanda subsides for the time being, contents herself with muttering, 'Those stupid friends of yours –' She can't abide them. Helen, Jocelyn, Audrey and Sylvia. They seem to her lightweight creatures who have rendered her Scarlet even more obtuse than was inevitable. Scarlet hasn't the energy to defend them but manages a little spirit on her own behalf.

'It isn't my fault,' she mutters.

'And whose is it, mine?' enquires Wanda.

'Yes,' says Scarlet, feeling pleased with herself and quite perking up.

'Christ,' says Wanda.

'You didn't give me a proper home,' says Scarlet, smugly.

'And what are you going to give that?' asks Wanda, pointing.

'Everything,' says Scarlet, with unexpected vehemence. 'I'm going to give it all the love it needs. I'm going to give it everything I never had.'

'I gave you what I could,' says Wanda, seeming quite impressed by this outburst. 'You can only give what's in you.'

'Other girls in my position would have had an abortion,' says Scarlet. 'At least I see things through.'

'You've got another twenty years to go,' says Wanda. 'I had three abortions in my time, which, come to think of it, isn't finished yet.'

'I don't want to hear about them.' Scarlet feels quite sick now. Is it the baby? Or her mother? Who's to say?

'Well you shall. I feel quite bad about them, if that makes you feel better. I used to think perhaps you were my punishment. If I'd tried one of the others instead of you it might have turned out better.'

'You are a revolting woman,' says Scarlet, and means it, and is tempted to tell her mother that she knows perfectly well who her baby's father is, and that he is everything that would most appal her. She makes do with, 'Father's new wife is younger than me.'

Wanda says nothing at first. Then, 'How do you know?'

'I asked him.'

'You mean you've seen your father?' Wanda is shaken.

'I spoke to him on the telephone.'

'Why?'

'Why shouldn't I?'

'You're wasting your time. He doesn't want anything to do with you.'

'I know,' says Scarlet, not without bitterness.

'Did you want to tell him about being pregnant? Break the good news? Was that it?'

27

'I was going to, but I couldn't. He talked about himself, he didn't seen to want to know about me. It was very formal and rather embarrassing. His new wife is called Susan. She is twenty. Do you think my baby is going to be a monster, mother?'

Wanda is surprised not only at being called mother, but by the panic in her daughter's voice: Scarlet seems to have stuck in her kneeling position. Wanda helps unfold her. Scarlet has tears in her eyes.

'I only wanted,' gasps Scarlet, 'I only wanted …'

'What?' asks Wanda, 'what did you want?'

'I only wanted to give you something to make up for all the other things,' says Scarlet, in desperation.

'Give me something?' repeats Wanda, incredulous. 'Like a baby?'

'Yes,' whispers Scarlet.

'You were born to make me a laughing stock,' says Wanda.

'What am I going to do?' asks Scarlet, panicking now at last. 'How am I going to live? What's going to become of me? Mother?'

The ribbon gives up its tightening process, postpones more strenuous activity for another little while. Byzantia, curled and cosy, drifts back into sleep.

'You'd better ask your father,' says Wanda briskly and astoundingly. 'Go on, ask your father. Why not? I'm finished. I have nothing to tell you, nothing to advise you. Go on. Get out of here. Ask your father.'

3

A Certain Sunday

Down here among the women. Is there no one nice, ordinary, and pleasant? Yes. There's Jocelyn, Helen, Audrey, Sylvia, Wanda, Scarlet and kind, kind Byzantia. Millie, Lettice, Lottie. It depends only on which of their words one chooses to listen to, which of their actions to overlook. And Susan, Scarlet's father's new wife, is nicest of all, slender of waist, and thick of mind, thick as the trunk of a kauri tree in the New Zealand forests whence she comes, and of which she is so fond, almost as fond as she is of Kim, Scarlet's mother Wanda's first husband and Scarlet's daughter Byzantia's grandfather.

Down here among the women who like to describe people by their relationship with others. It makes us feel more secure, or as if someone might notice when we die. So Sylvia says.

It is a momentous Sunday afternoon for everyone. What configuration of the stars is this?

Sylvia has gone to the pictures to see *La Ronde*. She sits in the ninepennies, near the front, for she is short-sighted, and a

29

little deaf in one ear. Jocelyn stayed at home to wash her hair. It is dripping wet when Philip arrives, slim, tender-mouthed, grey-suited, in search of his true-love Sylvia, and failing to find her tells his troubles to Jocelyn. He fears, really fears, that abstinence will ruin his health. What is Sylvia playing at? She slept with him once, then never again. Why? Jocelyn wraps a towel turban-wise around her hair and explains that Sylvia's mental balance is delicate beside her eyes and her ears being weak, and he must not worry her; and all the time her own flesh draws nearer and nearer to this unsuitable young man, who, being Sylvia's boyfriend, can only be illicit. She cannot help it; it is nothing to do with her; her soul cries out, but all it can say that she can hear is bully one, bully two, bully three and away, and it makes no sense. Now they are flank to flank, and her voice is telling him about Sylvia's schoolgirl abortion, while the world grows darker and darker with desire. And here they are in bed, while he consoles his disenchantment. How did they get there? The pillow is wet from her hair; now it will take hours to comb and curl. She takes this as evidence of overwhelming passion. She feels so bad about wronging Sylvia that she fails to notice how languid are the young man's habits – or that though flesh still calls to flesh, it is now from an irritated frustration rather than any aspiration to fulfilment. They are to marry, in the future. And serve her right, you might well say.

Sylvia returns from *La Ronde*, and finding her Philip still in bed with her Jocelyn simply blanks out conveniently and does not mind. It seems an extension of the film. Sylvia loses such small sense of the reality of her existence as she has so far managed to retain.

She closes the bedroom door, makes tea, takes it in to them and sits on the end of the bed and chats, telling them the plot, singing the theme tune, liberated from suffering. Philip decides that Sylvia is mad, and he has done the right thing. He is quite wrong. With Sylvia's tender mental balance and his tender mouth they would have been well matched.

Bully off, gels! Hockey One, hockey Two, hockey Three and away! Jocelyn played centre-forward at school. They wore their dark green bloomers and had hockey practice in a public park. Men in raincoats would gather to watch, but the staff did not seem to notice. Once Jocelyn's elastic had broken by accident. Once Jocelyn had broken the ankle of the opposing centre-forward, by accident. Jocelyn's life is dogged by accidents. Bully one, bully two, bully three and away! Faster, cries Miss Bonny, all long socks and tunic, faster! Out to the wing, gels! What, no one there? No one waiting? There is tragedy in her voice. No one waits for Miss Bonny, or only Jocelyn after school, and though Miss Bonny makes do, it is not what she wants. What all women want, Miss Bonny explains, is love. In the meantime, hockey one, hockey two, hockey three and away! Bully off, gels. How lovely life is before one catches a glimpse of death.

Helen is this afternoon busy encompassing her own, although it will be fifteen years before it matures and lays her on the floor in Wembley Park with little Alice there beside her.

Right how Helen sits naked, white, and rather blousy on a camp stool in X's studio. He stands and paints her. On the other side of the studio Y his wife, also at an easel, also painting Helen. X is good-looking, tall, brilliant-eyed and craggy. Y is rather plain, though they say a better painter than X. It was Y's idea that Helen should be there, should model; now Y is not so sure it was a good idea. X's real name is Alexis. Y's real name is Yvonne. Their friends – and they have many – know them as X and Y, never imagining a time when they might not be together.

'Do you have to wriggle?' asks Y crossly.

Wriggle? Helen turns her head to stare with her brilliant witch eyes at Y, whom she has thought until this minute she adored. She is angry. She turns back to face X, and catches his eye. Her pupils dilate: from now on she returns, whenever Y is not looking, the frank admiration with which she knows full well he looks at her. Naked or clothed about his house, she now moves languidly. She kisses his children, raises her eyebrows gently when Y fails to cope with them. Y should have kept her mouth shut. Death gets to her quicker than it does to Helen; having a straighter, smoother path to run. Y keeps looking over her shoulder to see how he's getting on, which one should never do. It takes only ten years from those five careless words for death to catch up with Y.

And Audrey? Audrey is being taken over the V. and A. by Paul Dick, a potter. He thinks he will change her name to Emma. It suits her better. She agrees, thinking he will have forgotten about it tomorrow. She would not dream of arguing with him. He knows so much, and she has so much to learn. Even sex, at which she thought herself well trained, now appears a mystery. He reads her pornographic books, observes and photographs. She has little opportunity to roll on French letters. After he has finished talking, indeed, she is usually too tired to care. Still, she is learning about art, pottery, wine and jazz. And what is she on this earth for? Why, first to fuck, and then to learn, according to Paul Dick. Such language is new to Audrey, and impresses her. Back where she came from f— was a swear word, not a description of an activity.

Scarlet's father Kim Belcher lives on the fourth floor of a red-brick Edwardian block of flats off Baker Street. Scarlet walks up and down outside for some few minutes. She is a conspicuous figure, for she does not own any maternity clothes. She wears an old skirt of Helen's, dating from the days when Helen was fat, and a Fair Isle jersey which Lettice knitted for Wanda decades ago, which Wanda did not like and would not wear. It is both unbecoming and indestructible, a terrible confection. Scarlet's coat is her own, and held together beneath her bosom by an ill-concealed safety-pin; it divides at this point over the swell of her stomach like a pair of theatrical curtains framing a stage. Her shoes are down at heel and her lisle stockings fraying where they have been darned. (Nylon stockings are for the rich and those with American connections. Only dancers wear tights. Ordinary respectable people have stockings which go into holes, not ladders, and are darned. The thread for doing so comes on cards of graded colours.) So Scarlet demonstrates her misfortune to the world.

She will go to her father, and she will say unto him, 'Father behold thy child.'

She has already said it on the telephone, mind you, and though he has been polite, he has not been encouraging.

Yet if she, his child, asks for bread, will she be given a stone?

Quite possibly. Kim, like Wanda, does not read the Bible. Kim has a strong sense of survival. Besides, Kim has replaced his daughter with a child wife.

Scarlet is nervous and feels like crying. Her legs will not take her up the steps. She gets cramp in a calf and has to stand on tip-toe and raise and lower herself two or three times before the pain goes. She is afraid of overbalancing. She is in a nightmare. Pretty soon, she thinks, if things go on like this, she will be obliged to wake up. What age is she, having this dream of a projected, impossible future? Six? Seven?

But her mother has said, 'Ask your father.' It is not just permission, it is a command.

She decides to telephone. She searches her pockets for three pennies. There are handkerchiefs (no tissues, they do not exist) a medical card or two, her blood grouping (O) and a half-crown and a couple of farthings which would be worth fifteen shillings if only she had them today.

Scarlet is obliged to go into two cafés and have two cups of tea and two buns before she can accumulate three coppers. It is not in Scarlet's nature to ask for change. Wanda has trained her too well to expect anything but nothing from nix. Scarlet herself will do a favour for anyone: and she can ask the enormous ones of others (look at her now, demanding recognition) but the little ones are beyond her. She cannot ask strangers the time or for change for the telephone. The buns – bright yellow from dried egg – give her heartburn.

Kim does not answer the telephone. He is out. Susan Watson answers it, in her refined little voice, with its careful vowels. Her mother voice-trained her on the voyage back from New Zealand – where they had spent the war – so as not to disconcert Mr Watson, Susan's father and now Kim's boss, with the closed nostril taint of New Zealand speech.

Scarlet is taken aback. She had assumed Susan to be a stage prop, not a real person. She has never answered the telephone to Scarlet before. Scarlet has accepted Susan in Kim's bed – a marionette to be wound up at bedtime and perform – but not as someone with power, opinions, or even feelings.

Susan too is taken aback. But she is welcoming, even eager. Kim is out. But why doesn't Scarlet come round? Scarlet says she'll be there in two minutes.

Susan has a pretty round doll's face, set in a sweet expression, and an obliging disposition.

Susan thinks it's marvellous to be married to Kim: she loves playing houses; she even loves Kim.

Susan despises Kim's former wives for having failed to make him happy.

Susan is envious that Kim has a past and she has not. Sometimes she worries lest she too, should become part of Kim's past.

Susan likes being so much younger than Kim. It is the same kind of showing off as she has always done, from puffed sleeves as a little girl when no one else had them, to passing round the telegram at school which said her brother had been killed in action.

35

Susan wants now to show off in front of Scarlet. She has so much; and poor Scarlet – daughter of Witch Wanda – has so little. She got to University, true, but when was a clever woman ever happy? So Susan's mother said when Susan failed her school certificate. Clever women don't make good wives, and in good wifedom lies happiness. So spoke Susan's mother, lying on a beach in New Zealand, while her husband did fire-duty thirteen and a half thousand miles away.

Susan runs round the flat like a busy little girl, tidying, plumping cushions, putting on bright orange lipstick.

Susan puts on the grill for toast – it's Sunday and tea-time, after all – and prepares to patronize Scarlet.

Susan is eight and three-quarter months pregnant. She has been married nine months. Kim had to marry her, not because they had f— (Susan has barely heard the word, ever) and she was pregnant but because she wouldn't before they were married.

Susan's mother said not to. Now Susan's mother knits little woollies and nudges her husband to make Kim a full partner in the firm; he has already done so but she never listens. Or if she does, she soon forgets.

Down among the women, if you are very very careful, and shut your eyes and ears, and keep your knees together nearly always, you can live really quite happily. Susan's mother does. It was Susan's brother, not Susan's mother's son, who was killed in action. That at any rate is how Susan's mother always refers to him. Poor Susan's brother. Not even Susan's poor brother.

Susan shows no outward signs of deserving pity. Even now,

as she opens the door to Scarlet, her face barely changes – she smiles sweetly on.

Scarlet faints.

Byzantia, noticing a change in her environment, prepares to abandon it. (Nothing will make Simeon – Kim's son, Byzantia's uncle, poor Susan's dead brother's nephew – leave Susan except the due processes of time, pressure and the conjugation of the stars. A ritualist now, and always will be, whatever the inconvenience to others.)

'Oh dear,' says Susan. It is her strongest expression. No wonder Kim, having lived through Wanda, is so devoted to her. He has not yet had time to grow bored. Presently he will get into the habit of saying he's going to die of boredom, and presently indeed he will. But that's a long way off.

Susan spent seven years in New Zealand, where girls are expected to be practical, so she drags Scarlet inside, and heaves her on to the couch. She has never seen anyone so untidy. Even Scarlet's stomach, Susan notices, is lopsided. Perhaps Scarlet is going to have a lopsided baby? Scarlet wears a wedding ring. It leaves a green stain. Woolworth's, thinks Susan, who is knowledgeable, as well as practical, as well as nice, and often shops at Woolworth's where you get good value for money. She has a streak of parsimony.

Susan feels a surge of pity for this poor messy Scarlet, her step-daughter, who has clearly ruined her life. The pity is maternal in its essence. And vengeful against dreadful Wanda, who not only once made Kim unhappy, but without doubt has failed as a mother.

Susan explained to the reviving Scarlet that Kim is out; he

37

will be back within the hour. In the meantime Scarlet, who looks dreadfully pale (she probably hasn't even been taking her iron tablets), must stay where she is and rest.

'I'm sorry,' says Scarlet vaguely, 'to inconvenience you.' The carpets here, she observes, are thick and soft. At home there is only green and yellow lino. Scarlet looks Susan up and down, and hates her for the following reasons, or if not reasons, feelings:

Scarlet has somehow believed she is the only pregnant woman in the world.

Scarlet, frankly, does not like girls who look like Susan.

Scarlet does not like girls who are married to her father.

Scarlet does not like her father's wives to be prettier and younger than her mother.

Scarlet does not like women who polish their shoes – she herself scorns to do so.

Scarlet does not like women with small feet and long painted nails.

Scarlet does not like women who live upon her father's money.

Scarlet does not like the thought of other women having more right to this flat than she does.

Scarlet does not like having a step-mother younger than herself.

Scarlet has a pain like a ribbon tightening round her middle which makes her feels sour.

Scarlet does not like the thought of this girl in bed with her father.

Scarlet does not see why the fuck (not for nothing is she

her mother's daughter) this girl's child should be legitimate while she, Scarlet, who is morally superior, should give birth to a bastard.

It is quite a long time before Scarlet speaks. Then all she says is, 'Mrs Belcher, I presume.'

Kim's surname is Belcher. It is the cross – along with the complications of his past – that Susan has to bear; she carries it bravely. Wanda reverted the moment she could to her maiden name, Rider, and Scarlet used this too. Every now and then, if Scarlet complains too bitterly of her lot, Wanda suggests she reverts to her father's name. Scarlet Belcher. Scarlet declines. Scarlet Rider is a good name and one of the reasons why the father of Byzantia took her home from a party, drunk and dismal as she was.

'Don't try to talk,' says Susan. 'Just lie a little. There's lots of time.'

Scarlet shuts her eyes and tries to contain her rage. Susan just sits with her hands folded and continues to smile.

Scarlet peeks.

She's working out a knitting pattern, thinks Scarlet.

But Susan is off where she always goes when she has a minute to spare, and times are tense. She is walking through the silent kauri forests of New Zealand. Clematis creepers trail down from the high branches. What light there is catches on its white starry flowers. The trunks are dark, smooth and immense. There is thick moss underfoot. It is primeval forest – no birds, no animals, no sound. Just Susan, back at the beginning of time.

Scarlet calls her back.

'I don't think there is much time,' says Scarlet enigmatically, more to frighten Susan than because she believes for one moment she is about to give birth. Susan enquires when the baby is due. No baby, surely, can be more nearly due than hers, in six and a half days.

'Last week,' replies Scarlet, as is her pleasure. Susan, for the first time, is put out. Scarlet's baby's aunt should surely arrive first. (She is as convinced she is having a girl as Scarlet is that she is having a boy.)

'You mean you might have it any minute?' her voice squeaks a little. She remembers her mother's training and lowers it a little. They had a dreadful journey back from New Zealand – in an unconverted troopship. Susan's mother caught dysentery and conjunctivitis but managed to ignore even these inconveniences. Still she paced the deck with the other mothers, released *en masse* from the dreadful provincial prison of war-time New Zealand, drilling offspring in 'The Rain in Spain', and other niceties of pre-war England. Susan's mother was not so much brave as obstinate.

'Any minute,' says Scarlet. 'I keep getting these pains.'

'We'd better get the ambulance.' Susan keeps her voice pitched low.

'They're only pains,' says Scarlet crossly. 'They'll go away. They always have before. I can't stand women who make a fuss.'

The only harsh word Kim has so far said to Susan is, 'For God's sake, don't fuss.' Susan is silenced. Scarlet swings her legs over to touch the floor and sits on the edge of the sofa, and smiles and smiles, which encourages poor Susan.

'Is this – um – just a social visit?' enquires Susan, with antipodean awkwardness.

'I have come to visit my father,' states Scarlet.

'Yes. Of course. How nice. But do you *need* anything?'

The question is too enormous for Scarlet to answer; in any case she has another pain and wants to go home; but Belsize Park seems too far away to be reached; and has not her mother sent her here?

The feeling grows that if she goes back home now she will never, ever get away. She continues to sit brightly, tightly upright and begins to dread her father's return. How can she explain herself to this stranger? If she stops smiling she will cry.

Susan makes a pot of tea, conscious of Scarlet's need, but praying that Kim will return and make everything all right again. Simeon kicks and she cries out, startled, and nearly drops the kettle. She has a vision of those white pure feet of hers raw, blistered and disfigured for ever. She trembles.

Susan hovers for a moment on the borders of that other terrible world, where chaos is the norm, life a casual exception to death, and all cells cancerous except those which the will contrives to keep orderly; where the body is something mysterious in its workings, which swells, bleeds, and bursts at random; where sex is a strange intermittent animal spasm; where men seduce, make pregnant, betray, desert: where laws are harsh and mysterious, and where the woman goes helpless.

Susan, in fact, nearly leaves the girls and comes down here among the women.

She thinks of her mother and survives, hauling herself out of the mire, using a lace doily as a foothold. She lays it on a tray and makes Scarlet lemon tea. There is a fine sweat on Scarlet's brow. Still she sits upright, tightly smiling.

What are people saying about Scarlet these days? All kinds of things. Byzantia bestows on this former invisible girl the mantle of existence, and thus makes her the easier to snipe at.

'I do think Scarlet went a bit far,' Audrey is saying to her potter, Paul, 'not even knowing who the father is.' They have gone on from the V. and A. to an anarchist party in Hampstead. There is a sheet hung out of the window saying, 'Only a sheep would vote'. The party has been going on since the previous night. The host has made beer in the bath. People queue outside the bathroom either to piss or vomit in the toilet, or take more beer from the bath. There is also home-made elderberry wine in the kitchen. At some time during its preparation it was contained in tin buckets, and is now mildly poisonous. A drunken rumour goes round that those who drink it die. No one seems to care; in particular not those who have recently visited the bathroom. Purple-lipped and black-toothed they drink on. Thus, in the vanity of youth, these reckless anarchs of twenty years ago rejoice.

Audrey and her escort prefer to see themselves in the role of spectators. The scene here is too like the home of her childhood, too unlike his, for comfort.

'I would like to meet this Scarlet,' he says.

'She has bad legs,' says Audrey firmly.

'Bad in leg means good in bed,' he persists.

'She's hardly in the condition,' says Audrey.

'In Poland they mate the cattle twice,' he says, 'once for

milk and once for meat. It works.'

'I don't know what that's got to do with it.'

'That proves your ignorance and lack of subtlety.'

So they bicker, but both are aware in their hearts that he knows better than she.

'I'm going to give her ten shillings a week to help out,' volunteers Audrey, defiantly. 'We all are.'

This silences him for a full minute. At the end of this time she is as nervous as once she was when she waited outside the headmaster's office to receive the cane. She had done a terrible thing. Brave then as now, she had crept into the boys' toilets to see what they were like and bear the news back to the waiting troupes of little girls. She'd been told on by a little boy. Discovered, Audrey is at her worst. She will lie, renege and squirm to get out of trouble. But undertaking the impossible, Audrey is magnificent.

At last he speaks.

'You – Audrey undertook to give her ten shillings a week. You – Emma may well wish to change your mind.'

Emma-Audrey is so overwhelmed by the masterful nature of this well-educated, cultivated young man that she betrays Scarlet instantly.

'I suppose it's not really doing her a favour,' she says, with hardly a moment's pause. 'She's got to come to terms with things, hasn't she?'

'Better,' he says, 'better. More my Emma, less my slum-child Audrey. Terrifying how deprivation fails to toughen, but merely softens. No one so mean as a man born rich; no one so spend-thrift as a girl born poor. Helen's taking you for a ride, too.'

But she won't have a word spoken against Helen, who moves like a grasping goddess through her life. He is put out, this young man with the clear cold blue eyes. She moves to placate him.

When he introduces her as Emma she abandons Audrey – or thinks she does. She joins him in abhorring the wine. He is used to better things, better parties, better orgies. He rips Emma's peasant blouse a little, thrusts in his hands and disorders her breasts.

'Do try and look more debauched,' he implores.

Emma-Audrey does her best.

His ex-wife (news to Emma) turns up later, red-haired and drunk, and makes a scene. He comforts her; assures her of his emotional if not his physical fidelity. Audrey-Emma, outraged, leaves the party with his best friend, an Australian teetotaller (astonishing!) with a very clean white shirt and asthma, a follower of Subud. There is a fearful row. It goes on for weeks. The ex-wife implores Audrey to stop tormenting her ex-husband. Audrey says my name is Emma, and pleads honest debauchery. The best friend sleeps with the ex-wife. Emma ends up in hospital with mysterious stomach pains, with the potter at her bedside – weeping tears of reproach, throwing away her prescribed phenobarb and replacing with herbal tablets given by a friend who as father-of-five is supposed to know all. My name is Audrey, says Emma, and worsens. He, seeing her slipping away, not just into Audrey, but into – he imagines in his conceit – death, offers to live with her.

Emma lies in her hospital bed and considers. Thwack, thwack went the cane in the hand of the tall grey man with

44

flapping trousers; it wasn't me, Audrey cried, it was someone else: and thwack, thwack, it went again, it wasn't me who wanted to look, it was someone else. Why won't you believe me? It's true. It didn't hurt in the least, and the honour of his attention was singular. He shoots hares, standing in the field like a scarecrow. Audrey skins and cleans them for him a two shillings a time.

Emma's life, in fact, is so rich and strange she has no time to think of Scarlet.

Those were the parties.

What is Jocelyn saying about Scarlet, as Philip sits up in bed and drinks the tea that Sylvia brings them?

'Of course if we give her ten shillings a week she's got to be honest with us. She's got to tell us who the father is.'

Jocelyn wears her bra in bed. She doesn't like the feel of her breasts flopping and bobbing. Neither, come to that, does Philip, but he's not aware of it yet.

'I suppose she knows who it is,' says Philip gloomily. 'I don't understand why you bother with her. She doesn't seem the right kind of friend for you two at all.'

Jocelyn and Sylvia enlist themselves on the side of the virtuous women.

'We can't desert her now while she's in trouble,' says Jocelyn, 'that wouldn't be fair. But she'll have to stop cheapening herself.'

Sylvia cries herself to sleep that night, but can't think why, except she would have liked Philip to have persisted in his wooing. She takes up with a Sales Director some fifteen years older than she is. He drinks a lot of gin, and is in the habit of

45

telling her in detail on the way home in his Riley of exactly what he wants to do to her, this way and that, in bed. Thus he expends himself and saves the effort of an actual seduction. Sylvia doesn't mind. She has a kind, if wispish, nature and is only too glad to be of service. He goes home happier to his wife. She sleepwalks back to Jocelyn.

Down here among the women, we do a lot of sleepwalking. The only way to get through some days is to suppose one will presently wake up. So says Wanda.

'They have no style,' Helen is complaining of her friends and admirers. 'Especially not Scarlet. It was a bad party, given by no one for nobodies, and now of course she's pregnant by someone no one's ever heard of. If one is to be an unmarried mother one should do it with a certain panache, don't you think?'

She is talking to Y, who is finishing a portrait of Helen. X is out lecturing students. The children ram and batter at the closed door which keeps them out of the studio. They are hungry. It is past teatime. Y ignores them.

'I don't think one should be an unmarried mother at all,' says Y virtuously. 'Children can't eat panache.'

'There's always National Assistance,' says Helen. 'I don't think women really need men at all. Fathers should be done away with. Men must be entertainment for women, no more'. She knows this will upset Y. She is quite right, it does. 'Women don't need men,' she repeats, 'not nowadays.'

'I do,' says Y, her large pale eyes unblinking, looking straight at Helen, who doesn't know whether she is being stared at as something to paint, or – which she would prefer – as a rival female.

'I would kill myself,' says Y, 'if X ever betrayed me with another woman.'

'How dramatic!' says Helen, as languid as she can manage, though Y sounds perfectly matter-of-fact. 'Do you really think a man like him can be expected to live the rest of his life with only the one woman? Surely, if you loved a man properly, you would want him to be happy, in his own way.'

'I wouldn't,' says Y, in whom there is not a small element of Wanda. 'I would want him to be mine, that's all.'

There is no doubt now but that she is looking at Helen, into the spirit of Helen. Helen is gratified. She feels they are hardly a match – Y so frail and mousy, she so bold and strong.

'I would kill myself,' says Y, 'and then I would kill the other woman.'

'In that order?' enquires Helen pertly.

Y shrugs. Helen is never to forget this conversation, never. At the door the children hammer and yammer. Y does nothing.

'Poor Scarlet,' says Helen. 'I don't suppose anyone will ever marry her now. She's rather plain and hasn't much to offer, except brains, and what man wants a woman with brains? Of course I don't believe in marriage, so it wouldn't matter to me, but she does. Not that I'd ever have a child if I really loved a man. Love's a full-time occupation, don't you think? And children are so distracting.'

She has to raise her voice to be heard above the din made by Y's three.

'And so very unerotic,' she adds. Y, in a fit of – what, rage, resentment, petulance, foreboding? – hurls a jam-jar of turps at the closed door, but still does not open it.

47

When X returns he finds Helen in the kitchen cutting jam sandwiches for three washed, brushed, well-behaved children, while Y paints on. He, who is accustomed to saying that the role of the artist is more important than the role of mother, is impressed, and feels a pang of purely bourgeois irritation with his wife. It enables him to kiss Helen in the pantry with a clear conscience, which is what she had in mind. For a girl of twenty-one she is not doing badly.

4

Scarlet is Brought to Bed

The ribbon tightener gets bored and Scarlet gets a backache instead, tedious, frightening and unnatural. She puts her legs back carefully on the couch, and groans. It is apparent now, even to Scarlet, that she is about to have a baby. She is panic-stricken. This was hardly what she had meant to happen. If she had only believed in a Heavenly Father she would have implored him now to take his gift back. As it is she can only mutter, after her earthly mother, oh fuck, oh shit, hell's teeth.

Scarlet has for some time been considered by her friends as a girl of loose sexual morality. It is not true. Until she went sulking to a party on the day she read in a newspaper of her father's wedding, actual intercourse had eluded her. Partly because offers were few, partly because those there were she ignored in order to annoy Wanda, who had fought so fiercely for the sexual rights of the rising generation. Who will believe that Scarlet lost her virginity and got pregnant on the same lamentable occasion? When she was, alas, so drunk she can hardly remember the incident at all? To be so pregnant and so unpleasured seems hardly fair.

She calls out for Susan, who, having made tea, is now on the telephone forlornly trying to trace Kim; who has been on the telephone trying to trace Wanda, who is out; who has inefficiently tried to call an ambulance – Scarlet having left her hospital card at home, naturally – and been informed that without the card ambulances can only be summoned by a doctor; who has tried to raise her own doctor, to be met by an answering machine – surely the first in London, and paralysing to the will.

(Susan is having her baby privately, at home, and the doctor, Mr Joseph Justice, is a rich and go-ahead man.)

Now there are messages for help left all over London but still Scarlet lies on Susan's couch and prepares to give birth. Susan is mismanaging the whole situation disgracefully.

And what will Kim say?

Susan goes to the bookshelves and takes down a book on progressive childbirth. It once belonged to Wanda. It was written in the 1920s and the photographs disturb her. The women look like her mother – the same swoop of hair over the forehead, the same small smile, the same hairless, marble limbs. She has wondered why Kim keeps it, wondered the more at herself for not throwing it away. For Susan does not believe in the written word, she believes in her Mr Joseph Justice. But alas, Mr Joseph Justice has gone fishing or whatever, leaving on an answering machine in his place. She turns to the section marked 'Deliveries *au naturel*' and returns to Scarlet.

'Get the police,' says Scarlet.

'The expectant mother often panics,' reads Susan aloud, 'and believes the birth more imminent than in fact it is.'

'Get the neighbours,' says Scarlet.

'Have the waters burst?' enquires Susan.

'What waters?' asks Scarlet.

'The womb is filled with a clear water-like liquid,' says Susan. 'Before you can have the baby it all comes out. Has it?'

'I don't know,' mutters Scarlet. 'I've no idea. I went to the toilet and everything seemed very wet but I don't know. My mother still wets her knickers, perhaps I just take after her.'

Susan winces.

'It doesn't sound like the waters,' says Susan.

'By the waters of Babylon,' moans Scarlet, 'we sat down and wept.'

Susan concludes she is wandering in her mind.

'Do you have a show?' she enquires, reading on.

'What's that?' asks Scarlet, who has read nothing about childbirth, believing herself to be so natural, normal, and healthy that the details can hardly concern her. Details are for neurotic and frightened women. It does occur to her now, with a shock that quite stops her feeling pain, that she may be both neurotic and frightened herself. Neurotic to be lying here upon her stepmother's couch; frightened, not just because it hurts and she has no idea what's happening to her, but because she has remembered that women do die in childbirth, and that the magic which protects her from disaster has lately shown signs of weakening. It seems quite likely to Scarlet now that Susan will let her die, either from stupidity or from malice.

'It says here a show,' says Susan forlornly, 'but it doesn't say what a show is.'

'You are a fool,' says Scarlet, and Susan feels indignation, until, reading on, she discovers that women in childbirth often show signs of irritation.

The pain in Scarlet's back evaporates. She feels better, gets up, walks about, announces it was a false alarm.

'Shall we get a taxi to a hospital?' asks Susan tentatively.

'No,' says Scarlet. 'I've never taken a taxi in all my life. I don't approve of them. I'm perfectly well and healthy.'

'Perhaps you'd better get home while you can,' says Susan, with dismal cunning. She, who once felt so possessive of Scarlet, so charitable, so condescending, can now hardly wait to get her out of her territory.

'Home?' enquires Scarlet. 'What home?' and watches with pleasure the blood surging into Susan's face. Perhaps Susan is going to cry.

'When you think of it,' says Scarlet, 'this is as much my home as anywhere else. My father's place.'

'You are not a child,' says Susan, made quite sharp by desperation. 'You ought to have a home of your own by now.'

Scarlet is dejected and deflated by the truth of this observation. She feels very strange in her body, and wants to go to the lavatory.

'I'll just go to the loo,' she says. 'Then I'll get the bus home.'

'Perhaps you should,' says Susan.

'You just want me to have it in the street, don't you?' complains Scarlet, going into the bathroom, where Susan's baby's pretty bath and Susan's baby's fragrant toiletries wait for the arrival of their user. Susan waits for retribution. It comes. Scarlet opens the door briefly and remarks, 'My baby's going to be bathed in the sink, along with the saucepans. We can't afford this kind of thing.'

52

Susan runs headlong into her dark kauri forest but it has shrunk: she is only there five seconds before she is out the other side and into brilliant sunshine again. It is Scarlet's fault. Susan is angry.

If Scarlet could only have been humble and grateful, had only asked favours, how happy Susan could have been, sharing baby vests, lending nappies, offering advice, arranging an adoption perhaps – even adopting herself, taking in instead of pushing away her husband's past – and all out of the public kindness of her heart. But Scarlet won't accept favours. Scarlet has come claiming her rights, and now Susan feels threatened, and frightened, and unprotected. Susan cries out in her heart against Kim for not being there when she needs him. Yet she dreads his return. She had wished to surprise him with her own generosity and understanding; she sees now that what she will surprise him with is a terrible, hideous encumbrance.

How neat and pretty her drawing-room (she was slapped on the boat coming over for calling such a room a lounge) seems without the voluminous presence of Scarlet. But why is she so long in the bathroom? Why must she be so extreme in everything she does?

Susan has a small and tidy pregnancy under a pretty spotted smock. You would never have known Susan was pregnant until well into the fifth month. Simeon curls tightly, tightly, never giving way, seldom flailing, only occasionally aiming an irritable blow against the pulpy walls of his confinement.

Susan nearly telephones her mother, but knows her mother will have 'flu or people round. There is a 'flu epidemic. Susan's mother is a sucker for minor ailments, thus preserving herself against the sudden major killers. Perhaps she'll live for ever, this bourgeois monster? Susan's mother would leave Susan in prams outside shops, sometimes for hours, going home by herself and forgetting she'd come out with pram and baby. On the day Susan got married Susan's mother murmured a languid prophecy about the consequences of marrying an older man, but forgot to do so until after the ceremony. She cared that her children should reflect credit on her: she did not care for her children. She did not care for her husband; she did not care for life itself. She played bridge and caught 'flu, and waited – for life to pass her by in as comfortable and orderly a way as possible. So Susan now realizes, sitting and waiting for the heaving Scarlet to emerge, wondering why she cannot after all be like other people as she had so hoped to be.

Poor Susan.

Lucky Susan.

In Susan's bedroom, next to the bed she shares with Scarlet's father – Susan, brought up in a world of twin beds, is still nightly disconcerted by the feel of another body next to hers – the white frilly crib waits for its occupant. There on the chest of drawers, above Scarlet's father's shirts and ties and underpants, above Susan's knickers and bras and scarves, are stacked the piles of Harrington's nappies – thirty-six towelling, thirty-six gauze – the six long Viyella gowns – size 0 – (no stretch zipper suits, this side of man-made fibres), the six Cherub woollen vests, the four bootees, the two bonnets, the rubber undersheet – (no plastic then) – the two shawls, the three coatees, the little jar of Vaseline, the baby brush, the rattle. They wait, in confident expectation of a healthy, well-formed, live baby.

And there on the table stand all the items required for a home confinement, as specified by Mr Joseph Justice, who with the assistance of Miss Taylor the lady midwife, means to deliver poor Susan, lucky Susan, of her planned and lawful baby. (Kim will wait in the room outside; he will not be asked in. It is not yet the custom.)

Scarlet is going to have her accidental baby in hospital, and take it home to the green and yellow lino. There are no ante-natal classes. She has no idea what is happening inside her, or why she now sits aching on the lavatory bowl. Her baby's crib will be the bottom drawer of the kitchen dresser, padded with crumpled newspaper and covered with white rexine. This crib has been Wanda's present to the expected baby, together with these words to Scarlet, 'Don't fuss.'

Scarlet is competing with Wanda in non-fuss, in which Wanda is an expert. Scarlet in any case has a blank where a future ought to be. The birth of her baby is a wall she hesitates to look over. She does not believe that because she is having a baby, she is going to go on having a baby. That it will presently get up and walk away and look back and jeer, having turned into another person, has not occurred to her. That it may live to carry tales of a newspaper-padded Rexine-lined dresser bottom drawer to others does not now concern her.

Scarlet comes out of the bathroom.

'Why were you so long?' asks Susan.

'I don't know,' complains Scarlet. 'I want to go but I can't.'

Susan had not wanted so precise an answer.

'I'll be off now,' says Scarlet brightly.

'Are you sure you'll be all right?' asks Susan, who simply

wants her out of here, quick, before Kim returns.

'Yes,' says Scarlet, who isn't.

'I'm sorry you missed Kim,' says Susan. 'Give him a ring and come round some time when you're feeling better.'

'Well,' says Scarlet. 'Tell him I came. Tell Daddy I was here.' It is the best she can do by way of attack.

'I will,' says Susan, and practically pushes Scarlet out of the door. She shuts it and puts up the chain. She goes and lies down on the bed. She closes her eyes. She wishes she was single again. She wishes she was not pregnant. She wishes she could go and drink some coffee without being sick. She wishes there was someone, anyone in the whole world she could trust. She does not want Kim to come home. He is too real for her now; his past has been going on too long: he has accrued too much strength from it. She sees him as a walking jigsaw, and every piece has been left by some other person, some other event, of which she knows nothing. And this monstrous jagged stranger, her husband, lies nightly like an incubus in the dark beside her, inserts his being into her, and grows his child within her.

Susan runs off into her forest, padding quietly over the moss. She comes into a sunny clearing, too sunny, too bright. Fallen trunks powder and flake. There is a magpie there, black and crowlike. 'Wardle ardle oode,' it gloats, gaping its angry pecking beak, in its tonsilly, warbly voice. 'Go on out,' it shrieks. Magpies in New Zealand learn to talk. Susan's mother had a pet one: kept it chained by its leg as a watchdog (it would frighten the cats and dogs away); trained it to say a few simple words. 'Go on out.' Susan evades the magpie and runs on. It is, after all, chained; it cannot pursue her. She is running hand in hand with Kim. He is all of a piece again; not jigsawed.

She sleeps, relieved.

Scarlet has got half-way down the stairs. She goes no further. She crouches on the stairs and groans. Here, returning, Kim finds her. He thinks she is a stranger, and is kind. He is a kind man.

Helping her up the stairs, he is not conscious that this flesh is of his flesh. Why should he be?

Kim is the envy of his pot-bellied friends. They are conscious of mortality; not he. He has pushed back the barriers of decline by twenty years or so. He has a young wife; he is starting again. Kim is slim, casual and happy.

Kim has known trouble in his time. He has known Wanda, and escaped. He has grieved for the loss of his daughter, and recovered. He has known fame, success, and wealth, and what it is to lose these blessings. He has been whirled to the centre of the world's affairs, and been for a time at its still, magic fulcrum: then flung out again, cold and penniless, to the crowded anonymity of the perimeter.

He has lost many things in his life, including six good years to the war and the Education Corps, where he laid land girls (What, your honour? A sheep? I thought it was a land girl in a duffle coat.) and taught illiterates. He has found many things too. He has found Susan's father, fresh from the Ministry of Food's propaganda section (the nation now cooks better, eats better, than ever before – children in the north are two inches taller in 1946 than they were ten years before).

He has found Susan. Scarlet's father starts an advertising

agency with Susan's father. Scarlet's father marries Susan, renews his life. If he saps her strength she surely has enough to spare. She is docile, sweet, pretty and admiring. Susan loves. Susan is young. Susan's father is rich. Scarlet's father loves Susan.

Where has Scarlet's father been this afternoon, thus allowing his wife to be so cruelly exposed to his daughter? He has been building the future, all our futures, talking to a new client, who works in a shed in the hills behind High Wycombe trying to dry and pulverize coffee beans on a commercially viable scale. There seems a future in it; Kim must be pleasant to the client, who likes to drink in the afternoon, but has nowhere in High Wycombe to do so, except at home where his wife is teetotal.

Kim takes his client round the drinking clubs of Soho and fixes him up for the evening with an available girl Kim knows. The client, he suspects, would rather go home to his wife but can hardly look a gift lay in the teeth. Besides, is he not growing rich? Are such things not his perks? Kim telephones the client's wife and says her husband is having dinner with him, and then retreats back to the safety of his own home as quickly as he can.

Kim keeps his painting past, his canvases, in racks in the attic. One day, when the Tate brings his two bought paintings up from their basement and hangs them where they can be seen, he means to sell the rest and grow rich, and thus encouraged, paint again. In the meantime he will put his faith in coffee beans.

When he first sees Scarlet on the stairs he thinks for a terrible moment it is Susan. He feels bad about lying to the client's wife, and expects retribution. Seeing it is not Susan, but someone far more mountainous, he is relieved. The groans of this stranger, he feels, are, though disturbing, at least not his fault.

They have gone but two steps upwards – she is very heavy and seems to have little instinct for self-help – when they are overtaken by Mr Joseph Justice, who has received a garbled message from his recording machine. The tape was set at the wrong speed and the words cannot be deciphered but he has recognized the timbre of his patient's voice and come at once.

Together they make better speed. They find the door on the chain and Kim rattles, shakes and shouts to wake Susan, who staggers sleepily to open it.

A three-part monster enters her home. She can make little sense of it at first. One speaks, crossly. It is her husband's voice.

'Why in God's name was it on the chain?'

She sees, now. Her doctor, her husband, her stepdaughter, united in monstrosity.

'Shall I ring for an ambulance?' her husband is asking.

'Too late for that,' her doctor replies. 'Get her in to the bed.'

Susan tries to stop them; she tugs and drags at the lumbering heap.

'You can't,' she cries, 'you can't!'

Her husband, horrified, shakes her off.

'You don't understand,' moans Susan, 'it's your daughter. It's Scarlet.'

Kim, though shaken, is deflected only for a moment. As for Mr Joseph Justice, he's delighted. He thrives on the bizarre.

Susan sits and cries in her chair while her stepdaughter's

child is delivered in the bed prepared for her child. It is Susan's doctor who smiles his expensive smile at the wrong mother and means it, for Scarlet is too terrified even to moan and so get mistaken for a brave good mother.

And who will pay the bill? Why, Susan's husband. He paces the room, consumed with rage, at Susan, at the world, at everyone.

Bitterness against Wanda, which he thought was dead, has been foxing him, lying dormant. Now once again it is seeking out the old pathways. Kim finds himself anxious: but then Wanda was always good at making him anxious: there is a pain in his chest: when he was with Wanda he was always in pain. And Wanda would infect him with the expectation of disaster – moral, financial, emotional, political and practical – and thus make him aware that he had always feared, somehow invited, calamity. Now she has sent this emissary, this daughter, yet surely no part of him, here to torment him and complicate his future.

He cannot find words to talk to Susan. She is too young. She cannot, will not understand. Look at her now, pouting and grizzling, incapable of any serious emotion.

In the bedroom Mr Joseph Justice holds Byzantia up by the heels and slaps her on the bottom. There is no need for it, since she is breathing perfectly well, but the gesture seems to reassure his patient. Besides, it is traditional. 'Take that,' says the doctor, in effect. 'And that! See if you enjoy it either!'

Byzantia cries.

'It's a girl,' he says to Scarlet.

'You're lying,' she says.

60

'A granddaughter for you, Mr Belcher,' sings out Mr Justice through the open door, hoping for a more reasonable response.

But there is silence. Susan stares at her old, old husband; and he stares into his soul and sees that it is no longer young.

'Say something,' whines Susan presently.

'Splendid, splendid,' he calls back to Mr Justice, which was not what she had hoped for.

'I could do with some help,' says Mr Justice, 'what's the matter with you both?'

'Go on,' says Kim, 'you're a woman.'

'You go,' says Susan. 'It's your daughter. It's nothing to do with me.' It is the first time she has defied him.

'I'm sorry about it,' he manages to say, 'but you knew when we married that Scarlet existed. I hid nothing. I wasn't to know she'd turn up.'

But he can't say anything right.

'You can't just shift the responsibility now,' says Susan. 'Go on in there.'

'I'm a man,' he says. 'It's no place for a man. Did she say who the father was?'

'No.'

'Didn't you ask?' His voice makes clear what a fool he thinks her.

'No, I didn't. I'm not supposed to be upset. In case you've forgotten, I'm having a baby any minute. Not that I suppose you care now. You've got a grandchild, haven't you? A girl too. What you wanted.'

It is true. He has longed for a girl. They both have. To replace the baby Scarlet torn from him so many years ago by

Witch Wanda. Scarlet is back now in the adult flesh, groaning, bleeding, space-consuming, troublesome. He doesn't, frankly, want any kind of baby any more.

He puts his arms round Susan. He lies bravely. 'Never mind,' he says. 'Never mind, It's your baby I want. Our baby.'

But Susan can only respond with petulance. She shakes him off, as her mother did to her, unforgiving, punishing. Twelve (waking) hours without talking for a minor offence: twenty-four (waking) for a major. Then a timed and calculating smile. Susan's face is set and cross. Kim is disappointed and fears for the first time the triviality of their future together. He takes away his arms, forlorn. He remembers the girl he left his coffee client with – as pretty as Susan, he thinks, and twice as generous, pleased only to give and be given pleasure. Why, the world is full of them. Full of pretty girls. What is the difference between one and another?

Susan's hand creeps into his. His tightens over hers. Then he goes in to help Mr Justice. She calls after him.

'Kim.'

He pauses. 'Well?'

'I think perhaps I should have my baby in hospital,' she says, hoping to drive home to him the enormity of the situation. But all he says is, 'Yes. Perhaps you should.'

Susan is hurt. She cries afresh. She hears someone coming up the stairs. The front door still stands open. Wanda comes in. She too has had a garbled message of desperate phone calls, and has come searching for her daughter.

Susan knows without being told that this is Wanda. And she in her folly has summoned her. Susan makes no move. It is all

62

too terrible. Wanda looks at her briefly, appears to dismiss her.

'Where is she?'

'In my bedroom,' says Susan.

'Is there a doctor?' asks Wanda, making towards the bedroom door.

'Yes. My doctor. And my husband's in there too.'

Wanda takes time off duty to smile a rare appreciative smile, and then goes into the bedroom.

'It's born,' says Susan, after her. 'It's a girl.'

How lucky, Susan thinks, to be Scarlet. Scarlet has everything, and deserves nothing. Susan wants her mother. Susan cries. Susan has a pain.

'I'm going to have a baby,' she says into the shambles of her life.

Susan has a slow and difficult labour. It lasts forty-two hours. She is taken to hospital because it seems simpler to the others than to turn Scarlet out so instantly, and besides, nothing at home is now ready for Susan. There is a 'flu epidemic at the hospital. They are short-staffed – Susan's in the ante-natal ward (no visiting, thank you) for thirty-five hours, with sporadic attention, then moved into the labour room. Here the system loses touch with her. She lies alone on a high hard narrow couch for six hours, forgotten. She rings the bell but no one comes.

They have gone to tea. She is afraid of moving for fear of falling off the couch. Time passes. The pains intensify until, each time, she is on the verge of fainting, then diminish, bringing her, as might some skilled torturer, back to full consciousness and ready for the next application. Presently she screams, though it scarcely seems to be her who is making this shattering noise. Someone comes running. Figures cluster and move. There is a feeling, she gathers, against anaesthesia. She strikes out at someone. Simeon dives into the world. She is surprised. She has forgotten she is here to have a baby. She has fifteen stitches; her legs strung up to poles specially devised to be fitted to the ends of maternity beds. She gets fearful cramps in her legs – there is a delay, a queue of women, legs strung in preparation for the student stitcher – while she waits, and thinks the pains are almost as bad as the earlier ones. But of course they aren't.

Poor Susan. Lucky Susan. Her mother, oddly, comes to visit her, almost immediately. She studies the poor lopsided little baby – Simeon was much distorted on his leisurely journey out, though of course the condition will right itself. Or so Susan has been told. Susan's mother speaks.

'Still, he's all right, isn't he? You never know, when the father's getting on in years. I was so worried.'

When Kim comes to visit her, Susan can hardly remember who he is.

5

Susan is Selfish

There will now be a short intermission. Sales staff will visit all parts of the theatre, selling for your delight whale-fat ice-cream whirled into pink sea waves at two shillings, or ten new pence, the plastic cone; at the apex of each you will find wedged a stiff syrupy strawberry. Or if you prefer, try a hamburger from our foyer stall at only two shillings and sixpence, or thirteen new pence; dig your teeth into the hot pink rubber sausage. The bread is hygienic and aerated (did you know?) with that same substance which creates the foam on your daily detergent.

Truly, yes, truly delicious. Or at any rate, all right by me. Time was when the children had rickets. More hens in the country now than people. Free-range for the hundreds, or battery for the millions, you make your choice. I know which I make. A good woman knows that nature is her enemy. Look at what it does to her. Give her a packet of frozen fish fingers any day, and a spoonful of instant mashed potato, and a commercial on the telly to tell her it's good. We swallow the lot, we mothers, and laugh.

Down here among the women, or up, up, up, in the tower blocks; those rearing phalluses of man's delight.

Down here among the women you don't get to hear about man maltreated; what you hear about is man seducer, man betrayer, man deserter, man the monster.

What did we hear last week, during our afternoons in the park?

Man leaves his wife, young mother of four. She is waiting to go into hospital for her cancer operation. He returns from a holiday abroad, stays a couple of hours, and leaves for good, saying, by way of explanation, he is tired of being married. He probably is, too.

Man runs off with secretary the day his son brings home his first girlfriend.

Man leaves home while his wife's in hospital having the baby. She comes home to an empty house and unpaid bills. Yet he visited her in hospital, brought her flowers and grapes … no one can understand it.

Man seems not so much wicked as frail, unable to face pain, trouble and growing old.

Yesterday L walked with me. A rich girl, clever, cultivated, desiring to marry M, an equally rich and cultivated person – if married already – much in the public eye. A suitable match for suitable people. How to dispose of the unsuitable wife, but kindly, without hurting her? Without mentioning L's name? For two whole years, I learn, he professes his love for his wife, whilst making himself as unpleasant to her as he can; finally, in her distress, it is the wife who asks for a divorce. The consummation to be wished. He acts his hurt surprise, his indignation, silent joy mounting in his veins. Rushing to the telephone. She's asked, she's asked! At last! Such kindness. Can you imagine such kindness? Yes, truly, they imagine they are kind.

Dear God, preserve us from such love.

Down here among the wage-earners, of course, we don't have that class of patience. Our love is less lofty. Money and law interfere. Let me quote a poem I know. It is called 'The Poet to his Wife'.

> *Money-and-law*
> *Stands at the nursery door.*
> *You married me – what for?*
> *My love was not to get you clothes or bread,*
> *But make more poems in my head.*
> *I've fathered children.*
> *God!*
> *Am I to die*
> *To turn them out as fits a mother's eye?*
> *I wanted mothering and they, this brood*
> *Step in and take my daily food.*
> *Money-and-law*
> *Stands at the nursery door.*
> *Money-and-law, money-and-law*
> *Has the world in its maw.*

Well.

Susan sits up in her hospital bed. Her father sends flowers: he's in the United States discovering more about instant coffee. Susan's stitches are infected. Movement is painful. Kim is kind but thinks she is fussing. Well, it isn't his first baby. There was, after all, Scarlet, a full twenty years ago.

Scarlet, they (Kim, Wanda, Scarlet and friends, but not Susan) have decided, may as well stay in the flat with her baby daughter until Susan returns with her son. Susan wants to return now, at once. But Susan is running a slight fever in the evenings. The hospital doesn't want to take any risks. And the baby is not yet back to its birth-weight. Susan's breasts are cracked and painful. When the baby sucks, male and searching, tears of pain and humiliation spurt from her eyes.

Susan's mother, and the ward sister, both say she should persevere in breast feeding for Baby's Sake. Susan perseveres, pumping her strength into the baby for her own sake, not his. She wants her home back. She wants her breasts back, too, for her own. She doesn't dare ask Kim on his nightly visit if Wanda visits Scarlet.

She won't decide on a name for the baby. 'I'd only thought of girls' names,' she says. 'What's Scarlet calling hers?'

Kim says he doesn't know. She doesn't believe him. Kim's sleeping on the sofa. She's not sure she believes that, either. But she must believe it, otherwise she's mad. Men do not sleep with their daughters, let alone when they've had a baby only days previously. Nevertheless, Scarlet is in her, Susan's, matrimonial bed, and Susan is deeply affronted.

Susan's baby develops an eye infection. He cries in that corner of the upstairs nursery reserved for infected babies. He with his sticky, pus-clogged eye, another with a dermatitis, another with dysentery; they lie in cots six inches apart. Mother isn't told. They wipe his eyes before he comes down.

Susan can pick out her baby's cry. It has a different note from the others. In the middle of the night, against all the rules, she hobbles and groans up the stairs to see her baby. She has never wittingly broken a rule in all her life; not even to run in the school corridors, not even to trap and sell for sixpence the miniature frogs, protected by law, which hopped and dived in her antipodean paradise of a back garden.

There is Simeon, segregated, cast out, threatened, eyes closed fast by pus. She clasps him, won't let him go, backs into a corner with him. Staff come running; they tug, she snaps and bites like a bitch with pups. She is astonished at herself. They think she is mad. So indeed she seems to be. They ring Kim, but he isn't at home. Wanda is. They tell Susan. They can't give her tranquillizers, it is too early in the world's history, so they try phenobarb; they even let her have the baby beside her for the night.

In the morning Kim comes.

'You shouldn't get so upset,' he says. 'Lots of babies get eye infections.'

'Take me out of here.'

'You're in no state to go, love. You need a rest.'

'Rest? Here?'

'Yes. You're still feverish at night. Sister said so.'

'Of course I'm feverish at night after what I've been through. If I stay, the baby will go blind.'

'Don't be so silly. They're looking after it perfectly well.'

'He's not an "it".'

69

'Very well, looking after him perfectly well. Don't be so irritable. Try and be calm and relaxed. Scarlet is, and look at the trouble she's in.'

Susan cannot think of anything to say for a while. Presently she does.

'Perhaps you'd like to keep Scarlet and put me into a home? She might suit you better.'

'I can hardly turn my daughter out, Susan, can I?'

'Yes,' she says.

'You are more like your mother than I thought,' he remarks.

'And what's that?'

'Self-concerned, Susan,' he says. It is an obvious euphemism.

'And you're more like my father,' she says, 'than I dreamed. You don't love me at all. You just use me.'

'Hush,' he murmurs – for their voices are raised and other women are looking, as if they did not have enough to stare at already. He had thought Susan so sound, so sweet, so sensible, so pretty.

Now here she sits, puffy-eyed, dismal, jealous and complaining. She might almost be Wanda but without, of course, Wanda's brain. He wonders whether this makes her more or less acceptable, and decides, after all, more. He takes her hand, pats it.

'You're a good brave clever girl,' he says, 'and I miss you very much. It's terrible for me at home without you.'

She is mollified.

'Please let me come home,' she pleads, 'Mr Justice can come every day.'

'Look,' he says, 'we get it all free in here. Mr Justice costs money and I have to pay for him looking after Scarlet. We're a bit tight, you know. I have more dependants than I had before.'

'I don't understand you.' Susan is aghast.

'I shall have to do something about supporting Scarlet and Byzantia.'

'Scarlet and who?'

'Byzantia. That's what the baby's called. I'm sorry, I should have told you before. Terrible name, isn't it? I stood out against it, but she insisted. She's a romantic girl.'

Susan buries her head in the pillow. She won't talk to him. It is all too much. He brings her water, smiles nervously round.

'You'll dry my milk up,' she says presently.

'You're a good strong healthy natural girl,' he says. 'Nonsense.'

'I suppose Scarlet just overflows.'

'She does rather,' he says.

'In my bed. Or does she spurt it at the walls? They do in here, showing off. It's disgusting. Does she have to be in my bed?'

'Where else can she be?'

'In her own home.'

'Who would look after her?'

'Wanda,' Susan utters the name with disgust.

'Wanda's out teaching all day,' says Kim.

'And with you all night?' Susan is sharp now; her eyes grow smaller in her head. Piggy-eyes, her mother used to call her.

'You're mad,' he says. 'For God's sake –'

'She was there when you rang. You weren't –'

'What would you have said if I was!' He laughs, ha-ha-ha.

He looks older and greyer, like every man pursued by nagging and doubting.

'Why was she there and where were you?'

'She comes in to give the baby its two-o'clock feed so Scarlet can get some sleep,' he admits at last. 'I was at the office waiting for a phone call from your father. Ask him if you don't believe me.'

'I believe you all right,' she says. 'You're never at home. It's just a hotel to you. If you'd been home last Sunday like an ordinary husband all this would never have happened. I suppose Scarlet has a nurse by day.'

'Yes,' he says. Silence again. Presently –

'And there's no money left for me? Your wife?'

'What else could I do?' he asks, piteously enough. 'One must do what one can.'

'You've managed not to for the last twenty years,' says Susan.

'One must face one's responsibilities.'

'It's her responsibility, not ours.'

'She went out and got herself pregnant the day we got married.'

'So it's all my fault?'

'It's not a question of fault,' he says lamely, but he feels yes it is Susan's fault.

Byzantia is a very pretty baby, with a clear pale skin and well-formed features. His son is a dark-red mottled sticky-eyed lump. He has been having long talks with Wanda. She has provoked him almost to the point of believing the time might be ripe for him to start painting again. But how can he,

72

now he has this influx of dependants? At least Wanda works – he can't see Susan ever doing anything but sit round waiting to be kept. Poor Susan. He smoothes her hair back from her forehead: it has wrinkles there he never noticed before. She is very tense. He wishes he didn't have these thoughts about her.

'Scarlet is part of our lives now,' he says. 'We must try and make the best of it, that's all.'

Nurses erupt from all sides; they move him to one side. It is not within normal visiting hours, so they don't count him as human. One wheels the baby off; another the locker. Susan watches while her flowers, her breakfast and slices of white bread and butter and raspberry jam disappear. (The hospitals are using up the war-time stocks. Jam is made of turnip pulp, flavouring, cochineal, and – in the popular imagination, at any rate – flecks of wood for raspberry pips.) Other nurses seize Susan's bed and wheel that off too.

He follows.

'Where are you taking her?'

'Ask Sister, please.' They are firm, brutal and kind all at the same time; armour-bosomed and sexually aware, these smiling girls who watch and observe the processes of motherhood.

He finds Sister in the store room, up a step-ladder investigating a forgotten shelf. She has discovered a false leg lying in the dust; she has not much concentration for Kim. Susan, however, she admits, has a post-puerperal fever.

'What's that?' he asks.

Sister is vague. But Susan is going into the isolation ward. 'Just to be on the safe side.' It's not dangerous, he enquires?

73

Good gracious no, she beams. And she can have the baby with her now, can't she? Without disturbing the other mothers.

Kim has to be off, back to the office, the three-roomed suite in Mayfair. Susan's father is away. Kim has to be entire creative and executive departments himself and he is very busy.

But he takes time off to have drinks at lunchtime with his friends in the pub in Oxford Street. Dylan Thomas holds the floor, with a supporting cast of poets. Penguin New Writing is into its fortieth and last edition. The beer is good, if warm; Scotch is back. The Welfare State is being wrought around them. In the Black Horse Kim drinks to celebrate his new fatherhood with friends on the whole rather younger than he is, not long back from the war, duffle-coated, seeking a congenial level – doorman today, BBC producer (radio) tomorrow, who knows? Painters, jazzmen, writers, the first sociologists – the original do-your-own-thing people, widening up the channels of culture for the masses to flow through.

Here Kim is a man of status: he earns enough to buy the drinks, he has two paintings in the Tate, albeit painted twenty years ago, albeit in the basement; now he has a baby. They are pleased for him. It is a time of hope.

Babies are welcome in this still rationed, still unpainted, barely photographed, rarely filmed, but lively world.

Kim is moved to tell them of Scarlet. He confesses to having a grandchild. They think it is a great joke. Why, they did not even know he had a daughter. There are more drinks all round. He understands he can be proud of and not alarmed by his new relatives. At closing time he takes some friends back to meet Scarlet and Byzantia.

In truth, he knows very little of Scarlet. She has hardly said a word to him. She is shy; but she glows at Byzantia – the perfect baby, who only sleeps to wake again and suck, and sucks to sleep again – and looks a good deal better than she usually does. He is pleased, for the moment, at any rate, to own her for a daughter.

During the course of the evening Scarlet's friends arrive to inspect the baby. It is quite a party.

Jocelyn brings Philip with her. While Jocelyn marvels at Byzantia, Philip says he would be interested in joining Kim's firm; he sees a great future for himself in advertising, but has failed the intelligence tests set by the personnel departments of the established agencies. 'More to my credit than otherwise, ha-ha,' he says. There is a good deal of drunken wincing at this, but Jocelyn does not notice. There are many things Jocelyn does not notice about Philip. Having trodden Sylvia's sensibilities underfoot, how can she afford to be critical?

Sylvia comes with Philip and Jocelyn – she spends most of her spare time with them, as if there was something to be learned from studying their behaviour.

She lets herself be picked up by an eccentric Scottish Earl (so he says) and be made very drunk. He takes her home to his studio, and there, in a specially constructed and padded box, in an effort to trap the forces of the orgasm, they copulate. Orgasm seems a very rude word to Sylvia, and indeed a rude thing – not that she is sure what it means. The Earl however seems satisfied, and presently rushes naked to his flask of sterile water – specially bought from Boots – to see whether bacteria have now formed. They have. He is overjoyed and kisses Sylvia with a real tenderness, very different from his previous humping fury; she would like to put her arms round him but he rushes off to tell his friends over the telephone that his theory is proved. Life springs from sex, not sex from life. Orgasm is at the heart of all things.

It would scarcely seem suitable, in the circumstances, for Sylvia to be hurt or offended. A scientific discovery has been made. He is a handsome, dramatic man, and she feels honoured that he has sought her out; included her, as it were, in not only aristocratic but creative circles.

She returns exhausted to Jocelyn – the Earl cannot spare the time from his investigations to drive her home – with instructions to return the following night. And Jocelyn encourages Sylvia to go, although she knows full well this earnest copulater is not a true Earl, but just pretending. She can't stand the sight of Sylvia, not just now.

Audrey comes to visit Scarlet, too. She admires the baby, cursorily, and talks about herself and her potter. He comes to visit nightly. It seems a good compromise. She is not sure she wants to marry yet. She keeps getting dreadful pains, far far worse, she is sure, than childbirth. Scarlet says in fact childbirth is dead easy, but Audrey isn't listening.

As for Helen, Helen can't come to visit Scarlet. Helen loves X. X loves Helen. They lie in the dark cupboard under the stairs where Y can't find them. The sloping roof has been papered at one stage with a white paper patterned with yellow stars. Helen stares up at it, at the circle made by the light of the torch. The memory remains with her as long as she lives. When she closes her eyes before sleep it is what she sees, and when she wakes, it is to this imprint of colour. Later, she is to buy dress material with yellow stars upon it for her little girl.

Of course Helen can't come to visit Byzantia. Later, Byzantia is to forget to visit Helen, and Helen dies. Not perhaps that it would have made that much difference. But it might.

Kim has drunk so much he forgets to visit Susan. Susan sits in splendour in the isolation ward. Her baby is beside her. They won't let her breast-feed the baby now; they bring her a bottle. They make her stay in bed. She feels splendid. When she doesn't walk her stitches don't hurt.

Doctors come and stare at her, and ask her how she's feeling.

'Fine,' she says, and they look bemused, and at each other, as they inspect, tap, and medicate. They don't understand it, and why should they? They have their test-tubes mixed.

In the ward another young woman drifts slowly off towards death, unnoticed. Would Susan mention the error, if she knew? Abandon the comfort and safety of her position? Fortunately, she is not called upon to speak up: she is not told till later. When Kim does not arrive that evening she decides he is angry with her for behaving badly and being jealous, and writes him a sad little letter of apology.

In the morning Kim lies groaning, hung-over, on the sofa. Scarlet gets up to make tea and collects the letters. He asks her to read the one from Susan. Scarlet does. Scarlet thinks Susan more of a fool than ever.

All the same, she thinks perhaps she should clear up before Susan's return; replace – if Kim will give her any money – the baby things she's used. She certainly means to.

Susan's ward, however, is abruptly closed, the infection – from which Susan has been saved, being in isolation – is rampant and uncontrollable. Susan is deposited back home without warning, still with stitches, and with Simeon underweight, unnamed, and sticky of eye. She hobbles in, to face Scarlet and Byzantia in her bed, and Kim talking about old times with Wanda.

Poor Susan. How flimsy her kauri trees seem these days. No protection at all.

Wanda and Kim have been arguing over Scarlet. Both want her. Scarlet wants neither of them. Scarlet has a vision of a little flat in South Kensington where she can entertain lovers and bring up Byzantia, in that order. She has decided she will never marry. She intends to be beautiful, romantic and sought after.

Lying here in Susan's bed, attended by a nurse by day and her mother by night, visited by Kim's handsome and exciting friends, enjoying her father's concern, all things seem possible.

Who will pay the rent? A detail, a detail. Does she not live here amongst fitted carpets? Kim does not worry about money. Why should she? Like father, like daughter.

Byzantia nibbles and sucks, containing in her strong little body all the energies of her past, to which – to name but a few – the following have contributed:

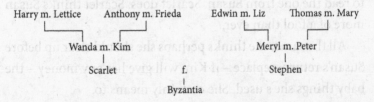

78

Scarlet draws the chart on her Basildon Bond (though she has to invent the names of Stephen's antecedents) and chants in her soul – 'The days of m. are over. Let the days of f. commence.'

Susan is approaching in her taxi to put a stop to such nonsense.

'You only want to keep her here to annoy me,' says Wanda to Kim meanwhile.

'Your annoyance or otherwise is a matter of indifference to me,' Kim says, lying in his teeth. 'I am only interested in Scarlet's welfare.'

'That makes a change,' says Wanda, with feeble sarcasm. Kim makes her self-conscious; she suspects he pities her for not being the girl that once she was.

'No,' says Kim. 'It does not. I was always concerned with my daughter, but I was not allowed to show it. You would not accept my money.'

'It was whore's money,' says Wanda. 'You prostituted your talent to obtain it. And anyway,' she adds, 'you only offered the once.'

'Money is money,' he says. 'You talk like a fool. Whether it's made from rich idiots or from teaching infants lies, as you do, it still buys the dinner.'

'I wanted Scarlet to grow up with a sense of integrity,' says Wanda, sounding quite lost and forlorn.

'Then you were impertinent,' he says, taking no pity on her. 'To impose such neurotic values upon my child. Look how it's turned out.'

'That's right,' she says, classically, 'blame me.'

'Oh I do,' he says.

'Your child, indeed! You never even paid her a visit. You took no interest at all.'

'I offered. The offer was refused. What did you expect me to do, go down on my knees, humiliate myself, in order to visit my own child?'

'The offer,' says Wanda, 'was refused because I was in prison where you had put me.'

'You put yourself there. I didn't ask you to slash my paintings. Why should I then ask the police to desist from arresting you? Why should you harm my paintings? I didn't harm you.'

'You had a mistress.'

'But you didn't know about her.'

Thus they take up the pattern of the row as they left it off, fifteen years ago. Nothing much has changed, except they are both older, and each year that passes makes strife the sadder.

'They weren't paintings, they were mockeries,' claims Wanda, getting into her stride.

'You know nothing about them. You were profoundly ignorant of what I was trying to do. You have a woman's eye, which means no eye at all. You just liked poncing on the art world. Your envy and your malice made you self-destructive. Jealous bitch that you were. It was your jealousy drove me to that other woman, what's-her-name.'

'Can't remember it, can you?' Wanda dances about with glee.

'No, actually.'

'Men!' she says. The force of the expletive shatters even her.

'Why do you say "men" in that tone of voice? You hate them, don't you? I think Scarlet should be saved from you.'

80

'I don't hate men,' she says, recovering her composure. 'I pity them. They are inadequate creatures. They cannot bear to be with their equals. They must always seek out their inferiors. In bed or in the pub, it's just the same.'

'I don't know what you mean,' he complains. He is a little shaken, all the same.

'Marrying this poor child Susan! It's nonsense and you know it is.'

'I love her.'

'Love is for equals,' she says.

'You know nothing about her.' He feels trapped. He remembers the feeling from long ago.

'I saw her, that was enough. I suppose she admires you.'

'Yes, she does.'

'She doesn't criticize.'

'No. Why should she?'

'What poor frail things you are, you men,' says Wanda, laughing, feeling quite cheerful, now she feels her point is proved. 'Why do you do these foolish things? You didn't visit her in hospital tonight. Why not? Does she bore you? Does she complain? Is she a nagger and a whiner, this child bride of yours?'

'It's her first baby,' he says, more defensively than he would like.

'I don't think you would be wise asking Scarlet to stay,' says Wanda. 'Scarlet would see through you in no time. And I hardly imagine Susan will appreciate the littering up of her love-nest with new-born relatives.'

'Susan is a sensible girl. Susan has always been in favour of renewing contact with Scarlet. Susan accepts the fact, as I do, that Scarlet is my daughter.'

'Scarlet is *my* daughter,' cries Wanda with passion. 'I gave birth to her. All these years I've looked after her. You can't just step in now and say she's yours. Fatherhood, as conducted by you, means nothing.'

'That's not what Scarlet thinks.'

'Scarlet hasn't got a mind to think with.'

'I would have liked to have been a father,' Kim compromises. 'You prevented me. You wanted her to yourself. I think you are very wicked, Wanda.'

'And I think you are incestuous,' says Wanda, beside herself with rage. 'You ignore her as a child. You wait until she's nubile and now you have her in your bed. The police might be interested in that. It would make a change for *you* to be in prison.' Kim is quite shaken.

'I thought I'd got rid of you years ago,' is all he can think of to say. 'Do you have no life of your own that you have to come creeping back into mine?' This hurts her.

'I am very sorry for you,' she says. 'You used to be quite a good painter. Now look at you. Advertising! It's hardly what you would have wanted for yourself. A pity to see talent go down the drain.'

'I thought you said they weren't paintings, they were mockeries,' he manages to say.

'Oh, that exhibition, yes. That was a disgrace. Cunts, tits and arseholes. Don't look so shocked. If you can paint them I can say them. I did you a favour, slashing them. I suppose *she* liked them.'

82

'Who?'

'What's-her-name. The female whose name you've forgotten. The one you were shacking up with when you were married to me and I was working fourteen hours a day to keep you in paint, and doing your shirts and emptying your ashtrays, when I got home exhausted at night.'

'And doing them very badly, as I remember,' he remarks.

She looks round wildly. He remembers the days when she would throw things. He flexes his thumbs, remembering how he could restrain her, pressing them into the two vulnerable nerve ganglions on her shoulders, until she cried with pain. He quite looks forward to it. In those days fights would end in lovemaking. Now he is not interested. The fight will be for the fight's sake, but it is a long time since he has had even that pleasure.

Fortunately Scarlet calls out, as she would call out from her bed when a very little girl, disturbed if not by the sound of battle, then by the tension in the air.

Now she wants, not water, as she did when small, but to be fetched the olive oil to rub into her tummy – it has the look of a deflated balloon, and she's not having that. She has her future as London's leading mistress to consider.

Wanda hands over the bottle – Crosse & Blackwell Olive Oil, used by the English in those days for cosmetic rather than culinary purposes. Scarlet could have stretched for the bottle herself, perfectly well. Wanda is grim-faced and silent. Scarlet is made uneasy and anxious. She wishes Wanda would go away, and leave her to empty chats with her father. She suspects that Wanda knows her fantasies.

83

When Wanda returns to Kim his thumbs have relaxed. He even smiles, amiably.

'Don't let's quarrel,' he says. 'We're too old for that.'

'I'm not quarrelling,' she says. 'I'm making statements of facts. If you want to support Scarlet I suggest you pay a banker's order monthly into my account.'

'You're joking.'

'Her account, then; though you know how impractical she is.'

'I don't, as it happens. Not having much of an acquaintance.'

'Well, will you?'

'Will I what?' He is being obstinate.

'Give some money?'

'No.'

'I thought not.' She is triumphant.

'Not if she's with you. Only if she's with me. It wouldn't be fair to Susan.' He smiles sweetly. He has a sweet smile. One would almost think he meant it.

'Oh no.' She is sarcastic. 'It wouldn't be fair to Susan. Bring her in when convenient, not otherwise. Poor bloody neglected little cow.'

'Susan's doing all right for herself,' he says, with a kind of rough and almost friendly conceit.

'There isn't room for Scarlet here.'

'A good deal more than at your place, I gather. Peter didn't look after you well, did he?'

'Peter?' She is lost.

'Peterkin,' he reminds her. 'Your lover.'

'Oh him.' He was lost a long time ago, lost in the misty past of lovers.

84

'He didn't last long,' remarks Kim.

'He had his uses,' drawls Wanda. 'He bailed me out, and he was good in bed.' She cannot remember whether he was or wasn't, but it serves to annoy Kim.

'Pity his wife died like that. From over-use, perhaps.'

'From abstinence, more like. She wouldn't.' They look at each other with a kind of alarmed sympathy. They are beginning to enjoy themselves.

'Quite like old times,' says Kim; he smiles tentatively.

'Yes,' she says, cool as can be. 'Do you have any good rows with soppy Susan?'

'No,' he says before he can stop himself, and is instantly mortified. He lapses into silence.

'I tell you what,' he says presently, 'let's ask Scarlet.'

'She shouldn't be upset,' says Wanda.

'You're frightened, aren't you? You've been a bad mother for bloody years and now it's coming home to roost.'

He is right. Wanda is scared stiff. She, who has longed, vociferously, for the day when Scarlet will leave home and set her free, panics at the notion that her wayward child might now not so much reject her, as actually choose her father.

Together they go to face Scarlet. She clasps Byzantia to her bosom and regards her parents as they enter the room.

'What a pity,' she remarks, 'that Susan exists. Otherwise we could all be together again.'

It is at this point that Susan, poor Susan, re-enters her home.

Susan does not have a key, having left the flat so hurriedly, and has to ring the bell. Wanda goes to answer it. Susan stands forlornly on the doorstep; Simeon is crying. He has a piercing, insistent cry.

Wanda takes the baby. Susan does not resist. She walks through to the bedroom and there finds her husband and her stepdaughter. Her face puckers.

'Darling,' says Kim, startled. 'What are you doing here?' He had thought her safe in hospital.

'They turned us out,' says Susan dully. 'People were dying all around me.'

'Dying?' enquires Scarlet sharply. 'What from?' Susan ignores her.

'Would you like me to go away again?' enquires Susan of Kim, with masochistic intensity. 'That is, if I'm in the way,'

'Darling,' he says. 'Darling. You should have rung. I'd have fetched you.'

'I wanted to give you a nice surprise,' says Susan dismally. Wanda pushes his child into his arms.

'Pity about its eyes,' she says, for Simeon's lids are still encrusted.

'Keep it away from Byzantia, if you please,' Wanda adds.

'What's wrong with its eyes?' Scarlet is sharper than ever in defence of her child, but no one replies.

'You should be lying down,' says Kim to Susan, and then to Wanda – 'she should be lying down, shouldn't she?'

'I'm perfectly all right,' says Susan, 'I just want to be at home.'

'She wants us out of here,' says Wanda.

'She wants nothing of the kind,' says Kim. 'Do you darling?' Susan does not reply.

'The baby's hungry,' says Susan.

'Then feed it,' says Scarlet. 'I feed Byzantia almost all the time, and she never cries.'

'I can't,' says Susan. 'My milk's dried up. It's on cow's milk and just brings it up all the time anyway. Really, I just want to jump out of the window. I mean, that would be the simplest thing for everyone.'

There is silence. No one disagrees with her. Susan's spirit begins to return. Since no one else is going to look after her and her baby, she will clearly have to do it.

'I'd like to get things organized,' she says firmly. She looks crossly at the disorder on the baby's table. In the hour since the day nurse has left Wanda and Scarlet between them have created powdery and greasy chaos amongst the unguents and cotton wools. 'And I must have somewhere to put the baby,' she adds. 'In fact,' she says, 'there's only really room for one baby in this flat.'

She trembles. She has never made so definite and aggressive a statement in her life. She doesn't like herself for being unpleasant, but she knows when she has to be. She stares obstinately at the ground.

'I expect you are right,' says Kim sadly, his vision of future entertainment evaporating. He puts his arm round Susan. He has undertaken her. He will go through with it. The prospect of himself tormenting Wanda, and laying Scarlet's girl-friends, departs. Susan snuffles cosily into his shoulder.

Scarlet, Byzantia and Wanda leave. Byzantia snuggles down in the dresser bottom drawer.

Kim lifts Susan's face to welcome her home properly.

'Don't touch me,' she says. 'Just don't touch me.'

She has never said a thing like that before.

'Anyway,' says Scarlet, 'Byzantia would only have caught some terrible disease from that baby.'

'Her uncle,' remarks Wanda.

'The relationship doesn't reflect much credit on her, I'm afraid. Did you see its eyes? And such a funny-shaped head. Do you think it's all right?'

Wanda has never before heard Scarlet speak so disagreeably of strangers.

6

Problems and Solutions

Down among the women. There's a flasher in the park, a poor pale middle-aged man, who lets his trousers down to little girls. The little girls are shock-proof, or appear to be. 'Seen better than that at home,' they cry, and jeer, and he slinks off. They don't tell their mothers, whom they know will get upset and phone the police. And though the children like excitement and the sudden rush of policemen and dogs into the park, they quite like the flasher too; he carries his own excitement with him, stepping out unexpectedly from behind trees, and they don't wish to forgo it. Not yet, until they're bored.

Two of the little girls pass by. I know them well, infant thieves. Cat-toothed Christine, six, and squinty-eyed Theresa, five. They wear their mother's shoes, her shrunken jerseys; they carry toy handbags; they wiggle their hips. 'Blood everywhere,' Christine is saying, 'under the table and over the telly and they had to take a hose to the ambulance.' And Theresa nods, sage and horrified, as her mother would, and says, 'They sewed me up with stitches once because my arm was coming off.'

'How many?' asks Christine.

'A thousand,' says Theresa.

'That's nothing,' says Christine, 'I had seven hundred and thirty-two when my head nearly came off.' They enjoy themselves. They will never join the girls. They were born down here among the women. They were born scavengers and vultures. Christine and Theresa, one day, tiny, dusty and old, will fight each other at the jumble sale; not for an old jersey for sixpence – who wants that? – but because they don't want the other to have it.

Alice and Regina pass, sisters. They aren't whores. They don't get paid. They're on drugs, I think. I know their mother, she's going mad with worry; she keeps threatening to put them in care. Alice is fourteen; Regina sixteen. Camp-followers, groupies, gangsters' molls, revolutionaries' birds, what's the difference? The perks are much the same, and one is being useful to and used by those one most admires.

A well-dressed woman passes. I don't know her. She is middle-aged and hatchet-faced. She is talking to herself, mutter, mutter. She is angry. She wears a flowered hat. I think I know what she wants. She wants to hang, flog, behead, draw, quarter, stone, shave, guillotine. She wants her revenge. If she came across the flasher she would have him publicly castrated, and wield the knife herself.

I am sure her house is clean. I am sure there is not a speck of dust anywhere. The cleaner the house the angrier the lady. We are the cleaners. We empty the ashtrays which tomorrow will be filled again. We sweep the floors which tomorrow will be dusty. We cook the food and clean the lavatory pans. We pick up the dirty clothes and wash and iron them. We make the world go round. Someone's got to do it. When she dies it will be said of her, she was a wonderful wife and mother. She cooked a hundred thousand meals, swept a million floors, washed a billion dishes, went through the cupboards and searched for missing buttons. She muttered, but we will miss her.

Down among the women, we don't like chaos. We will crawl from our sickbeds to tidy and define. We live at floor level, washing and wiping. If we look upward, it's not towards the stars or the ineffable, it's to dust the tops of the windows. We have only ourselves to blame.

'Yes, God,' we say, 'here's your slippers and your nice hot dinner. In the meantime just feed us, keep us, fetch the coal and say something nice while you're about it.'

Audrey and Helen share a flat. Audrey doesn't do house-work. She is something of a slut. She will clean if she has to, for the sake of a quiet life, but her heart isn't in it. Men, observing her domestic habits, feel there is something unnatural here. Women feel the same. They resent her freedom. Such cleaning as she does is man-orientated: when the man drifts away, so does Audrey's capacity for domestic action. Dirty knickers pile up on the bathroom floor; bread gets cut on the sideboard and the crumbs are left for the mice.

Helen, on the other hand, has a gift for domestic grace. Where she moves, there is beauty. She will put one flower in a jam jar and make the arrangement remarkable; she will open her trunk and bring out embroidered oriental fabrics with which she will cover cushions and make curtains. She will lay a table nicely and fold paper napkins into pretty shapes. The food tastes better.

The arrangement, by which Audrey pays the bills and Helen blesses the flat with her orderly presence, works well enough while, as it were, it is not overlooked.

But now Paul is complaining to Audrey – not without justification – that Helen is exploiting her, and X is complaining because they have to pass through Audrey's bedroom to reach Helen's – thus being confronted by what he feels to be the mating of inferiors – and tensions arise. Harsh words are spoken, not to each other, but to mutual friends. Helen says of Audrey, 'She is a mercenary slut,' and implies it is Audrey's lack of breeding that makes her complain that Helen keeps the electric fire on all night, so that X will be able to step out into a warm room.

(Y has entered an art competition. It rather looks as if she might win it. There is a prize of £1,500. X would have liked to compete but clearly can't enter into direct competition with his wife. She put her entry in without telling him. He is nervous and angry, and only feels at ease and himself when immersed and active in Helen. He does not tell Y where he goes at night: he is angry when questioned. And Y, who feels she has done him a great wrong by entering the competition, does not have the heart to persist in enquiry. At least he comes home in the morning, and has had breakfast, so she does not have to make him coffee and delay starting her work. She has never worked better. He, so far as painting is concerned, is alternately frenetic and apathetic, and accomplishes very little.)

Audrey says of Helen, 'If she can afford new clothes, she

92

can afford to pay the electricity. Why doesn't she get a proper job? And he's a married man, she should think of that.'

All the same, in bed with Paul, listening patiently as he talks, Audrey watches X's dark figure as he goes through to Helen in the inside room, and she envies. X, she knows, she feels, will not demean himself with words, as Paul does. X belongs to a romantic world; she cannot aspire to it. Audrey was born below stairs with legs, she rightly fears, too short even for Emma-Audrey to be able to climb to more rarefied regions, where Paul cannot pursue her. Yet she longs; she desires; she finds X's brief disdainful presence by her bed more erotically stimulating than a whole half-hour of Paul's patient verbal stirring and dextrous manipulations. To be taken, seized and left is all she wants.

Paul finds these midnight intrusions insupportable. He is no painter, no writer, no poet – his pottery is stern and practical; he tries and tries, but cannot achieve more. He makes do with creative diatribes against X's painting – and affords Y faint praise. He despises and lusts after Helen, and prophesies that she will come to a bad end.

His proposal to Audrey still stands, but he does not press it. Why should he? He has, rash fellow, got her a job on a woman's magazine. She loves it. She is animated, heady with competence. She sneers at the editor, the caption writers, the art directors – alters copy and headlines as she types. She can do better than anyone, she knows. Paul listens and laughs. At the office she is known as Emma. He feels quite safe. In the evenings he teaches her to cook, how to listen to music; he gives her exercises in pornographic writing and marks them out of ten. She models for nude photographs, but finds that this gives her stomach pains. These frighten him; he desists.

One day Emma's Editor sends a memo round the office saying the magazine is to carry no more fiction. Up and down the corridors there is uproar. The Editor, quite clearly, has misinterpreted the findings of the new Readership Research Department. Will anyone tell him? No, he is too bold and angry a man. He hires in a minute, fires in a second. What's this? Little Emma? Pattering up to the Editor's desk, telling him he's a fool? He smiles, re-instates fiction, and promotes Emma. It's like a fairy story. Now she's head of the story section. She takes writers out to lunch. At home, she is found to be intolerable. She talks of nothing but interoffice politics; Helen yawns, X declines to turn up at all. (Y thinks 'you see, patience and tact has won him back'.) Paul gets fearful headaches from nervous irritation. This is not what he had meant at all.

Paul asks Emma to marry him. Of course, she will wish to stop work. If they are to be together, it must be totally, inseparably, day as well as night.

Emma hesitates. Emma has written home boasting about her new job. She's making good. Her parents reply with a crude request for £53, money they once had to send to supplement her County Award while she was at college.

Emma agrees to marry Paul. Emma needs shelter. Paul won't let her send a penny home. Emma, he says, must break off all relationship with her family completely, start life anew. She is only too glad to do so. They will move to the country, to Suffolk (no editors in Suffolk, no lunches, no taxis, no expense accounts, none of the seductions of office life); they will run the pottery business together. Emma's good at typing and invoicing. She will be very useful. They will live as near to nature as the U.S. Air Bases in the area will allow. She will bake home-made bread, and have a herb garden. He will have a little conservatory for humming-birds – always his ambition. It sounds entrancing. Emma hands in her notice.

It is a Registry Office wedding. Audrey dreamt in her vulgar way of hymns, a choir, white veils and bow ties; Emma knows better. She scoffs and giggles quite openly at the Registrar's few kind words, as he misguidedly tries to make the ceremony more than a legal transaction. Her mother wanted to come – Paul won't let her, and Emma is grateful.

Paul's brother Edward is there – a schoolmaster with bad asthma. He seems to find Paul mildly ridiculous, which upsets Emma. Scarlet is there, her ring finger greener than ever. She carries little Byzantia. Helen comes; so do Jocelyn, and Sylvia and Philip. So does Paul's first wife. Who asked her? Why, Paul.

On way and another Emma is glad when the day is over, and she can retire to bed with Paul, who celebrates the occasion by making love for an hour and a quarter, timed with his stop watch; including preliminary love play of the duration of, from the first pinch of the ear lobe to the last blow into the nostril, and the final delicate fingerings, an hour and twelve minutes.

Truly he is remarkable.

After a few months of Suffolk life Emma either stops getting stomach pains or grows used to them. Presently she stops dreaming of X.

Helen cannot afford to keep the flat going, now that Audrey

95

has gone. She confides her troubles to Y, of whom she now sees a lot. She loves to wander in X's territory when he is not there, to wash his coffee cup, read his letters, hide her head among his clothes, sit in his chair, see his family as he must see them. She loves Y because she is part of X. Sometimes she loves X because he is part of Y. Y seems to her more and more beautiful; a pale, quiet, thin woman with light eyes fringed by lighter lashes, and long thin legs. Her paintings are sad and powerful. Helen wants to smooth Y's wispy hair out of her eyes, make her cups of tea, help her relax, smile, be happy. Yet when X appears she is in a frenzy of impatience, waiting for him to find some dark place and overwhelm and satiate her.

Y no longer suspects Helen. She believes X has lost interest in Helen, found some other newer light of love, and is now even sorry for her. So she puts up with Helen's continual presence in her household; Helen talks too much in too naïve a way, Y thinks, but she is useful with the children.

'If I had any money I would help you out,' says Y to Helen, 'but I haven't. Not unless I win this prize, which isn't likely.' But she knows in her heart she will win it.

Helen stays for supper quite often. They all eat black-eyed beans and bacon, talk of art and artists; of teachers at the Slade, Camberwell and the Central. There are lots of friends, there is lots to drink, they make their own beer and wine. They live cheaply but well. They strip the paint off unfashionable furniture and discover the beauties beneath. They are young; there is a duffle-coated resurrection in the air.

Presently, of an evening, X will get up and leave. No one asks where he is going: they know he likes to work at night, anyway. And then when the others go, Helen goes too.

Or sometimes she stays a little longer to comfort Y.

'You mustn't worry about it,' says Helen. 'It means nothing. It's you he loves. There is so much in him to give, it's not surprising he needs more than one woman to keep him going, is it? How can a man like that, a major creative talent, be expected to keep bourgeois rules? It would be death to his painting. You are so lucky to be his wife,' adds Helen, and Y smiles her tight, small, faded smile and says nothing.

'You're all so talented,' complains Helen. 'I wish I could *do* something. I'm a parasite, that's all. I must have a symbiotic relationship with the great, or die.'

'The great? X, great?' Y is amused.

'Oh yes.' Helen is quite serious. 'So are you,' she adds as an afterthought.

Y denies it. But she looks at her husband a little differently after these talks with Helen, and is even less inclined to challenge him. How can she, so small, so ordinary, so everyday, have the right to the totality of his being? She must be grateful for what he can bestow: she must not feel distress when he seems to need more than she can offer. Sexual jealousy is a mean, horrid, destructive emotion. Helen keeps saying so.

'If you really love someone,' Helen keeps saying, 'you want them to be happy and free.'

And presently Y hasn't the courage to reply, as once she did, 'No. I want them to be mine.' She tries to be generous and noble. X makes love to her as frequently as before, but she feels he is angry – whether with himself or with her she cannot tell.

'The sensible thing for a wife to do,' says Helen, 'is to make

97

it easier for a husband to take his extra-marital pleasures when and where he feels inclined. I mean, what is the real danger for a wife? Not that the husband will be unfaithful, but that he will find love elsewhere. Men don't leave home for sex, they leave home for love. And we all know that sex denied soon turns into love. A husband's infidelity should be seen as an enriching of the marriage, and encouraged. He brings something extra home.'

'Oh, yes,' says Y, sarcastic, 'so long as it isn't V.D.'

'Penicillin,' says Helen, 'will put an end to V.D. once and for all.'

All the same, in spite of the knowledge that Helen is young and foolish, Y is influenced. A letter arrives. Y has won the prize. £1,500. Y hides the letter for days. But it will be announced in the newspapers soon. Y will have to tell him. She waits till he is in a good mood and Helen is out of the house. She has the feeling that Helen's presence irritates him.

'I have a present for you,' she says all at once. 'I have won that prize, I have the cheque, and I have bought you a studio flat. It is just around the corner.'

'A flat? What for?' He is astounded.

'You might find it easier to work there,' she says. 'And models, and girls and things.' Her tongue can scarcely get round the words, but she manages. 'Really, you see, I don't mind. You mustn't think I do. I'll go on loving you. It's just a kind of nervous twitch, really, with you. I know. This sex thing with other women. Well, I mean, it's you, isn't it? I married all of you.'

She stops talking. He says nothing. She can't make out whether he is pleased or angry.

'It's a nice flat,' she says. 'With a lovely studio stove. A Pither. I've polished it up. It's brass.'

'It's good about the prize,' he says, eventually. She has forgotten all about that part of it.

'It doesn't mean much,' she says. 'I mean they've got no judgement, really, have they? People who give prizes.'

There is silence between them again.

'Well, thank you very much,' he says.

'I won't go round there,' she says, 'ever. It's your private place.'

Thus retreating, accommodating, placating, she safeguards her marriage. Helen stops complaining about the rent.

Jocelyn is employed! Jocelyn has found a job at last. She is a temporary assistant clerk in a Government Department. She gets only £62.0. a week. She grumbles, although, unlike her friends, she has a private income of her own, the interest on money left her by a grandfather, and expectations of even more.

Jocelyn went to the Marlborough Street Employment Exchange to get the job. There, amongst the kitchen hands and machine sewers, she joined a queue of girl arts graduates. No one wishes to employ them. Why should they? Conceited, self-important girls, with nothing to their credit except a knowledge of Middle English or Diplomatic History, sulking over the filing? Uppity, graceless girls, leaving to get married like anyone else, and in the meantime, troublesome?

Jocelyn's talents find her out, however. She ends up in a branch of the Foreign Office, still on £62.0. a week, sifting refugee reports, and monitoring radio broadcasts from the

Eastern Europe Communist Bloc. She writes papers which are read by Churchill and for which her Department head takes credit. When she is not otherwise occupied she makes tea, and files top-secret documents in the crumbly bathroom where the secret files are kept. (The Department is housed in a Georgian mansion in Central London. A few partitions have been built, but otherwise nothing has been changed, except that the water supply to the bath has been cut off, in case important documents get damaged by steam. In the secret files are kept memos from ambassadors, mostly asking for more sherry, or more blankets, or complaining about Embassy Central Heating; and of course the staff's hats and coats.)

Sometimes staff are asked to keep to their offices for an hour or so. On one such occasion, peering through the keyhole, Jocelyn sees a group of anonymous and forgettable men, all wearing raincoats although it hasn't rained for days. Spies, she concludes.

Jocelyn, writing her reports, interprets the truth as her employers would wish. She does not lie, but neither does she tell the truth. Either way, she does not care. She is preoccupied with her inner world.

For Jocelyn wants to be married.

Byzantia, when she reaches nubile age, can be heard to say, 'I don't want to get married. Why should I get married? I don't want to be some man's wife. Moreover I do not subscribe to these outmoded bourgeois formulae. Children? No, the world's too terrible a place.' She means Vietnam and so on, brought to her daily on the telly, before which, in the security of her mother's house, she sits in protein-fed beauty and laments.

But Jocelyn wants to be married. She wants to have a white wedding and a reception with a wedding-cake, local photographers, envious ex-boyfriends, a weeping bustling mother and a hoarse-voiced conscientious father. Her parents are rather elderly. They live in a cosy house in a country town, tend the garden, and already consider Jocelyn off their hands. She would not mind reminding them, in this forcible way, of her existence.

She wants people to say, 'What a lovely girl. She used to be rather plain, too. Do you remember that hockey phase?'

She wants to ask Miss Bonny to her wedding. She promised herself this when she was fifteen. She wants to have a London flat, to have an account at Harrods, to be known as Mrs. She wants to entertain.

She wants a wedding collection at the office. She wants everyone to know that she, Jocelyn, is truly female, truly feminine, truly desired, is now to be married and complete.

She would like Philip as a husband. He is young, suitable, gentlemanly, of good executive stock, smart appearance, and public school background. (He has his job in advertising. He works for Susan's father after all; he is junior executive at Watson and Belcher.) She knows she loves Philip because she suffers such anxiety when he stays away from her bed on Sunday, Monday, Tuesday, Wednesday, Thursday and Friday nights. On these nights he sleeps at the flat he shares with two rugger-playing friends. Jocelyn thinks his reluctance to commit himself, on any night other than Saturday, is due to Sylvia's presence in the flat. She feels she cannot bring the subject up.

'Perhaps I've been foolish,' she confides to Helen, who is

supposed to know about men. 'Perhaps I shouldn't have agreed to sleep with him. Perhaps now he thinks I'm too awful to marry, and wants a virgin bride or something. He lost interest in Sylvia, didn't he, quickly enough. But then if I hadn't, he'd just have found someone else. And anyway, if we hadn't, there wouldn't have been any relationship at all. I mean, we met in bed, if you see what I mean. London is a terrible place. If we lived at home everyone would know exactly what was happening, and he'd have to marry me. Helen, do you think if I had held out he would have asked me to marry him?'

'I daresay,' says Helen, who has a low opinion of Philip. 'But would you then want to marry him? If you have to resort to sexual blackmail to get a man to marry you, he is surely not worth marrying.'

On the evening before Audrey's wedding to Paul, Jocelyn leaves the office early to buy a dress. Her looks have improved. Her legs have lost their hockey nobbles. Her waist is agreeably small. Jocelyn cries at Audrey's wedding. Partly from envy and partly because the brevity of the ceremony upsets her. She is not upset because Audrey is married in the name of Emma. She thinks such devotion to a man is admirable: she predicts a happy future for them. Everyone does.

When she gets back to her gold-leafed room in the Foreign Office there is a Security reception to see her. Three grey unsmiling men stand beside the dark green tin cupboard in the bathroom. It has been sealed with a blob of red sealing wax the size of a dinner plate, solemnly imprinted with the Foreign Office seal.

'But there was nothing secret in there,' says Jocelyn.

'That is beside the point,' they say.

Jocelyn loses her job. They are sorry to see her go, for seldom has someone worked so hard for so little money, but the rules are the rules.

Philip, always the gentleman, offers to marry her.

7

Scarlet Shows Off

Byzantia's first birthday falls on a Sunday. Driven by anger, rather than by family feeling, Scarlet takes her child and once again visits Kim and Susan. She does not telephone first. She wants it to be a nice surprise.

Kim is not at home, and in her heart she is glad. But Susan and Simeon are there, suitably unprotected.

Byzantia is dark, grubby and bright. Scarlet has dressed her in her shabbiest, most-washed clothes. Byzantia dribbles constantly – she is teething – and her nose runs a lot so that there is one sore reddish patch around her mouth, but in spite of all, Byzantia is beautiful. She is walking well, too.

Scarlet is glad to see that Simeon, in her eyes a withdrawn and stodgy child, still only crawls. Byzantia has at least a few words to offer the world. Simeon has no desire to converse with anyone. He likes his meals at precise intervals, and his sleeping times to be regular, and that is the sum of his present desire. If his routine is not strictly kept, he is fretful and troublesome. He does not like strange places. He does not like other people. Thus Simeon holds Susan prisoner. She is resigned to her captivity. She devotes her life to looking after him. If Kim wants to go out she says, 'You know what he's like with baby-sitters.' If Kim wants to make love she says, 'No, Simeon always wakes up at the wrong moment.' If Kim wants to hold his baby and bounce him, she says, 'No. You'll overexcite him and he'll be sick.'

Susan is not happy but she has the consolation of feeling she is in the right. It would be difficult to fault her, and she knows it. She keeps the flat beautifully: she dresses neatly; she cooks from a cookery book and not from memory; she keeps strange cats, strange dogs, strange people, strange germs at bay. These days she does not wander in her secret forests, she has forgotten them. She is the chained magpie. 'Go on out,' she screams in her soul, and wakes in the night with an angry fluttering of black wings about her.

She doesn't smile much, and she blinks rather a lot. She knows, but she cannot feel, that Kim has a right to share her child, her bed, her home, her life. She wants to push him out, and would be shocked at the very notion.

Watson and Belcher, Practitioners in Advertising, are prospering, which is as well for Kim, since surely he deserves some pleasure in life. Their offices now occupy six rooms. There is a creative staff of four, led by Kim. He has to work late, and many of his weekends are spent at the office. He refers to his young wife and baby son with affection, and shows photographs of them to his friends in the pub, but rather as if he had to keep reminding himself that they do indeed exist.

He does not send money to Scarlet. He suggested once to Susan that perhaps he should, but she grew pink in the face and said that if there was any money to spare it should surely go into an Education Policy for Simeon. He agreed with her. He is aware that her distrust of him was born when he took Scarlet in and talked to Wanda, and he feels bad about it.

His secretary, Alison, however, attracts and distracts him from such dismal thoughts. He devotes much of his emotional energy trying to come to intimate terms with her, without Susan's father knowing. Not so much because Susan is his daughter – Mr Watson has his own fairly public diversion, a pleasant young designer he first took up with in the Ministry of Food when his wife was in New Zealand and can hardly point a censorious finger – but because this Alison of his is over forty and plain, and Kim feels he has a reputation to keep up.

He cannot bear, these days, to be alone, idle or sober for long.

Scarlet drinks the lemon tea which Susan, with barely disguised reluctance, offers her. Byzantia and Simeon sit on the floor and stare at each other.

'Working weekends, is he?' says Scarlet. 'He must be raking it in.' She's as crude and brash as she can be.

'No,' says Susan firmly. 'The agency is going through a tricky time. It's very new, remember.'

'You understand financial matters, do you?' says Scarlet, who does, or at any rate could if she put her mind to it, which she won't. She likes to believe that Susan is not only ill-educated, but stupid. Susan does not reply. Byzantia hits Simeon. Simeon looks bewildered. Susan picks him up protectively.

'So you called him Simeon, did you,' remarks Scarlet. 'Uncle Simeon. Well, it has a dignified ring. They're just about exactly the same age, aren't they?'

Byzantia walks over to her mother and holds out her arms to be picked up. Scarlet obliges. Scarlet knows she is behaving badly, but she can't stop herself. She is almost physically conscious of the knot of resentment in her chest.

'I see you have a new carpet,' says Scarlet. 'Didn't you like the colour of the other one or something?'

'No,' says Susan, who is beginning to feel angry. 'I didn't.'

'What did you do with the old one? Give it to the poor?'

'I gave it to the dustmen, if you want to know.'

'Can Byzantia have a biscuit or something?' asks Scarlet.

'I'd rather she didn't,' says Susan coolly. 'Simeon will see and want one too, and I don't let him eat between meals.'

Scarlet looks at Simeon with obvious pity.

'Poor little Simeon,' she actually says. Susan sits very upright. She is flushed.

'Actually,' says Scarlet, 'I clean a carpet like this every day. I go out cleaning when Wanda comes back from school.'

'Cleaning other people's homes must be quite interesting,' says Susan eventually. She is taken aback. She sees Scarlet as a lifetime's burden.

'It isn't,' says Scarlet. 'But what else can I do? There's no one to help me. I'm quite alone.'

Susan curls Simeon's hair into a quiff. She smiles at him.

'Perhaps,' Susan observes, 'you should have thought of that before. I mean, what did you expect to happen? If you have an illegitimate child it isn't easy, is it?'

Scarlet doesn't reply at first. She too is pink.

'Tell you what,' she says eventually. 'If I came and cleaned for you and my father, you might pay me a shilling or so above market rates.'

'We have a daily help already,' says Susan stiffly.

Scarlet laughs.

'I was only joking,' she says. But of course she isn't. She wants nothing for herself. She is anxious for Byzantia. She is always anxious, these days. Anxious when Byzantia cries, when she has a cold in the nose; paralysed with fear if she runs a temperature; nervous of asking Wanda to baby-sit; alarmed by her own irritation with Byzantia's grizzles, nappies, fads and habits; terrified (though why should she be?) lest Wanda turn her out and she is left homeless and helpless. She does not feel twenty-one, she feels as old and battered as the hills of the moon.

Like Jocelyn, she wants to be married. But she is moved by desperation, not ambition. She wants security and respectability. She wants to be looked after. She is tired of being pitied. She wants her dignity back. But who would want to marry Scarlet? She is a mess; she knows it now. Over-weight, spotty, untidy, angry; there is only one thing to be said for her, and that is her devotion to Byzantia, her burden.

'If I was pretty and smart,' she says suddenly, 'my father would acknowledge me.'

'He does acknowledge you,' says Susan, embarrassed. 'He just can't afford to keep you. Frankly, I don't think he sees why he should. Wanda behaved very badly.'

'But I'm me. I'm nothing to do with Wanda.'

'To him you are. You had years when you could have got in

touch with him. But coming only when you want something from him ...'

'Please try and explain to him –' but Scarlet's voice fades away. She knows it is no use.

'See him yourself,' says Susan.

'No,' says Scarlet. She has not the heart. Her father, to be frank, frightens and embarrasses her. She is not accustomed to the company of men.

'Can't the baby's father help?' enquires Susan. Scarlet shakes her head. It has at last occurred to her that from Byzantia's point of view any father is better than none. She has tried to get in touch with the young man responsible, but he has left his bed-sitting room leaving no address – or at any rate none which is available to sad-voiced females.

She, once so indifferent, now searches Byzantia's unformed features for traces of this young man; who once took a girl called Scarlet Rider home from a party, spent four hours in bed with her, and then rose, and shaved, and put on a tie, and went to spend Sunday with his fiancée's parents.

Not that Scarlet wants him now, not really. Scarlet wants no interference. Scarlet will be father and mother both to her incestuous child – for let there be no mistake about it, and to quote her lady analyst years later, Scarlet, all unknowing, wanted her father's child. And that is why, in this particular version of events, she is bashful of Kim, and is frightened of Wanda, and why she must now quarrel with Susan on anniversaries.

She is hardly being reasonable.

She is causing trouble to everyone.

No one loves her, not even Wanda, who is bored and tired. Only Byzantia looks at her with pure love in her eyes.

Scarlet snatches up Byzantia and rushes away. Byzantia lets herself be startled and does not complain. Simeon, subjected to similar stress, screams with fright. Scarlet allows herself a second in which she can be seen to sneer. They do not meet again for years.

Down here among the women, there is a sour and grim reality about money as Wanda points out.

So, you choose your degradation, as Scarlet does, and go out scrubbing. So, you lose your purse in Woolworth's because you want to lose your mother. But you get paid money for scrubbing, and if you leave your purse in Woolworth's you can't pay the rent. The bailiffs either come and put you on the streets, or they don't.

Scarlet worries about money. Scarlet's fear is that the State will step in and take away Byzantia, her unlawful child. So, it is free-floating anxiety. So, the Council Homes are full of children whom Children's Officers feel better qualified than any natural mother to care for.

Perhaps they are right, thinks Scarlet, staring with despair at Byzantia, as the child shrieks and stamps with joy upon the floor, and the people in the flat below bang with a broom upon their ceiling, and Scarlet, paralysed with depression, knows that presently she will have to confess to Wanda that it has happened again; and even worse, go down and face them and apologize.

If the people in the flat below complain to the Estate Agents, Scarlet and Byzantia will have to go. There is a 'no baby' clause in the lease. And where else will they find to live? Scarlet comes out in spots.

Wanda had the same concerns years and years ago. They bore her now. She looks at her spotty and apathetic daughter, and laments the waste of her own youth, spent nurturing a child who has grown up no better than she.

'The thing about having babies,' she says sourly, 'is that you can't. All you ever have is just more people.' And from the sound of it she doesn't much like people.

All the same, when Scarlet isn't looking, Wanda croons to Byzantia, and weaves magic to make her smile, and be content, and good. She is better with Byzantia than Scarlet is; but then of course Byzantia expects more of Scarlet, seeing her mother as an extra limb which will do her bidding, and becoming frustrated and furious when it fails to live up to her expectations, or shows it has a will and purpose of its own.

Wanda earns £10 a week. She worries less about poverty than her daughter, having spent longer with it, and moreover she does not have her daughter's capacity for running up debts. The rent is £3 5s. 0d. £3 goes on food. Byzantia, one way and another, costs another £1 a week. Other household expenses, including fares, heating, light and hot water come to £4 a week.

Scarlet, working as a cleaner, earns £2 10s. 0d. a week.

There is 25/- a week left over for the three of them, after necessities have been met. This ought to be enough, except that Scarlet, to her mother's rage, will buy lipstick, cigarettes, toys for Byzantia; and Wanda, to Scarlet's rage, will buy rum.

Wanda has taken to drink. She has discovered its pleasures

late in life. She cannot afford to buy much, but she goes to pubs, leans against bars, and men buy her drinks. She is at her best in pubs. She looks battered, used, available and lively, and in no way a source of reproach, being normally in worse condition than her drinking companions. She builds up quite a pub life. Scarlet is horrified.

'And you a primary school teacher,' she says. 'You'll lose your job if you're not careful.'

'You can be as drunk as you like,' Wanda claims. 'What they can't stand is politics.' And she adds gloomily, to frighten Scarlet, 'Wait until they catch up with that.'

She is right. Teachers with communist pasts are suspect. Some have already lost their jobs. Supposing they subvert the children? Or indicate that all might not be well with the world? It is not so much political opinion that is feared, as the spirit of restlessness. No one mocks, in 1951. Stalin is not yet dead.

Wanda is horrified by the way Scarlet goes to parties in a low-cut black sweater and does not return till morning, dusty, tired and bitter.

'Like a cat on the tiles,' she complains.

'I thought you were all for sexual freedom,' says Scarlet.

'Not for mothers,' says Wanda. 'You've had your fling. You should be at home looking after your brat. How can I keep working if I have to get up at two, three, four and five o'clock in the morning?'

It is true. Byzantia has stopped sleeping through the night. She needs entertainment at more frequent intervals than she does food. She will cry as if pierced by a nappy pin or threatened by a rat until the light goes on and a face appears. Then she will giggle, gurgle and rejoice; and only cry again when the face goes away and darkness returns.

'You grudge me my pleasures,' says Scarlet. 'How am I supposed ever to get married if I have to stay at home in this dreary flat? It's not as if I could ask anyone home. I'd be ashamed.'

'Pleasure!' says Wanda, who observes that Scarlet's all-night absences merely increase her depression.

'You think sex is dirty and nasty,' says Scarlet. 'You try not to but you can't help it. That's why you're always so crude. It isn't honesty and frankness, it's sheer terror.'

'I don't think sex is dirty and nasty,' replies Wanda, quick as a flash, 'I think you are.'

And it is true that Scarlet begins to feel ingrained, though not so much with dirt as with despair. When she's not thinking she wants a husband, she's thinking she needs true love.

Alas, neither seems available – she herself is the only thing which is. There are more than enough men to go to bed with – and each one she hopes, will fall in love with her and save her. She feels she has a great deal to offer. She opens her heart and her soul when she opens her legs; but alas, only the latter are of practical use, and men, she decides in the end – experience reinforcing Wanda's training – are only interested in practical matters.

'The awful thing is,' she says to Helen, who drops by one day to visit, 'if I was morally corrupt, if I was a calculating person, if I played men like fish on a line, if I had had an abortion instead of Byzantia, if I was cold, hard and unfriendly – then I would be pursued by men.'

'To be pursued by men,' says Helen, casting Scarlet down

to depths from which it takes her years to emerge, 'you have to be beautiful.'

Helen is both sorry for and irritated by Scarlet. Helen lines her love-nest with silks and downs, plucks the hairs from her legs one by one, learns poetry like a child, and entertains her lover. Y pays the rent, and never calls.

Scarlet, messing about with old saucepans on an ancient gas stove, serving coffee in cracked mugs, seems to Helen to have abandoned youth, hope and beauty. Scarlet, Helen thinks, can sink no lower. Little does Helen know.

Jocelyn is giving an engagement party. Scarlet is asked. Scarlet assumes she will be able to go because it is on a Sunday evening, which is the day Wanda holds her Divorcées Anonymous meetings. Thus Byzantia can be safely left at home. On Sunday evening she is disconcerted to see Wanda putting on the brooch which is her one concession to dressing up for an outing.

'Are you going out?' she says.

'Yes,' says Wanda.

'Where?'

'Is that your concern?'

'But it's the lady divorcées' meeting.'

'We're holding it in the pub,' says Wanda smugly.

'But I'm going to a party,' wails Scarlet.

'You're not,' says Wanda. 'You're going to stay home and look after your baby.'

Scarlet is in despair.

'They'll hate it in the pub,' she claims.

'Why? They say they want men. Pubs are full of men.

Drunk, red-nosed, miserable men in old creased trousers, married mostly. Impotent, crude, greasy-necked, smelly, stupid men with swollen bellies – you can hear the beer swilling in their stomachs when they walk, did you know? Let alone when they try to copulate – but men, none the less. They say they want men. Men they shall have.'

Wanda is irritated by her ladies. She has tried to indicate to them that life without men is possible, even desirable, for women past child-bearing age, and that in fact the sum of human happiness and achievement would be increased by apartheid between the sexes, but still they persist in longing for the company of men; reject lesbianism as a solution to sexual frustration, curl their hair, put on lipstick, and try to look younger than they are. Why? Because they can only seem to exist in relationship with men. Wanda takes them to the pub to punish them and to be disagreeable to her daughter.

'You should have told me,' says Scarlet.

'What, that you want a cheap baby-sitter?'

'You knew I was going out.'

'I did not. You didn't ask me.'

'But the card's been on the mantelpiece for weeks.'

'A card! What kind of party is it you get asked to by a card? What a funny girl this Jocelyn of yours must be. Does she wear a twin-set and pearls?'

'She's a bit dull,' says Scarlet, 'but she likes to do things the proper way. And what's more, she asked me.'

'Why, is she sorry for you?' asks Wanda.

'Yes,' says Scarlet, 'she is. She is very sorry for me because I have to live with you.'

And she stomps off. The relationship between them deteriorates still further. The evening at the pub is disastrous. The membership is embarrassed, leaves early, and thereafter loses its trust in Wanda. Only Lottie remains.

'They don't really even want men,' says Wanda in disgust, but cheered because her point is proved. 'All they want is status. They want to have men to tote round on leads. They're not unhappy because they've lost their husbands. They're just peeved. How I do despise women.'

'Shall we dress up as men?' enquires Lottie. 'I've got so thin lately I'm sure I'd pass. And as for you –' she stops.

'I've always been half a man,' says Wanda. 'I know. Well, I wish to God I had a wife to clear up after me, that's all.'

They don't dress up as men, of course. Something in them revolts. What? Men's underpants? Men's trousers? And the more intimate the two of them become, emotionally, the more careful they are never, never, to touch one another. Wanda speaks badly of Lottie behind her back, but is in fact devoted to her.

Scarlet gets the better of Wanda by taking Byzantia with her to the party. That means she can't go home with a man, and has to get the last Underground train home, with a grizzling baby in her arms. She has a sudden panic fear that she will be reported to the Child Welfare Officer for having a child out at such an hour. She almost wishes now that it will happen. She feels she cannot go on. The craving to live her own life is so strong she imagines she cannot act reasonably any more. She is frightened of damaging Byzantia.

116

Jocelyn's engagement party is remembered for its dullness. Philip has asked his young executive friends, who only talk of cars and salaries. Helen is ashamed to expose her artistic friends to such a bourgeois gathering, and doesn't even come herself, let alone ask anyone else. Sylvia brings a group of middle-aged Sales and Research Directors, who drink too much and go round fondling the bosoms of the girls, who are respectable in low-cut, tiny-waisted, full dresses, with hair swept back from the face and well curled. Audrey is in Suffolk with Paul and can't come up – or, as rumour has it, isn't allowed to. Scarlet, of course, brings her baby, which cries, and depresses the young men with a vision of their future.

Fatherhood is not yet fashionable. Men are not present at the births of their children, if they can possibly help it. They do not shop, push prams, design the home. Marriage to the unmarried male is a trap, and sex the bait, which by stealth and cunning may yet be won. Poor passive outnumbering middle-class girls do indeed manoeuvre, lure, plot and entice in order to bring men to the altar. Not, of course, Scarlet, 'Look through the surface of me into my soul,' she begs of all comers, 'see what's there! See how I can love, feel, respond, love, oh love. If you will just accept –' But why should they bother? Why take the trouble to inspect a dismal soul when there are a myriad glittering surfaces to attend to? Scarlet's surface does not glitter. Even her low-cut black sweater is dusty: her shoulder-straps dirty.

Philip cannot stand her, or so he tells Jocelyn. He disapproves of their friendship. Jocelyn – although she sleeps with

117

him on Saturday nights, which he is prepared to overlook – is good wife material, a virgin at heart if not in fact. Scarlet is just a slut.

Yet he drifts over to talk to her. He tells himself it is because she is Mr Belcher's daughter – although he must know that a good word put in for him by Scarlet would do him no end of harm.

She baffles him. She speaks well. She seems to come from the middle-classes; why then does she live the way she does?

'All your men friends are sorry for you,' observes Scarlet.

'Why?' he asks, taken aback.

'Entering your life-long prison,' says Scarlet. 'Marriage. You're the first to go.' She puts on a Welsh voice. 'Getting married and not pregnant? There's posh for you!'

'They're just envious,' he says.

'No, they're not.' What an uncomfortable person she is.

'Of course they are,' Philip insists. 'And why not? I'm going to get my meals cooked, aren't I? Clothes washed. Housework done. The days of discomfort are over.'

'Is that why you're getting married?' she asks. 'Shall I tell Jocelyn?'

'Are you a mischief-maker as well?' he asks.

'As well as what?'

He doesn't reply. He smiles, he looks her up and down in a way he has never regarded Jocelyn. Clean, fastidious, well-mothered as he is, she attracts him. She is, in his eyes, delightfully degraded.

'I've got to get a good job,' she says. 'I've got to earn lots of money, that's the only way out. Do you know of any?'

'I know a night-club where you could be a cigarette girl,' he says.

'Don't be silly,' she says. 'Me? Look, I've got a brain. I got to University.'

In his mind he undresses her, baths her, curls her hair, dresses her in long lace stockings, high heels, black corsets, slings a tray beneath her bosom and sends her out selling cigarettes to the rich and lascivious. His fantasies take him no further. His mother steps in, even here, good, smiling, pure and kind, and makes him feel ashamed. He's only just kept his mother away from this party by the skin of his teeth. It is fortunate that his mother likes Jocelyn. Or is his mother just being good, smiling, pure, kind and polite yet again?

Scarlet, bored by his silence, which she takes for obtuseness, wanders off, and talks to Sylvia.

'There are two sides to Jocelyn,' she complains. 'There's the conventional side and the human side, and I'm afraid the wrong one is winning. Bed's one thing, but marriage! He'll be playing golf on Sundays any minute now.'

'There is nothing wrong with sport,' says Sylvia vaguely. There is a little frown between her eyes. Jocelyn and Philip are going to share the flat. She will, she supposes, have to leave, although it hasn't been mentioned by the other two. She doesn't want to think about it. She is, in any case, drinking with Philip's friend Butch, who is six foot three inches, plays Rugby and works in the sales department of a vacuum cleaning firm. He enjoys her misty-eyed delicacy; and fills her up with gin and bitter lemon. And now she speaks well of sport, which she has been accustomed to despising.

119

Butch has a wife, but a disagreeable one. He has had to leave her. He weeps. Sylvia is sad on his behalf. She likes his simplicity. Later on, in bed, she tells him things she has never told anyone else, and barely acknowledges herself. She tells him how she loved a boy at fifteen, and let herself be seduced, and became pregnant, and how her mother took her out of her English literature lesson to have an abortion. She wets his shoulder with her tears, and he comforts her in his lumbering way. 'If I found that boy,' he says, 'I'd beat his brains out.'

'It wasn't like that,' she pleads. 'It wasn't his fault. It wasn't anyone's fault. It was just something awful that happened.'

'I'd cut his balls off,' Butch insists. He was born Christopher but is always known as Butch. He is more subtle in his lovemaking than seems likely. He has discovered, all by himself in a world not yet acclimatized to it, the pleasures of oral sex. In the morning they don't want to leave each other: sit with bodies touching, he such a lumberer, she so delicate.

Philip nobly warns Butch against Sylvia. She's fine for an easy lay, he claims, but not the sort to get entangled with. Her morals are weak, along with her eyesight and her hearing. He is glad when Butch sweeps away the warning. It will be easier now to ask Sylvia to leave.

'She's been a bit upset,' Butch says. 'She's had a bad start. She's going to be all right now.'

After the engagement party, Philip gives a stag party. His father offers to pay. Philip's parents are shadowy figures, even to their son. Philip's father is gruffly amiable and waves a cheque book to prove his good intent. Philip sees his mother more often in his fantasies than he does in life: she appears ladylike in flowered prints, to damp his ardour and spoil his concentration, and make him feel guilty. In real life she runs the W.I., does Church work, and is always calm and good. He has only once seen her cry. That was when he was sent away to school to be made a man of.

Philip, made a man of, now gives a stag party. Philip goes to an agency and orders a stripper to add gaiety to the occasion. The agency takes his money but the girl does not turn up. Philip is relieved. The mechanics of the matter have played upon his mind since he made the arrangement. He will have to open the door to this girl, give her instructions, pay her, send her home. How, in a taxi? Supposing she is elderly, scraggy and unpleasant? Expects more than money? Is one of his friend's sisters? (There is a high-class brothel in South Ken, so they say, where girls from high-class families turn the odd penny. A Guards' Officer is reputed to have been shown into the room where his sister lay waiting, naked on the bed. 'Why, Amanda, old girl!' 'Why, Jonathan, old chap!')

No, the idea of a stripper is far, far preferable to the actuality.

After the wedding – which takes place in Jocelyn's village church, with all the trimmings she wished for, except her mother did not cry and her father's voice was not hoarse, but at least it was too far away for her friends to attend – Philip gets more and more angry with the agency, which he feels has got money from him on false pretences. He threatens to sue. The agency maintain his complaint is against the girl. He sends her a solicitor's letter, asking for his money back.

Jocelyn, casually informed, is aghast. First that he should

have wished to employ a stripper; then that he should seek vengeance. He tries to explain.

'But it was my stag party,' he says, smiling in his remote masculine may. 'My last fling as a bachelor. I wouldn't do it now.'

'You're not a different person,' she says, 'just because you're married.'

'No, but I've got to behave now,' he says. He thinks he is pleasing her. She doesn't look pleased.

'But what's the point of watching a strange girl take her clothes off?' persists poor innocent Jocelyn. 'I'll take my clothes off for you.'

After hockey she and the girls would strip and shower. She was never shy. She always enjoyed her body.

'Take them off then,' he says, conventionally, but of course she won't. She is offended by the mysteries attendant upon his desires.

'And you shouldn't be so vengeful,' she complains. 'I don't understand what is the matter with you.' And she doesn't, and neither does he.

'We need every penny we can get,' he ventures. It is true. They have overspent his income and some of Jocelyn's capital. They have had the flat painted, and furnished after the style made fashionable by the 1951 exhibition. Jocelyn stalks over green and yellow carpets, wonders why Philip still only makes love on Saturday nights, and then so languidly, and is put in mind – for no reason she can think of other than a general feeling of depression – of Scarlet's mother's green and yellow lino. The curtains are brown and yellow; the ceilings pink and the wallpaper patterned with orange geometric designs. Can this be what she meant by it all? Is this the feel, the heart, the texture of married life? She hasn't the heart to write to Miss Bonny. It even crosses her mind that she could join a team and play hockey on Saturday afternoons while Philip plays Rugby, but she knows in her heart that those times are past, those sources of solace unavailable.

'Do you think it's because he plays Rugby that he always seems tired on Saturday nights?' she asks Helen.

'If he didn't play Rugby on Saturdays,' says Helen, 'I doubt you would have the opportunity of knowing whether he was tired or not.'

Jocelyn looks at her blankly.

'It's those Rugby songs,' says Helen, 'they get him going. And he needs something, I'm afraid.'

Jocelyn is quite pale.

'They're so horrid,' she complains. 'There's no *feeling* in them. I never listen.'

'If you want feeling,' says Helen, smugly, 'you must take up with an artist. The only whole men in the world are the artists.'

Helen lives a strange and isolated life in the studio where X works by night and which Y pays for. X keeps his liaison with Helen sporadically secret. He assumes both that Y must surely know about it, and that his friends don't. In fact, of course, he is wrong on both counts. Both X and Y wonder, on the rare evenings when Helen joins them for supper, why their friends are now so rude to her.

X does not like strangers in the studio, so Helen has either to entertain secretly or not at all. She is driven more and more into the company of Jocelyn, Sylvia and Scarlet, with none of whom, these days, she has much in common. She does have the pleasure, however, of having her opinion asked, and she thrives in the golden glow of sexual reputation. She is idle. She writes poetry, goes to poetry readings, tends her little home, and waits for X. She grows riotous pot plants. She waxes white and odalisque-like. X spends some four nights a week with Helen, some three with Y, which is surely a victory for Helen.

He is working well. Y, after the interlude of her prize and a patch of acclaim, has fallen into a trough of non-appreciation. But she is glad that X is working well. The studio was a good idea. She suspects he has girls there from time to time, but does not wish to know for sure. At any rate, he is happy.

Y is grateful to Helen for having helped her improve her life. Helen calls sometimes in the afternoons – when she knows X is out teaching, Y notices – and they drink coffee, talk about men in general and X in particular, and Helen will help put the children to bed. Y is defeated by, and X uninterested in, his children. X tried to paint them once but couldn't catch their essence. And although he had fed them phenobarb to keep them still, they would wriggle. Nothing will stop them wriggling or grizzling. Not threats, shouts, bribes, smiles or drugs.

'You must take a lover,' says Helen to Jocelyn now. 'An artist or a poet. I'll see what I can do. These are the worthwhile men.'

Jocelyn is indignant. She regrets having confided her difficulty to Helen. She feels she has been unloyal to Philip.

Next time Helen rings she is abrupt and unwelcoming, and Helen does not ring again for quite a time.

Jocelyn opens her account at Harrods, and overspends wildly. She buys hoop earrings in solid gold which everyone takes for tin.

There is no answer from the stripper to Philip's letter demanding the return of his ten guineas. Just a rude, humiliating silence. Philip broods. He feels his friends are watching and waiting for him to resolve the situation.

One Saturday night, after a hard afternoon's Rugby playing and two inflammatory hours in the pub, Philip takes a taxi to the girl's flat, instead of home to Jocelyn, to exact payment in kind.

'You can't be made a fool of by a whore,' Butch had said to him in the changing-room that afternoon, when they were both slippery with soap and sweat and seemed to be sharing a moment of truth and intimacy. 'It's the kind of thing you remember all your life.'

So now Philip bangs and crashes at her door. The girl, who is neither scraggy, elderly, nor his best friend's sister, but plump, young and badly spoken, allows him in and concedes victory. Philip acquits himself well enough, but has the feeling she is laughing at him. He slaps her around a little.

Philip returns to Jocelyn confused and depressed. He tells her all about it and asks to be forgiven.

'I forgive you,' she says (what else can she do? She has been married a month), and sits on the floor by the gas fire while Philip snores off into a healing sleep on the sofa. She cries a little, but not much, and for her situation rather than for

Philip's infidelity, which seems, now it has happened, to have a cosmic inevitability. She has always expected the world, if not to betray her, certainly to ignore her plea for happiness. Youth had perhaps blinded her to the truth for a year or so; now she is back to a more pertinent vision of reality. The gas fire is faulty. It pops and plops, and one jet burns blue and tiny, instead of golden and powerful. Jocelyn turns the gas off at the main tap in the kitchen, and cleans the jets. When she is next in the kitchen, she turns the main gas tap on again, but forgets that she has not turned off the fire itself, until the cat, asleep on top of the bookcase as is its habit, moans and falls off, unconscious.

There is very nearly a nasty accident. Jocelyn's life is full of them.

Philip tells the story for years, of how the cat fell off the bookcase and saved his life.

Next Saturday he plays Rugby with more than normal violence, and cracks Butch on the side of his head with his heavy boots. Butch is concussed, and when he is out of hospital, Sylvia has to move into his flat to nurse him.

This suits both Butch and Sylvia. They lie wrapped in each other's arms, afraid to move for fear of aggravating Butch's injuries. Their passion, thus repressed, becomes transmuted into a golden glow of love, which stands them in good stead if not for years, at least for months.

Jocelyn, forgiving, and Philip, forgiven, resume their married life. They are polite to each other, and kind, and perhaps a little embarrassed by the intimacies of married life. Jocelyn finds she is more bashful of her body than she had ever believed possible, and undresses in the bathroom. He, so happy, soapy and naked, amongst men, presently does the same. He is a considerate and loyal husband. He and Butch are never to play Rugby together again. By the time Butch is fit and back in the field, Philip has given up. He takes up tennis instead, so that he and Jocelyn can take their Saturday sport together. They take it in unspoken turns to win.

Presently Philip is made Group Executive at the fast expanding Watson and Belcher, and presently, when the bedroom is redesigned, sleeps in one of the twin beds. There was almost an embarrassing moment when the change from the double bed was made, and almost a spoken protest from Jocelyn, but the moment passed. Philip takes care to join Jocelyn in the other bed at least once a month, and more often, sometimes, if he has taken a client to a blue film or a strip club, and the memory still looms in his mind.

Jocelyn, out of kindness to her husband, trains herself in sexual disinterest, even distaste. Presently she is apologizing to the world for her frigidity.

She strips the Festival papers from the walls, distempers them pure white, and begins to buy antiques. She is proud of her home. She gives coffee mornings; has some nice lady friends, all with accounts at Harrods. Still she does not write to Miss Bonny, although she hears that Miss Bonny now lives in a little cottage in Westmorland, which she shares with Miss Tippin, Jocelyn's Classics teacher.

Stalin dies. Jocelyn thinks of the office, and wonders what horrors they will live off now their demon has gone. She considers going back to work, but Philip is not enthusiastic.

Monthly, Philip and Jocelyn drive to visit one or the other sets of in-laws. The young couple stay overnight in twin-bedded spare rooms which, in both houses, are remarkably similar. They have pink bedside lamps, twin beds, and chintzy curtains, and look out over well-kept flower gardens. Philip's father nudges him in the ribs and asks about the strip clubs; Philip's mother offers Jocelyn pot-plants and noticeably refrains from asking why Jocelyn is not pregnant.

Jocelyn's parents say practically nothing.

Jocelyn writes to Miss Bonny, and tears it up. She never liked Miss Tippin. Hockey one, hockey two, hockey three and away! Sunny winter afternoons, the ground still crisp and crackly with frost, the edges of the park misty. Is it all then to come to nothing more than this?

She becomes rather thin. 'She will ruin her life if she goes on like this,' writes Audrey to Sylvia, signing herself Emma, 'she can talk of nothing but hairdressers and hats.' They should move to the country, Audrey-Emma maintains. Philip should give up advertising before his soul rots completely away. How can people hope to be happy while they live such unnatural anti-social lives? Audrey-Emma is sure, moreover, that Jocelyn and Philip drink too much coffee, which everyone knows is bad for the liver.

Sylvia won't be drawn. 'I don't see much of Jocelyn and Philip these days,' she writes. 'We live rather far out.' In fact Butch has finally quarrelled with Philip – having no patience with a man who opts out of Rugby in order to play tennis with his wife – and makes it difficult for Sylvia to maintain the friendship. Sylvia feels tired and ill. She is pregnant, and Butch is not happy with what he sees as her bloated and perverted shape. He calls her 'fatty' in public, and marvels to friends and pub acquaintances at her increasing size. Butch's divorce is going to be long, costly and complicated. He and Sylvia now have a tiny little rented house in Dulwich; it is hard to keep going financially because Butch's wife's solicitors have insisted on interim alimony of a third of his salary at the vacuum cleaning firm.

Sylvia does editorial work at home for an accountancy journal. She has to struggle to understand its contents, and is pale from strain and boredom. But they do have a television set – the BBC broadcasts live shows in the evenings. It has an eight-inch screen. Sylvia does not like television much, but Butch waits anxiously for the programmes to begin. They do not have much conversation these days, and something has to sop up the silence.

129

8

Scarlet Goes to Market

Down here among the women.

I have company on my park bench. Two young girls collapse, all giggles, next to me. They plonk down the parcels and ease their feet out of their boots. They are friends, and look alike. They have the same slight bodies, long straight hair, round fleshy faces, docile eyes and unhealthy skin. They are animated and happy. They look at me out of the corners of their slidy eyes, as if they expect me to slap them down. Why should I? I like them.

One is getting married. She has the bridesmaids' dresses in a carrier bag. They are yellow see-through.

'That'll give the priest something to think about,' she says, with satisfaction.

They chatter. They gasp and squeak. The bride is pregnant and glad to be. Her only worry is lest her wedding dress doesn't fit on the day. They talk of the ceremony, the reception, the clothes, the presents. They talk of everything and everyone except the groom. Oh, blessed pair.

In ten years' time – no, don't think of it. The tower block

where I live is full of women who were once girls like this, now off to Bingo, desperate, with their children left locked up; pale, worried and ageing badly; without the spirit any more even to tuck a free-gift plastic daffodil behind the ear.

At least the priest accords them a soul. At least like Mayflies they have their brief dance in the sun before they go down into the darkness.

They gather up their parcels, wriggle back into their boots, eye me with a certain curious friendliness – they don't understand why I sit by myself, quiet and respectable, without a friend – and pass on into their future.

I sit on my park bench and cry for all the women in the world.

I think perhaps we are in the throes of an evolutionary struggle which we must all endure, while we turn, willy-nilly, into something strange and marvellous. We gasp and struggle for breath, with painful lungs, like the creatures who first crawled out of the sea and lived on land.

The sun comes out. An old woman, a felt hat on top, and black Wellingtons below, passes by and laughs into the wind, and proves me wrong. Her face is ruddy, lean and cheerful. She seems to be what nature intended. But I do not think Byzantia will look like that when she is seventy-five.

I cry for my own malice, cruelty, self-deception and stupidity.

The children come up. 'What's the matter?' they ask. 'The wind in my eyes,' I say. 'Shall we go home?' I ask. 'No,' they say. 'Not yet.'

Where did we leave Wanda and Scarlet? Back in the early days and on bad terms, aggravated by Byzantia's wakefulness.

Wanda is antagonistic to the world. Scarlet is fat and spotty. Byzantia is teething.

But rescue is at hand.

Wanda has a boyfriend.

There has been trouble with the Education Office. Wanda's job is in jeopardy. Not, as she had predicted, because of her political past, but because she explained to a class of nine-year-olds how babies are born. She has drawn a diagram on the board. Parents have complained. The press has become involved. The fact that Scarlet is an unmarried mother is cited in anonymous letters to the local Education Authority as proof of Wanda's unfitness for teacherhood.

'They are quite right,' says Scarlet. 'You aren't fit. Anyway, why should children know the truth when it's all so revolting? I would far rather believe I came out of a doctor's black bag than out of you.'

'Go and live with your father,' says Wanda. 'I don't want you.' It is her normal retort when Scarlet goes too far, and can be relied upon to silence her daughter.

Wanda's boyfriend is a Schools Inspector who has been delegated to investigate the incident. He is a tall, pleasant-faced, rabbit-mouthed, stooping man, with flabby scarecrow trousers and pockets full, Scarlet feels, of string and white mice. He is a stamp collector, and plays the spinet. His wife has left him recently. She has run off with another man.

He shows Wanda photographs of his wife. She is not unlike Scarlet to look at, only the spots. Wanda remarks on this, and

Edwin Barker, who is fifty-five, looks at Scarlet with increased interest. He has a semi-detached house in Lee Green, which is an outer London suburb.

Edwin takes Wanda out three Sunday afternoons running. He forgives her for being a divorced woman, for teaching children the facts of life, and for having an unmarried mother for a daughter, but Wanda is not interested in his forgiveness. He takes her to amateur theatrical productions and for rides into the country in his little car, but she is not interested in amateur drama, and can see no merit in countryside for its own sake. He saves her job, and this she does appreciate. On the third Sunday he parks the car and tries to kiss her, but Wanda finds the prospect distasteful and refuses. He is hurt, and bewildered. All the way home he talks about how he was cheated out of £3 10s. 0d. by a stamp dealer.

The next day, Monday, Edwin telephones Scarlet while Wanda is at school and asks her and Byzantia over for the day on the following Sunday. Scarlet accepts, but is frightened to confess to Wanda that she has done so.

Six days of thinking about Skinny Winny – as Wanda refers to him – and fearing Wanda, and she is practically in love with Edwin. Well, there is no one else to attach her feelings to.

On Saturday she is particularly nice to her mother, makes her breakfast in bed, tells her how good she is with Byzantia, offers to sew on her buttons, until Wanda asks her what the matter is. They are very fond of each other, these two; they resist their attachment, circle each other at as great a distance as unkind words can put them, but still must orbit round each other.

'Skinny Winny has asked me and Byzantia over tomorrow,'

Scarlet admits. 'Well, he likes Byzantia, and he doesn't want to lose her, and he knows you can't stand him. So he has to ask me.'

Wanda just laughs.

'He wants a wife,' says Wanda. 'He wants promotion and married men stand a better chance in the rat race than single men do. He resents paying income tax, too, at single rates. He could claim a child allowance on Byzantia. On the salary he's getting now, it would work about the same whether he had my wages coming in, or you and Byzantia to claim as dependants. He worries about things like that. You're a very good bet to a man like him, and he will enjoy forgiving you.'

'You mean you don't mind me going?' Scarlet sounds disappointed.

'Of course not, my dear,' croons Wanda, 'off you go, have a good time. Fuck yourself silly if it's what you want.'

Scarlet is most put out. But she goes. She and Edwin get on well. She makes tea and butters scones. They hold hands. Scarlet likes the comfortable mediocrity of Edwin's home. She likes the thought of the toaster. She likes being forgiven. She likes the way he takes Byzantia upon his knee and plans her future. She likes the fact that he is respectable. She longs for respectability.

Later, she discovers that she likes being seen out with him. People stare. He is so old and thin, and she is so young and fleshy. They are mistaken for father and daughter, until he takes her hand, or puts his sinewy arm round her, and proves otherwise. That amuses her.

She even likes it when he parks the car and kisses her. He is

134

so old. She is conscious of his past, stretching back and back, of the whole great mysterious sum of his existence, now being offered to her through the pressure of his lips.

It is not desire that is stirred, it is her imagination; but how can she know this? She feels she loves him. When she thinks of him kissing her, she is simply enchanted.

No one can understand her.

Edwin calls at the flat every day, nods in a slightly, but only slightly, embarrassed way to Wanda, and continues his wooing of Scarlet. He won't let her go out cleaning any more. Silently, every week he hands her £2 5s. 0d.

Byzantia laughs and chuckles as he bends over her, his faded blue eyes crinkling. He is a kind man. He is an old man. His back is weak – he has mysterious pains in his spine, for which he consults doctor after doctor. Byzantia doesn't know this. She holds out her arms to him. He picks her up and tries not to wince. They love each other: old flappy legs and plump, curly, brilliant Byzantia.

Byzantia will not stay in her cot. She will not go to sleep. She is an exhausting child. Wanda is tired. Wanda is tired of Edwin, tired of Scarlet, tired of life, tired of lifting Byzantia back into her cot while Scarlet and Edwin drive down leafy lanes and kiss in their mis-matched way.

Wanda snaps and snarls. Wanda keeps her children in after school.

Edwin proposes.

Scarlet accepts.

People talk. Kim makes a phone-call to Wanda. 'Don't interfere,' says Wanda. 'Either support her, or keep out of it.

Look, he's a man, he can give her a home. God almighty, I think she loves him.'

Kim keeps out of it.

'She's made her bed,' says Susan, unforgivably. 'Now she'll have to lie on it.' And Susan repairs to her own with a migraine, taking Simeon in beside her, clutching him and moaning in pain. He smiles, thinking she's playing, because it is his time for playing. She hates him, slaps him, and wants her mother. When she remembers that these days it is she who looks after her mother – for Mrs Watson has discovered the existence of Mr Watson's lady friend – Susan cries. She is having a terrible time, and is sorry for herself.

Audrey writes from the country, to give her blessing. She signs herself as Emma, and mentions that the pottery is giving way to a free-range whole-food chicken farm, says marriage is bliss. She is making a patch-work quilt. She will send it to Scarlet for her marriage bed.

She is glad everything has turned out well at last. Children need fathers. (Audrey is six months pregnant, and appears to be rejoicing in her state. Though Jocelyn, visiting her, complains of an atmosphere of chicken feathers, wholemeal bread, and despondency.)

Jocelyn tries to dissuade Scarlet. 'If you marry him,' she says, 'you will become a Lee Green housewife.'

'I will remain myself,' says Scarlet, 'only more comfortable, and without my mother trying to ruin my life.'

'But you don't remain yourself when you marry,' says Jocelyn. 'You take on your husband's level in the world. You take on his status, his income, his friends and his way of life. His class, if you like. You become an aspect of him. It's all right for girls to marry above them, but they should never ever marry below.'

'You are a terrible snob,' says Scarlet.

'Don't be cross,' begs Jocelyn. 'I don't want to see you ruin your life, that's all.'

'It's pretty ruined already,' states Scarlet. 'Anyway, how do you know it's like that? Perhaps I won't take on his way of life. Perhaps he'll take on mine.'

'He's twenty-five years older than you,' says Jocelyn. 'It's not likely, is it?'

'Thirty-two,' says Scarlet smugly, and Jocelyn is shocked. 'Anyway, Byzantia needs a father.'

'But not this one, Scarlet. I'm sure he believes in early potty training and discipline, and shutting children in dark cupboards.'

'Look,' says Scarlet, 'I'm sorry you don't like him –'

'It's not that I don't like him,' pleads Jocelyn. 'It's just he's so unsuitable.'

'He may not be – well, widely cultured, and he's not really interested in abstract matters, but he's kind. And by God, he wears trousers and he wants to marry me.' Scarlet's voice rises to a shriek. Jocelyn keeps a parrot, which begins to squawk in sympathy.

The cat's lungs were weakened after the incident of the gas fire, and it died a few months later. Philip bought her the parrot to cheer her up.

'I can always leave him,' adds Scarlet presently, and Jocelyn is even more shocked. Jocelyn believes marriage is forever.

'I can't go on the way I am,' Scarlet tries to explain. 'Sleeping around. I don't really like it. I've got to settle down. And I am so tired of worrying about money, and the rent, and Wanda, and everything.'

It is a plea for support and understanding but Jocelyn becomes even more remote, icy and disapproving.

'It's all so messy,' is all she'll say. 'You're not going to be happy.'

'Byzantia is,' says Scarlet, pleading mother love. Jocelyn is unmoved. She raises her eyebrows, crooks her little finger and sips tea. She doesn't take sugar. Scarlet does. Jocelyn has put salt in the sugar bowl and forgotten she has done so.

'What would you know about being a mother, anyway?' says Scarlet, when her tea has been emptied down the sink, and a fresh cup poured, and the explanation and apologies are over. Jocelyn sees this remark as an unprovoked attack, and they part on cool terms.

Scarlet asks Jocelyn and Philip to the wedding, but they don't come. Jocelyn gets the date wrong. When they discover the error, they are relieved rather than distressed. Jocelyn does describe Edwin to Philip, and he takes a prurient interest in the union of these two such disparate bodies, but he is really not concerned in Scarlet's fate. In his view, she long ago turned into a slut and opted out of the world of serious people. He hopes her marriage will keep her more out of Jocelyn's way. He does not like to associate with unfortunate people. He fears the ailment may be catching, like measles.

Sylvia is glad that Scarlet is getting married. She sees marriage as a desirable state. Butch's divorce drags on and on. But she won't come to the wedding. She is frightened that Jocelyn will be there. Butch has made up the quarrel with Philip. Now it is Sylvia who hangs back. Butch has expressed recently an unnerving appreciation of Jocelyn's arse – Sylvia finds his language these days, crude. Once she had found it stimulating. She is very thin, and her eyes dark and wide.

Helen simply says of Scarlet, 'She is doing the proper thing. He will be a good father to her.' And of Jocelyn, 'The more frustrated the lady, the more expressive the backside.'

Wanda can hardly bring herself to speak of Scarlet. Was this what she has endured so much privation for? To see her daughter in the hands of this grey and stooping philatelist? To lose Byzantia to the back streets of Lee Green?

In the schools, her reputation goes before her. 'Miss Brown is ill. Miss Rider's coming.' The absentee rate soars. Little children clutch their stomachs and convince their parents they are ill.

Elderly Edwin takes Scarlet to see his even more elderly father, a retired railway worker with a gold watch to prove it. The old man can scarcely see Scarlet, for his eyesight is failing, but what he does see he does not like. He cannot comprehend the existence of Byzantia. He thinks, in his confused way, when they try to explain her, that she is some foreign visitor who refuses to leave.

The wedding arrangements proceed. Edwin cannot understand why Scarlet's father does not pay, since surely the bride's father bears the cost of the wedding? Scarlet begs and pleads with him not to approach Kim, but Edwin does. Edwin writes to Kim asking for £57 10s. 0d. Kim, too astonished to resist, sends a cheque for £50. Edwin refrains from asking again for the £7 10s. 0d., and points out to Scarlet, at length, his generosity and understanding. She believes him.

A slight difficulty arises for Scarlet, however. Edwin, relating after the fashion of lovers the high-spots of his life, tells Scarlet an anecdote of how, as a young man, he and a friend both managed to seduce and make pregnant a farmer's wife – and then left the district. As they had given her false names, the woman had no means of tracing either of them, and thus trouble was avoided. He tells this story as an example of his ingenuity and presence of mind.

Scarlet pushes Byzantia in her pushchair for hours and hours, trying to recover her love for Edwin. Byzantia has holes in her woollen bootees. Her little pink toe pushes through. Even as Scarlet watches, another strand of wool gives, and lo, there is half Byzantia's naked, chilly, infant foot. Scarlet recovers her love for Edwin.

Wedding plans proceed. Edwin takes Scarlet away for a week's holiday. They book into a boarding house on the south coast under a false name – 'Johnson, to make a change from Smith,' explains Edwin. 'We couldn't have gone abroad, you see. They ask for passports.' He is delighted at the subterfuge. It affords him an erotic pleasure, and they make love on the first night they are there. 'The non-event of the year,' Scarlet describes it to Jocelyn years later. But the next day he has bad back pains – the cold sea winds, he supposes – and asks the landlady if they can be transferred to a room with twin beds.

'So I'm not tempted,' he explains to Scarlet.

On the way back to London he stops the car to relieve himself. Scarlet watches his tall grey stooping figure – back carefully to the wind – suffers total revulsion, and knows she is mad. But she won't stop. She won't.

The wedding day comes. It is a dismal affair in a registry office. The Registrar, or so Scarlet likes to think, looks dazed. He is used to marrying rich and vigorous older men to pretty young girls, but Edwin looks like a death's head. Edwin's pain is bad on his wedding day.

Scarlet thinks he won't last long. She is horrified at herself. She takes his hand, presses it, willing him health and happiness, protecting him against evil. Yet she would like that little Lee Green house all to herself. It has carpets, red Wilton patterned with yellow zig-zag stripes.

Wanda doesn't come to the wedding, either. She says she will stay home and look after Byzantia.

The reception, in a Lee Green hotel, is a forlorn affair. There is warm sweet wine, slices of ham, potato salad, and trifle. People stay for as short a time as possible; leave without discussing the marriage. There is nothing to say.

The marriage is not consummated for some months. Edwin discovers undisclosed debts of Scarlet's – £30 run up on a Budget Account at a department store – and takes the view that she has wilfully deceived him. He sulks for days. Scarlet offers to go out to work to pay the debt, but that makes him angrier still. No wife of his goes out to work. It is the first time Scarlet has heard of this.

She looks into a blank future. But at least Byzantia has a

little room to herself; and Edwin has bought a frieze of dancing lambs to go round the picture rail. Scarlet puts it up. They are crude and vulgar lambs, but they do dance; and Byzantia, Scarlet thinks, will need all the gaiety she can muster in the coming years.

Edwin passes out of his sulk into another attack of back pains. Scarlet asks for details. 'The doctors are fools,' he says. 'They know nothing. There's some foreign body pressing between a couple of discs. I know there is. I can feel it. Something that ought not to be there. They say there's nothing. They say I imagine it.'

'But if it hurts, there's something wrong,' says Scarlet.

'Of course there is,' he says. 'But try getting them to admit it. I even got sent to a psychiatrist once.'

'What did he say?'

'He? It was a she. The world's gone mad.'

'What did she say, then?'

'She said I was a repressed homosexual.' And he laughs. He can laugh. He has a sweet smile, in fact, like a little boy's, who knows only too well how to be endearing. Scarlet laughs too.

'What would having a pain in my back have to do with me being a repressed homosexual, even if I was, which of course I'm not? How extraordinary people are! Why, I've been married twice.'

'What kind of thing do you think it is, trapped between your discs?' asks Scarlet.

'A bit of grit, I should think. A little bit of dirt. Probably something quite tiny. I'm sorry. Not much of a honeymoon for you, is it?' and he laughs nervously. He feels friendly

142

towards her, and protective, and has forgiven the £30 altogether, now that his back is hurting, and he is relieved of his sexual obligations.

For a time Scarlet does not mind. She sleeps in Byzantia's room – Edwin says it would be better. His tossing and turning might disturb her. Scarlet makes toast in the toaster. She takes Byzantia to the swings. She shops in the high street. She smiles graciously to the neighbours. She, who is accustomed to feeling worse than other people, now feels better than they. As an educated, cultured girl, she is superior to her husband, who is old and ill, superior to her neighbours, and superior to her fellow shoppers.

Edwin leaves the house at 8.30 in the morning and returns at 5. He is a man of regular habits. He pays bills the day they come in. Her housekeeping money is regular. Sometimes he travels the country for the Education Authority, but always makes sure she is properly provided for in his absence.

She feels well looked after.

It is not surprising, she thinks, that he is an inspector. It is in his nature to inspect. He runs a finger over door-ledges; he turns down the gas flames as he comes into the kitchen. He cannot bear to see them high. He inspects Byzantia's hair, nails, neck for dirt.

Scarlet waits for him to die.

Months pass.

The marriage is consummated, astonishingly, rapidly, one night, in a south coast boarding house. Edwin and Scarlet have gone to visit a spiritualist healer who is an old friend of Edwin's. Scarlet presents herself to him with confidence thinking that if this old man has any kind of extra-sensory perception at all he will perceive that she is an exceptional person. But the spiritualist responds to her badly. He clearly does not like her. He is on Edwin's side.

Scarlet is depressed. The consummation of the marriage – though the event is not repeated – does not cheer her up at all. On the contrary. It means she now can't get the marriage annulled.

Edwin becomes more critical, more anxious to find fault. They have rows. He does not take baths. They hurt his back, he sits for hours and hours on the lavatory.

'You impotent dirty old man,' she screams.

'You oversexed whore,' he snarls.

When they are calmer he claims that sexual activity is a small part of normal life. Her experience of life to date has been faulty. She has simply associated with a peculiar and perverse group from which he has rescued her. He cites various couples he knows, in their fifties, who, to use Edwin's language, 'never do it'. His parents never did it, either.

'How did you come to be born?' asks Scarlet.

'There was only the one occasion,' Edwin claims. 'That was not for pleasure, that was to conceive a child. You don't want another child,' (he asserts, though he has never asked her). 'Byzantia is quite enough for you as it is – and incidentally, when she goes to nursery school don't you think she should be registered under a more normal Christian name? Linda, for example. It's not just that one does not wish to underline her somewhat unconventional start in life, for her sake – but she does bear my surname, and is known as my child. No, I don't really understand your complaint. You must be a strange person. If you do feel yourself to be sexually deprived I can only suggest you go out for the night every now and then. It will break my heart,' he adds, 'but if you feel like a whore that is my cross and I must bear it.'

At other times he feels he has failed her. Tears come into his eyes. (Edwin cries easily. He is a sentimental man, easily moved by kindness. He cries when Byzantia – who is fond of him, in spite of his inspectoral habits – draws him a birthday card, or makes any gesture of affection.)

'I know I am no good to you,' says Edwin. 'But I am an ill man. I haven't much longer in the world. Be patient with me just a little.'

'Yes,' she says, and is.

At other times he accuses her of waiting for him to die in order to inherit his money. £400 in Gilt-Edged. The house, worth £2,500 with a £1,500 mortgage still to pay. Or at other times he suspects her of trying to send him mad, by twisting his words. When he speaks like this he sounds like a madman, and she could dismiss him as such, except that she knows that what he says is true.

She wishes him to die: she wants him locked up, put away, buried, gone.

Yet when he is in fact taken to hospital for an exploratory operation, she visits him daily, prays for his recovery, fights doctors, sisters, nurses for his comfort, worries for him, feels for him, nurses him back to health to the limit of her capacity.

He has a little song he sings while he convalesces; a cheerful time. Scarlet has been good to him and he is happy:

'Uncle Alf and Auntie Mabel,
Fainted at the breakfast table.
Let it be an awful warning,
Never do it in the morning.'

And he looks at Scarlet slyly to see if she is shocked. She is. Her mother sang rude songs. Must this man do the same?

Scarlet's friends do not visit her. Lee Green is a long way, and besides they cannot get on with Edwin. They write to her, sometimes. Scarlet does not reply. Jocelyn gives parties, and asks Scarlet. Scarlet does not turn up. She does not want to be pitied.

Edwin and Scarlet see very little of Wanda. Wanda has joined the C.N.D., thus frightening Edwin. And she is brisk and formal if they do meet, thus frightening and upsetting Scarlet.

Wanda can only be happy when she is not thinking about her daughter. It is not too difficult for her not to think, these days, for she has a lover. He is a twenty-year-old lorry driver she met in the pub. The liaison offends everyone – Kim, Susan, Scarlet, Edwin, even Lottie in her last few months – which gives it a cheerful momentum. Scarlet thinks if she can, I can – but she doesn't.

Wanda is further displeased with her daughter's behaviour when, instead of justifying her existence by starting a Lee Green branch of the C.N.D. (though can you imagine Edwin allowing any such thing?), Scarlet joins the Lee Green branch of an anti-communist organisation.

For Edwin has discovered that Wanda was once a communist, and though he could forgive her teaching innocent children the facts of life, he cannot excuse her political past, which, the times being what they are, puts his own position in jeopardy.

Edwin accuses Scarlet, yet once again, of concealing information detrimental to his interests. Edwin points out, at length, long into the seven nights of a full week, that she has married him on false pretences. He, a much respected man with a position in the community, has out of the kindness of his heart seen his way to marrying a fallen woman and taking her illegitimate daughter into his own home. Is this how she repays him?

Scarlet is perfectly happy to join the anti-communists if it will stop Edwin talking. Wanda can't forgive.

Years pass.

Scarlet walks like a zombie. Regard Scarlet's personality as if it were a plant. Come the winter it goes underground. Come the spring it will force its way up, cracking concrete if need be, to reach the light.

Scarlet's spring seems a long time coming. No sun rises to bathe her world with warmth.

She is deserted by, has deserted, Wanda, Kim, family, friends. She makes no new acquaintances here in Lee Green. They think she is snobbish, and they are right.

Only Byzantia smiles and grows and talks, beginning to feed back to her mother the nourishment she has sapped for so long.

Suez. English, French, Israeli troops – shooting at Egyptians?

147

It seems, in those naïve days, incredible, monstrous, dangerous, unfair.

Scarlet is frightened. She thinks the nuclear holocaust is imminent. She wants to take Byzantia and flee to Cornwall, where she imagines she will be safe. Edwin won't give her the fare money. Edwin is shocked.

'You are mad,' he says. 'If there is any danger, which there isn't, it is your duty to stay here.'

'Why?' she asks.

'You can't run away,' he says, indignant.

'But I want to,' she says.

Suez passes, nations subside; but the fact that Scarlet wants to run away, once spoken, stays in her mind. It feeds, grows, nourishes the roots of her being. Is spring coming?

A stall-holder at the Saturday market where Scarlet shops, a dealer in fabrics, forty, a short, fat, lively villain, propositions her as she buys elastic for Byzantia's knickers. Scarlet is shocked; she laughs it off. He renews his request the following week. She refuses. But she quite likes him. He is insistent.

'Why me?' she asks.

'You're my type,' he replies.

'A fat, spotty, dreary housewife?' asks Scarlet – and indeed she is all these things, and looks a good thirty-five as well – 'Your type?'

'You're posh,' he says. 'I've got a little room round the corner –'

'I'm not like that,' she says. 'I'm a married woman.'

'What do you want? Money?'

'No,' she says, shocked.

'I'll tell you what,' he says, 'Nylons.'

She looks down at her stockings, as he does. Stockings are always a problem to Scarlet. When Edwin goes through the accounts, he questions the amount she spends on nylons, and reproaches her for not taking more care of them. She goes round, always, with laddered stockings.

'All right,' she says.

Spring is coming.

They rendezvous one evening, the barrow boy and Scarlet. She has told Edwin that she is going to the pictures: she has checked the stills outside the cinema during the day to make her story stick in case she is questioned later. The film is *The Nun's Story*. She likes that. Deceit comes easily to her.

Alone with this stranger in a neat clean chintzy bed-sitting room in a private house, she talks nervously about his wife, which disconcerts him.

'We didn't come here to talk,' he says. 'Take your clothes off.'

She does.

Two pairs of cut-price nylons the richer, Scarlet walks the Lee Green streets, until it is time for the cinema to end. Then she joins the crowd as it leaves and walks home.

Scarlet feels she is at last a whore. She need no longer resist Edwin's accusations. She can accept them gracefully and have some peace.

The next Saturday Scarlet goes to the market seeking her client, who, apparently pleased with her performance, has asked her thus to meet him. His stall is empty. Where once the gauzy laces and the brilliant trimmings dangled, is now just a

149

bare dusty platform. He has gone. Gone to another market, another part of London, to buy another posh lost lady housewife for two pairs of cut-price nylon stockings.

Scarlet walks home with Byzantia holding her hand. Scarlet cries. Scarlet sings 'Tammy's in love' to Byzantia. It is a commercial love-song. It was playing on the radio – he had turned the volume up so that his landlady, of whom he seemed nervous, would not know he had a visitor – while he obtained his nylons' worth from Scarlet.

Scarlet loves her client. Scarlet will love anything, anyone, so long as it's impossible and not actually Edwin, whom she married for what he could give her and now finds that this is nothing.

Poor Edwin. To grace him with her presence in his house, eating his food, spending his money, though wearing her own nylons, is hardly enough.

Scarlet cries herself to sleep for a full week. Tears water the ground. All is ready for the sun.

It doesn't dawn.

But one day there is a knock at the door. The milkman? Scarlet shuffles down, wearing Edwin's slippers. It is Susan.

Susan has driven to visit her in her Utile Morris Minor. Simeon sits in the back, a neat clean little boy, even neater and cleaner than his mother or his grandmother before him.

Scarlet asks them in. Scarlet looks round her house with their eyes. It is a dim and dusty place. Edwin will have nothing in it changed. When she Hoovers the carpets she must put the furniture back exactly where it was before. The legs of the three-piece suite (1932) have worn twelve small neat holes through the carpet in the living-room.

Byzantia trips Simeon up. She is not used to other children in the house. Edwin does not encourage them.

'This is *our* house,' he will say. 'Not a stage-post for strangers. You, me, Byzantia – shall we call her Edna? – we are happy just by ourselves.'

Simeon, tripped, does not cry. It is not man-like.

Susan cries.

'It's all my fault,' she says. 'I've felt so bad about it. Scarlet.'

'Bad about what? I'm all right.'

'You're not all right,' says Susan. 'You're fat and miserable and you live in this horrible place with that horrible man.'

'How do you know he's horrible?'

'Wanda says so.'

'You talk to each other, then?'

'Yes, actually.'

Susan has had a nervous breakdown. She trembled and cried, and could not stop. Kim took her to a psychiatrist; she still visits him weekly; now she visits Wanda and talks to her instead of to her mother. She feels better these days. She dreams about Scarlet, and feels she must make amends, somehow.

'It was me would never let Kim send you money,' says Susan, in an agony of remorse. 'It was me made him so nasty to you. I was angry about Byzantia.'

Scarlet is baffled. Susan explains she is seeing a psychiatrist and Scarlet assumes that Susan is a little out of her mind.

'You've got to get out of here,' says Susan.

'Why?'

'It upsets me too much,' complains Susan.

151

Susan cannot escape, these days, in the manner she used to. Just before her breakdown, when she fell asleep it was as if her eyes stayed open. The night worlds would be closed to her. She would sleep, that was all. And waking in the mornings in her new house – for Kim has grown rich and they have moved to Kew – she would think she was still back in Baker Street and would stumble round the bedroom trying to find her bearings. Now at least she knows where she wakes, and she dreams of Scarlet, and has steeled herself to come visiting.

Edwin returns, and is introduced to Susan. Susan leaves as quickly as possible, but not before Edwin has reminded her that her husband owes him £7 10s. 0d.

'It is not the money,' he says. 'It is the principle. A father must take responsibility for his daughter, whatever the daughter may be like. I am sure I will take responsibility for Marjorie –'

'Marjorie?' asks Susan, confused.

'My name for Byzantia – although she is not even mine by blood. I take it Scarlet *is* Kim's daughter, although knowing Wanda's habits one can forgive him for perhaps doubting it? Was that why he failed to pay me the £7 10s. 0d? I have sometimes thought so.'

Susan writes a cheque. Scarlet is humiliated.

It takes Scarlet a week to move such belongings as she has out of the house, suitcase by secret suitcase, to an astonished Lee Green neighbour. Then she steals seven pounds from Edwin's wallet in the middle of one night, wakes Byzantia early in the morning, and they leave together.

She means never to return.

9

On The Move

Down among the women. If all else fails, we can always be useful.

Angling story:

Two men sit fishing on a river bank, raincoated, morose, silent. Eventually one speaks.

1st angler: You weren't here yesterday, then.

2nd angler: No.

1st angler (*presently*): Something hold you up, then?

2nd angler: Got married.

Silence.

1st angler: Good-looker, is she?

2nd angler: No.

Silence.

1st angler: Got money, has she?

2nd angler: No.

Silence.

1st angler: Sexy, then?

2nd angler: You're joking.

Silence.

1st angler: Good little housekeeper, is that it?

2nd angler: No. She's blind.

Silence.

1st angler: Then what you want to go and marry her for?

2nd angler: She's got worms.

The girls are on the move. That same manoeuvring star, which once led them trooping up the stairs to offer help to Scarlet, which then dispersed, antagonized and rooted them down for years – like children playing Statues, caught when the music stopped – that same star now takes another turn and sets these young women in motion once again.

Helen turns up at Jocelyn's house in the middle of the night. (It is fortunate that Philip is away on business.) Jocelyn lives in Chelsea now. She is a cool, chic, childless young lady. She has a built-in kitchen, new American style. Her cushions are covered in Thai silk, and tastefully arranged in a cool, chic, childless drawing-room. Her bathroom is pink and orange, and the soap and towels match. Her drinks tray contains bottles of every imaginable form of alcohol. Her accent she sharpened into Upper English Chelsea. Shopgirls pay attention when Jocelyn walks in: it seems an achievement.

To live so graciously costs a great deal – more, probably, than Philip can afford on his salary. They do not, of course, discuss money, or sex, or politics. Jocelyn, made nervous by the amount of her Harrods' bill, has been obliged to spend some of her capital. One suicidal impulse, as it were, leading to another, she then takes the rest out of Gilt-Edged and re-invests in Insurance Companies. She does not tell Philip.

The parrot has died. Jocelyn left the window open one frosty night, and forgot to move the cage, so that it caught a chill, wilted, and expired, reproaching her. Now she has a highly-bred dachshund with a bronchitic cough, and a limp, creased body.

Jocelyn, opening the door to Helen, wears a pretty white and blue fur-edged housecoat and white fur slippers. (Central heating is not yet fashionable. Hot bedrooms seem sinful and over-luxurious.) As for Helen, she has walked half-way across London in her night-gown, and the night is not warm, and her face is battered, but still she smiles with condescending grace at poor, dull, chic, bourgeois Jocelyn.

'You can't have come dressed like that,' is the first thing Jocelyn says.

'I walked boldly,' says Helen, 'with my head held high. I assumed I was wearing evening dress, so others assumed it too. No one remarked on anything unusual.'

'Not even a policeman?' asks Jocelyn, leading her friend to the bathroom.

'One can tell you're a rate-payer,' says Helen. She surveys the cleanly lustres of the bathroom, and manages to make clear that it is not to her taste. Jocelyn bathes Helen's eye with cotton wool. (We are not yet into the era of plentiful tissues, and the toilet paper is still hard and shiny, made by puritanical Northerners.)

Helen's face is quite badly battered. Jocelyn is nervous, and her hands tremble, but Helen stands still and docile, as if accustomed to being tended.

'What happened?' asks Jocelyn. 'Was it an accident?'

'No,' says Helen. 'You are the one who has accidents, not me. It is a private matter actually.'

And she peers at her face, and the swollen purplish flesh around her eyes.

'It gives one a slightly oriental look,' she says. 'It might please decadent tastes. What a pity Philip isn't here.'

This remark puzzles Jocelyn. A lot of things about Helen puzzle Jocelyn. Jocelyn is not stupid. Let us say she is going through a stupid patch, as people will when they are attempting to evade unpleasant truths; and Jocelyn, these days, maintains that she is happy.

Helen thinks Jocelyn is a pain in the neck, but has, frankly, nowhere else to go.

Jocelyn, for her part, welcomes Helen kindly, even though it is the middle of the night, both for old times' sake, because X is by now one of the country's leading painters, and artists of all kinds have a cachet down here in Chelsea, and because she has not the courage to turn Helen away. Helen makes such vibrant demands of the world, it seems to Jocelyn, that other people's wills and wants tend to dissolve in her path. Only X faces her, implacable, and refuses to be manipulated.

Helen and X have quarrelled. Or rather, Helen and X have been discovered by Y, and X, it transpires, can live without Helen but not without his wife.

Picture the scene in which Y, paler than ever, and trembling, arrives at the studio and stands at the end of the bed in which Helen lies surprised, helpless, and even righteous – for on that particular night X has worked late and fallen into bed too tired to even put his arms round her. Helen stares, and then smiles politely. Y takes off a shoe and starts to beat Helen about the head and face.

X wakes, slips out of bed, goes into the bathroom and locks the door. Y abandons her victim and batters the door with her shoe.

'Coward,' she cries, 'come out of there.'

There is silence.

'I want you to come out of here,' she shrieks.

'Momma don't allow no female-fucking here,' he sings, in his powerful voice, 'Going to fuck that female any old how, cos momma don't allow no females here –'

Thwarted, Y takes up a kitchen knife and goes round the room slitting canvases. Helen emerges from under the bed-clothes, and struggles long and silently with Y to take the knife away.

X emerges from the bathroom.

'What are you doing here?' he asks his wife. 'You promised me you would never come. What kind of person are you, to break a promise like that? How can I trust you again? And what are you doing up in the middle of the night? Shouldn't you be asleep? I hope you haven't left the children alone?'

Y squirms free of Helen and advances on X with her knife raised. Helen rushes into the bathroom and locks the door.

X disarms Y, easily.

'How can you!' says Y, inadequately enough. 'And with Helen!'

'But you know I have girls here,' says X. 'You have never minded before. I'm sure you have your own diversions.'

'But I haven't,' says Y.

'Is that the trouble then?' asks X. 'Shall I arrange something for you?'

He is very angry at his wife's intrusion. He does not like his actions questioned, or his liberty challenged.

'It's not like that,' says Y, helpless, and already beginning to feel she is in the wrong. 'I only want you.'

'That is your misfortune,' he says. 'Do not burden me with it.'

'But Helen!' she says. 'I had no idea it was Helen. You've both been cheating me.'

'You are mad,' he says. 'First, you practically drive me away from home and push me into bed with other women. If you remember it, it was your idea I should have this place. I didn't want it, God knows – I was happy at home. Now you object when I use it. What proper wife behaves the way you do?'

'I love you,' says Y. 'I want you to be happy.'

'Love?' he says. 'What's that? You wanted me out of the way so you could pursue your career, that's all.'

Y gets her knife back and starts slitting more of Helen's paintings, and breaking Helen's best glasses and china.

'Stop her, stop her,' bleats Helen through the keyhole, but X makes no move.

'Stop, stop! Let me talk to you, let me explain,' begs Helen, but all Y does is slit on, and smash on, and say, 'What a lousy painter she is! What crude and amateur stuff. An amateur artist and an amateur whore. What an insult she is, what a parasite, what a nothing.' And X just sits and watches. He seems amused, now, as if watching the antics of a performing animal.

'I am going to hand back the lease,' says Y, pale and vicious. 'Tomorrow. You have cheated me long enough. Why should I pay for your filthy pleasures?'

'Don't do anything so rash,' says X, moved to nervousness at last. 'I have an exhibition next month. I can't move out now, not without spoiling everything.'

'It's you who've done the spoiling,' says Y. 'If you see anything good or noble, you can't wait till you have spoiled it. Why should I put up with it? This is my place. I command you to leave now, or I will call the police.'

'Helen will leave, if it all upsets you so much,' says X. 'I never meant to upset you. I honestly thought you didn't care.'

At this Helen opens the bathroom door, looks at X with no little contempt, and walks out of the studio and into the street.

Thus Helen makes her exit, and once out in the street wonders where to go. Scarlet is lost in limbo, Sylvia weeping in Dulwich, Audrey plucking feathers in Suffolk. Only Jocelyn lives sensibly in central London.

'So he's finished with you, has he?' says Jocelyn not without relish, pouring Helen brandy.

'Of course he hasn't,' says Helen, who is wrapped in a blanket. 'He is only trying to keep his wife quiet. What a spoilt and dangerous woman she is! How terrible it is that the wrong people always have the money, the power and the glory.'

'She earned the money,' says Jocelyn. 'And it must have nearly all gone by now.'

'She didn't earn it,' says Helen. 'She won it. And I daresay she slept with the judges in order to do so. I wouldn't put it past her. She is a vile, scheming, neurotic woman. How desperate she must be to have recognition. She is a remarkably inept painter.'

'I thought she was supposed to be rather good,' murmurs Jocelyn.

'I hardly imagine,' says Helen, looking round the paintings on Jocelyn's walls, 'that you are an expert. And now if you don't mind I will go to bed. My face is beginning to hurt.'

Jocelyn leads her friend to the spare bedroom and helps her into bed, for Helen is trembling violently.

'Shall I call a doctor?' she asks.

'Ring X,' says Helen. Jocelyn is horrified.

'What, me?'

'Ring X at the studio and tell him he can get hold of me here.'

'But supposing he doesn't want to?'

'Don't be so stupid,' says Helen. 'Of course he does.'

Jocelyn telephones. To her relief there is no reply.

'You see,' says Helen. 'He is walking the streets, looking for me.'

'Shall I try his house?' asks Jocelyn, fearfully.

'He won't be there,' says Helen, with total conviction, and falls asleep. Jocelyn goes back to bed.

Helen is wrong. X is back home in bed with Y, as Helen finds out the next afternoon when she goes back to the studio with Jocelyn and finds her belongings out in the street, and X, silent and craggy, stacking her paintings, slashed and broken, behind the dustbins.

He will not speak to her. Not a word. Y is there, though, and she says quite a lot. Jocelyn tugs and drags at Helen, gets her back into the car, and takes her back home. Jocelyn too is trembling. She had not known educated people could speak to each other like that. She goes back later for the paintings, but the dustmen have taken them.

Helen lies on the bed in Jocelyn's spare room, silent and frightening. She will not eat. She spends her twenty-sixth birthday staring at the ceiling.

Jocelyn is bowed down by responsibility. Helen has no parents, no family, no friends. Where does she come from, this mysterious creature? No one has ever been quite sure.

On the second day Philip, who is flattered by having his spare room occupied by someone so exotic, tries to cheer Helen up. He puts on a false moustache and does his imitation of a Jewish miser. Helen turns her face to the wall but sheer astonishment seems to work some healing in her, for on the third day she speaks.

'How like your dog your husband is,' she says to Jocelyn, who is dusting round the ornaments. Jocelyn wears rubber gloves for the dusting, feeling she has to choose between the ornaments and her hands. Many is the nice piece of glass, the pretty piece of china she smashes. But what else can she do? She doesn't trust the cleaning woman Elise, though Elise – who is a middle-aged mid-European refugee fallen on hard times – looks in the dustbins at the wreckage and marvels; she who has seen so much broken in her life that she now treasures and cherishes the smallest thing.

'What do you mean?' asks Jocelyn, surprised. 'Like a dog?'

'Oh, never mind,' says Helen, and closes her eyes and appears to go to sleep, until the crash of Jocelyn tripping over the lead of the vacuum cleaner prompts her to speak again.

'We all have our own ways of surviving,' she remarks. And she talks of her past, while Jocelyn puts the electric plug back on to the lead. Her parents were Berliners, communists. They sent her out of Germany to a British family just before the war, and that was the last she saw or heard of them. The family – rich Hampstead communists – sent her to Australia, and then were themselves wiped out by a flying bomb. At seventeen, she married. At eighteen she divorced her husband, who was a schizophrenic. Helen relates the tale calmly.

'I never knew,' says Jocelyn. 'What a terrible place the world can be! I have so much to be thankful for.'

She puts the plug into its socket and turns on the switch. There is an explosion and all the power in the house goes off, though Jocelyn does not realize this until the evening when she tries to put the lights on. Philip roars and bangs through the house in rage, and Jocelyn, going into the darkness of Helen's room, hears what at first she thinks is sobbing, and then realizes is laughing. Helen does not often cry.

On the fourth day Helen talks about X.

'He is a man without a name,' she says. 'He is any man, he is interchangeable with other men. All men are the same. So, he can paint. So, because he is a great painter does not mean he is a great man. It was his painting I loved, not him. As for Y, she is meaningless. I thought she was gentle and kind, as I remember my mother, but she was hard and cruel and violent to me.'

All the same, she cries a little. Jocelyn has never seen Helen cry. She is awed.

'They were my family,' says Helen, eyes enormous and swimming. 'Y had no right to be so unkind to me. I never meant to harm her. I loved her. I only took from her what was left over. She didn't need it. Why did she grudge me such a little part of him?'

She sits up in bed. She combs her hair. She looks at her face in the mirror.

'I am beautiful,' she says. 'I am talented. Y is nothing, nothing. That is the whole trouble. A man can only be happy with his inferior.'

'What a strange thing to say,' says Jocelyn.

'It is perfectly true,' says Helen. 'That is why Philip will never be happy with you.'

Jocelyn leaves the room.

On the fifth day Helen gets out of bed and stands naked before Jocelyn. Not as the girls at school would stand naked and shivering under the showers, but like some goddess, arms up-stretched towards the heavens, as if they were her natural home.

'Well,' says Helen. 'I am still alive. So, while we wait, let us live.'

Helen goes through Jocelyn's wardrobe, without enthusiasm, and finally condescends to wear a lambswool sweater and skirt. She wears no bra, which shocks Jocelyn, who is alarmed by the sight of nipples through stretched wool, and disconcerted at the way Philip's eyes are riveted while they eat dinner. Philip plies Helen with wine. Helen talks of painters and paintings, and scandals in the art world. Jocelyn forgets that she ought to be jealous. Already she cannot bear to think of the world without Helen.

On the sixth day Helen takes Jocelyn shopping. They go to Liberty's, and Helen feels fabrics with her sensitive fingers, and regards clothes with an eye that seems only to be pleased by what is very expensive, and very precious. Helen adopts a haughty attitude towards material things. It is as if they have to try very hard to please her. Jocelyn, for her part, tends to feel inadequate in the face of objects, as if it was she who failed in the appreciating, not they in the pleasing.

Helen buys clothes, and a real leather trunk to put them in. She spends over seven hundred pounds. Jocelyn does not like to ask where the money comes from. But Helen, on the way home in a taxi, offers the information.

'I came into some money,' she says. 'Reparation money from Germany because of my ruined life.'

'Is your life ruined?' asks Jocelyn.

'Not in the way they think,' says Helen, 'but yes, my life is ruined.' She seems resigned, almost cheerful.

'Is it a lump sum?' asks Jocelyn, awed by someone who's life has been so disturbed that even governments take notice. 'Not a pension or anything?'

'A small lump sum,' says Helen. 'I spent most of it this morning.'

'On clothes!' Jocelyn is shocked.

'If one has to be poor,' says Helen, 'one can at least be poor in style. One must never accept what is second best. Even in degradation, one can choose. The gutter one lies in must be the deepest, dirtiest, freest-flowing gutter of them all. If one eats weevils, let them be curly, plump and strong.'

And she promises to take Jocelyn to Harrods the following day and advise her on new fabrics and furnishings for her living-room. Helen's presence has made Jocelyn worried lest her home might be tatty, vulgar, and tasteless.

But by the seventh day Helen has gone. Not back to the studio – though she has tried, only to be faced by Y, who has moved in and is now working there with X – but to live with Carl, a man whom Jocelyn never even knew existed. Carl is a rich man, and an art collector – a patron of X's. His desire to be part of the creative process is so strong that it stretches to include even Helen. Nightly he makes love to her, and feels that this above all is art. Here he roots and plunges, hour after hour, conscious not so much of her, but that here X has gone before.

Helen endures, for the sake of the porcelain out of which she sips her morning coffee, and daily brushes him out of her consciousness, like crumbs from the breakfast table.

As for Jocelyn, she recognizes now that everything about her life is second-best, and has been for a long, long time.

Butch has gone to Germany to play rugger. Sylvia, six months pregnant, again – the last child was stillborn – goes to stay with Audrey-Emma and Paul in Suffolk.

The house, crumbling, unpainted, but picturesque, stands alone in a stretch of flat and boring countryside. It is a wet autumn, and to look out of the kitchen window, Sylvia thinks, is as rewarding as holding a wrung-out dishcloth before the eyes. Audrey-Emma and Paul, however, talk about the satisfactions of living next to nature; and about the rhythm of the seasons. 'The children have a real feel for the country,' says Paul. They are not allowed to look at television, talk to corrupting estate children, eat white sugar, read comics, or, in theory, say please or thank-you.

They are pale, pretty, withdrawn children (a boy of four and twin girls of three) with pink runny noses and bad chilblains, and clothes which seem for ever caked in mud. Audrey-Emma does not often wash clothes – let alone iron them – but Paul's family, understandably anxious for his children's welfare, have for years been sending monthly parcels of old clothes, and Audrey-Emma herself likes to buy at jumble sales, so, though always muddy, the clothes do change from day to day.

When Paul requests her to wipe a nose or sweep a table, or spray the cockroaches, she is too busy – either baking 100% wholewheat stone-ground compost-grown bread or reading Beatrix Potter, aloud – to oblige. She chides her husband for his bourgeois soul. As Paul's interest in anarchy, old films, Chinese pottery, and health foods wanes, so does Audrey-Emma's increase.

Paul is kind to Sylvia, who is gentle, female, passive and never answers back. She both lays the table for meals and clears away afterwards, which is something Audrey-Emma never does, although she must get up and down twenty times during each meal, and each time she does so she looks at Paul and sighs, either reproachfully as if to say, 'Look how hard I have to work and it's all your fault,' or, on good days, virtuously, as if to say, 'Look how sweet and domestic I am being.'

During Sylvia's stay, deprived of this outlet for her feelings, sitting quietly at the table eating, she feels restless and discontented. She tries to persuade Sylvia to leave Butch.

'I'm pregnant,' says Sylvia. 'How can I?'

'Women can have babies by themselves,' says Audrey-Emma. 'Look at Scarlet, she manages all right. It was only when she was married she had such a hard time. And then again, look at me. I bring my children up single-handed, practically. Paul takes no notice of them at all. I think he is what is called a rejecting father.'

Outside, Paul labours through the mud towards the hen house, tall, pale, and bearded, with a pail of chicken-food in each hand, his three children rolling in the puddles around and behind him, so he has difficulty in walking. There seems total trust between them. Sylvia says nothing.

'You don't even know Butch is going to marry you,' says Audrey-Emma. 'This has been going on for years.'

'It's his divorce,' says Sylvia. 'Something is always going wrong. But he won't leave me. He has to get his gear washed. All that mud every week.'

'Don't talk to me of mud,' says Audrey-Emma, with bitterness. 'I have it every day.'

'I thought you liked living in the country,' says Sylvia.

'I couldn't bear to live in a city,' says Audrey-Emma, automatically. 'Filthy, sooty, nasty places. Do you know that when Londoners die their lungs are black with embedded soot?'

There is no heating in the house that day. The electricity

has been cut off because the bill has not been paid. But there are candles, and rush-lights and an oil stove to cook on. Audrey-Emma cooks four-course meals upon it; dishes up home-grown vegetables, omelettes made of fresh eggs, cottage cheese made from sour milk hung up to drip in stockings in rows in the kitchen; sponge pudding made with heavy brown flour and black strap molasses. A meal will take her three hours to prepare, but nothing puts her off.

'You'll just have to wait,' she says. 'We can't let the Electricity Board get the better of us. People have lived without electricity for centuries; so can we, and what's more we'll live well.'

Her family sit down at midnight, exhausted and shivering. The children stay up. 'Families must eat together,' says Audrey-Emma. 'That's what you said, wasn't it, Paul, when I left my horrid job in London and we came down here? People must be together, totally, within a family. Live together, work together, sleep together. Eat together, even if it is a bit late.'

Audrey-Emma likes to have the children in bed with her and Paul. If he protests, she goes and sleeps with them in their bedroom.

There are bee-hives in the garden, but the swarms succumbed to a disease of some kind last year. Paul says jokingly, 'Emma ill-wished them.' Sylvia finds dusty, curled-up bees in corners everywhere. 'Now Emma has ill-wished the hens,' he adds.

And indeed the hens, in the previous few weeks, have been hit by illness. Moulting fowls huddle in the unkempt garden. 'Before that,' Paul complains, 'she ill-wished the kiln. It overheated and cracked. I've never been able to raise the fifty quid to mend it.'

Emma-Audrey laughs at her husband's jokes, but breaks crockery in the kitchen after he has made them.

'He overheated the kiln on purpose,' she explains to Sylvia eventually. 'I'd started to do pottery myself, and frankly I was better than him. So of course he had to go and crack the kiln.'

Meanwhile the rain pours down outside, and in through broken tiles inside; the children draw on the walls with chalks and press plasticine into their hair; Paul sits in the study writing poetry; Sylvia chops fresh vegetables on the dining-room table with a patent Victorian vegetable chopper (soon the vegetable will boil brownish pink from traces of old varnish from the table's surface); and outside a hundred and seventy-seven hens have not even the energy to seek shelter.

Soon after Sylvia departs, the man from the Ministry of Agriculture turns up. Emma-Audrey prepares to do battle with broken bottles and an air-rifle but Paul, who seems dispirited, and lacks his old ferocity, lets him in, answers questions, and fills up forms.

Emma-Audrey is angry and bewildered.

The Ministry claims the birds have Fowl Pest. Emma-Audrey proves to her satisfaction, by consulting Victorian text-books, that they have an obscure infection which is transmitted by ailing bees, and is curable by dietary control.

The Ministry has the hens destroyed. Emma-Audrey wishes to go to law. Paul will not allow it. Emma-Audrey sulks. So does Paul.

Presently he has talks with his Bank Manager and sets up a battery unit, and produces eggs and chickens by intensive farming methods. He pours penicillin into the mash. The birds, in their tiny cages, have not room to turn around, least of all to peck their neighbours. Their chests are naked, pink and swollen where they have rubbed against the mesh.

Emma-Audrey weeps for all trapped creatures, sleeps nightly with her grubby, restless children, and starts buying her vegetables canned. She has more housekeeping money these days.

10

Sorting Out

I went to a party the other night. At midnight, the host escorted a woman guest to her home. By five in the morning he had not returned. The hostess continued with her hostessly duties, smiling politely. What else could she do? She is fifty, intelligent, and nice, but she is fifty. She has been trained to behave well, and not to shout, scream or murder, and that is the only training she has had, besides cookery and housecraft at school. Her husband is rich; if it were not for him she would not be able to give a grand party, and in any case he will be home for breakfast which she will have the privilege of laying on the table before him. So what is she complaining about? What does she expect?

The woman guest needs comforting. Can one grudge her a simple sexual drunken pleasure? Her husband has just left for Norway on business with his secretary, who has long blonde hair and what her husband describes as laughing eyes. The secretary in her turn needs comforting because her boyfriend has become engaged to a plain fat girl who cooks *Apfelstrudel* and piles it high with whipped cream, and who came top in housecraft at school. 'A man needs two women,' maintains the boyfriend who is all of twenty-two, 'one to cook and one for bed. I love you but I shall marry her. As life goes on, sex grows less important and dinner more so.' The secretary, indignant as who would not be, zooms off to Norway in the woman guest's husband's Jaguar, for a month's straightforward affair with the boss, with a little shorthand thrown in. She prefers office work to cooking.

The hostess, fifty and at the end of the line of distress, smiles politely and offers hot soup to departing guests. Soon she will be a grandmother. That seems comforting, down among the women. One wishes marriage for one's daughters and, for one's descendants, better luck.

Wanda, Byzantia's grandmother, feels first relief, and then a spasm of fright when Scarlet leaves Edwin. The period of her reprieve is over. If Scarlet has rejected wifehood, Wanda must presumably resume motherhood. Wanda knows that Scarlet has left home only because Edwin telephones her, and accuses her of a conspiracy which, he maintains, is punishable by law.

'She is your wife,' says Wanda, recovering her composure quickly. She does not like to show surprise. 'She is your responsibility. Nothing to do with me any more.'

'She is your daughter,' he retorts. 'And you've been egging her on to this. You're a man-hater. I hold you responsible. I shall divorce her and sue you for enticement.'

Wanda shrieks with drunken laughter, her hand jovially diving for the crotch of her lorry driver, who is a young out-of-work alcoholic History graduate grateful for a temporary home and someone to buy him drinks.

'No one who married a man like you,' she says, with glee, 'is any daughter of mine.'

'I shall get Byzantia away from you,' says Edwin. 'You're none of you fit to have a child in your care. You'll be hearing from my solicitors.' And he slams the phone down.

Presently Wanda looks out Scarlet's old telephone book, traces some of her friends, and telephones them. But no one has seen or heard of Scarlet.

Edwin rings again. He is crying. He apologizes for being rude. He wants Scarlet and Byzantia back. He loves them. The house is silent and empty without them. If he has behaved badly he is sorry. He will go down on his knees if anyone wants him to. He pleads with Wanda to allow him to speak to Scarlet. It is a long time before she can convince him that Scarlet is not with her.

'Then where is she? You're her mother. Where else would she go?'

'Perhaps she has a lover,' suggests Wanda.

'Who?' he is very sharp.

'Now how should I know? You haven't let her speak to me lately; if I can't give you any information you have only yourself to blame,' says Wanda unkindly.

'So long as it's no one local,' he says. And then, with real feeling, 'Supposing she's in some trouble? I only ever wanted to look after her and little Rosemary.'

'Little who?' asks Wanda.

'I used to call her Rosemary. I never liked Byzantia as a name.'

Wanda's heart, which had been softening towards Edwin, hardens again.

'If I hear from her I'll let you know,' she says, 'and in the meantime please stop pestering me with phone calls. You bore the piss out of me, if you want to know.'

There is a short silence. Then Edwin says, coolly, 'I shall have to report certain things to the Education Authority, you know.'

'Report away,' she says, 'report away!' and puts the phone down.

'Poor bloody sod,' she says to her lorry-driver. 'I suppose Scarlet drove him mad. He was eccentric when she married him. Now he's fucking mad.'

But she telephones Kim, all the same, to tell him his daughter is missing and ask him what he means to do about it. Kim, as usual, is not in, so she speaks to Susan. Susan, lately, has been in the habit of visiting Wanda, although Wanda does not know why. Susan on a visit tends to just sit around, and smile in a vague and worried way. She talks very little, except about Simeon's education – he goes to a school for young gentlemen behind Harrods and wears a curious cloth cap which rests on his infant ears and all but covers his dull eyes. Simeon is very clean and well-behaved, and Susan is proud of him.

Now Susan, hearing the news, begins to cry. 'It's all my fault,' she says, 'I shouldn't have told her I was seeing you. Now she's out and she'll murder me.'

'She hasn't been in prison,' says Wanda. 'Merely resting. Now Byzantia's five, life can start for her again.'

'It's nothing to do with the child,' sobs Susan. 'It was what I said to her. I should never have interfered. Now what's going to happen?'

What happens is that the next day Scarlet turns up, her hair blonde and permed, at Wanda's flat and asks if she can leave Byzantia with her mother for an hour or two.

'Off whoring?' asks Wanda. 'Already?'

To which Scarlet retaliates by turning to the lorry-driver and saying, 'If it's a mother you're after you've come to the wrong address.'

('I don't know what happens to everyone,' Scarlet says to Jocelyn later. 'The older we get the more we become ourselves. We were nicer when we were younger and all little bits of other people.')

Wanda sends the young man out to get fish and chips and enquires where Scarlet is living. Scarlet replies, haughtily enough, that she imagines that this is a matter of indifference to everyone, especially to her mother.

'Not to your loony husband,' says Wanda. 'He wants you back.'

'Which is more than you do,' says Scarlet. 'Don't worry. I shan't be a burden to you.' And she snivels. She does not like to see her mother in the company of this young man.

'Oh, for God's sake grow up,' says Wanda. 'You're a grown woman, not a little girl. If you don't want to tell me where you're living, don't. Only don't use me as a dumping ground for Byzantia while you go off to parties.'

'You can't stand it, can you,' says Scarlet. 'You can't stand me having a good time. You and Edwin ought just to have got married and left me out of it.'

Byzantia stops staring at the television (a twelve-inch screen these days) and begins to grizzle. She is very tired,

175

having spent the previous night in a strange boarding-house, the morning in a hair-dressing salon and the afternoon in a domestic agency.

Wanda scoops her up in her arms. Byzantia likes her grandmother, and is instantly happy. She smiles benignly and falls asleep. She has lost her infant plumpness; she is now long-legged and wide-eyed.

'Well,' says Wanda, giving in. 'Here we all are again, then.' She feels, surprisingly, happier than she has for years.

'Except you've got that awful boyfriend,' says Scarlet, 'and it's revolting at your age.'

Having got that out, she too feels better. She tells her mother she has taken a job as a living-in maid, in a household where they will take Byzantia too.

Wanda clasps Byzantia and glares at Scarlet. 'Over my dead body,' she says.

'But it's all arranged,' says Scarlet. 'Anyway since when were you such a snob? I'm sure Byzantia doesn't mind being the maidservant's child.'

'You're mad,' says Wanda flatly. 'We'll have to get you treatment.'

Wanda rings Edwin and tells him Scarlet has turned up.

'She is of course mad,' she says to him.

'I had been thinking just that,' says Edwin. 'I have been sitting here in this lonely house thinking just that. I took her out of the gutter and showed her every kindness. She has behaved wickedly; she has deprived Annabel of a settled home, and a status in life; she has ruined my happiness completely, and for what? Because she is sexually insatiable. It is a kindness to believe that she is mad.'

'Quite so,' says Wanda.

'How thankless as a serpent's tooth,' he says, 'to have so sharp a child.'

'Quite so,' says Wanda. 'Have you been drinking?'

'I don't drink,' he says. 'It prevents me thinking carefully. I have a terrible, terrible pain. I am in agony and even little Pussy' (his name for the big Alsatian dog next door) 'is missing her footsteps in the house. You are quite right. She is mad. I shall come straight over and explain that she is mad.'

'I shouldn't do that,' says Wanda. 'But what about getting her cured?'

'Committing her, you mean?' he asks, with a not unwelcome vision of a screaming Scarlet being carried off in a strait-jacket by while-coated orderlies.

Wanda suggests that Edwin pays his runaway wife ten pounds a week, on condition that she is under psychiatric care. 'It would be a very kind thing to do,' she says, and rather to her astonishment, and certainly to Scarlet's, who has already cast poor suffering Edwin in the villain's role, he agrees. He says it is for Annabel's sake, and so it is.

'Just when I'd decided on a good name for her too,' he laments, the next time he comes to deliver the money. He brings it in cash, in an envelope marked 'Scarlet and Annabel' every Friday evening at 6.30. He brings, in fact, £9' 17s. 6d., for he is claiming repayment, in easy stages, of the £7 she stole from him. Every Friday Wanda must delay going to the pub in order to receive the money. Every week he asks if Scarlet is nearly cured, for he is certain that when she is, she will want to come back to him. How could she not?

'He is a nice man, really,' says Wanda to Scarlet. 'Or if not nice, good.'

'Yes, he is a good man,' agrees Scarlet puzzled. 'How can anyone be so good and yet so awful?'

'It must be terrible for him to be without Byzantia,' says Wanda.

'You mean Annabel,' says Scarlet, but with rather less conviction.

'Oh yes, Annabel,' says Wanda, remembering. 'It wouldn't really do, would it? The most important thing in the world is to be oneself.'

'Quite,' says Scarlet.

Scarlet and Byzantia live in a tiny flat round the corner from Wanda. They are glad to be on good terms with each other again. Wanda drinks rather less. The next time her lorry driver, angered by her foul tongue and evil temper, hits her, she asks him to leave and he does.

She stares at her face in the mirror and says, 'I'm nearly fifty. I reckon that's really that. With my build and on my form.'

'Ha bleeding ha,' says Scarlet.

'I never thought I'd get that last gentleman,' says Wanda. 'What did he see in me? I make a lousy mother.'

'I know,' says Scarlet. 'I wish you weren't so proud of it.'

'I wish,' says Wanda, 'if we're talking of wishing, I had led a different life. I should never have left your father.'

'Oh, I don't know,' says Scarlet indulgently, 'I can't see you being happy with fitted carpets and six matching dining-room chairs. Not as an ad-man's wife.'

'If he'd stayed with me,' says Wanda, 'he wouldn't be the way he is now. He's done the whole thing to demonstrate just how much he needs me.'

'But he put you in prison.'

'I shouldn't have slashed his paintings.' Scarlet has never before heard Wanda express regret for something she has done. 'It was a terrible thing to do. He was very young. So was I. We both were. He thought I was trying to destroy him, but honestly, truthfully, I wasn't. Only his paintings.'

'If you'd stayed,' says Scarlet, 'he wouldn't have married Susan, and that would be wishing that infant creep Simeon out of existence.'

'He hardly exists how,' says Wanda unkindly. 'I expect that's why. Somewhere along the line something went wrong. I don't believe Simeon was *meant*.'

'You're going to end up an R.C. convert,' says Scarlet, 'the way you talk these days.'

'It's old age,' says Wanda. 'I'm mellowing. I am finished with sex and see wheels within wheels. But I could wish things had been different.'

'Well,' says Scarlet, 'all one can do is act according to one's nature. It's not a question of blame or praise.'

'Yes, it is,' says Wanda. 'Don't be so sloppy. That's your whole trouble. You behave as if you were some kind of stupid puppet and fate is pulling the strings. You should cut them loose and dance round a bit of your own accord. That's another thing, I would have liked more children.'

'What?' says Scarlet, unbelieving. 'More like me?'

'You're not so bad,' says Wanda, and means it. Scarlet is

179

pleased, and that evening cuts her hair very short, getting rid of the frizz. She looks boyish, now, and her spots have gone. She becomes quite thin and lively. All kinds of things please Scarlet now; from spring blossom to Byzantia rushing off to the local school by herself. Scarlet goes to see a psychiatrist once a week. She tells him what she thinks he would be interested to hear. She is waiting for a vacancy with a National Health psycho-analyst, which the psychiatrist, rather to her surprise, has recommended. She does not believe she needs treatment, but feels she owes at least this much to Edwin.

She goes out with Edwin in the car on Sundays. She sits in the front, Byzantia in the back. Edwin picks them up at two, and they drive round the outskirts of London, while he catalogues railway bridges – his latest hobby – until five-thirty.

Now his life has fallen into ritual again he seems quite happy, or at any rate not unhappy. He worries about Byzantia's school, however.

'I know it's very modern,' he says, 'but it's not for Annabel.'

'Well, that's all right,' says Scarlet, 'because her name's not Annabel, it's Byzantia.'

'That's what it says on her birth certificate, I know,' he says, 'but what sort of birth certificate is it? Certainly not one to be proud of.'

'If you don't call her Byzantia,' says Scarlet, 'I will never come out with you again on these boring and ridiculous rides.'

'I never knew you minded,' he says. 'I thought it was rather jolly calling her different names. It was like having my own child. You are much younger than me, so I tried to be jolly. But if it pleases you I shall call her Byzantia. When you're better and we live together again, we'll discuss the matter once more. In the meantime, I don't think the school is right for Byzantia.'

'It's very free,' she says, 'that's what I like. And Byzantia can't get there soon enough. She runs all the way, and sometimes I have to run after her with her shoes.'

'She can't read yet,' he says. 'She'll be behind when the eleven plus time comes.'

'I don't care about exams,' says Scarlet.

'Well,' he says, 'that's very modern of you, and I know it's the latest theory, and I'm sure it's the way your mother thinks, but take my word for it, a small child is best sitting at a desk learning, not crawling about on the floor playing with sand and water. As for these rides of ours being ridiculous and boring, you are quite wrong. You would find them very interesting if you would bring yourself to concentrate on patterns of building and subtleties of Victorian brickwork; and besides, it keeps us all in touch with one another, until this tragic patch of our lives is over.'

'Yes, Edwin,' says Scarlet.

'All the same,' says Edwin, 'we could go further afield, I suppose. We could go visiting country houses. That would be very educational for Byzantia. I could pick you up at ten in the morning.'

'No,' says Scarlet. 'Really, it's all right.' And adds brightly, 'Our Victorian grandfathers had some wonderful bridge-builders, didn't they.'

'I have reason to believe,' confides Edwin, reassured by her interest, 'that a remote ancestor of mine designed Tower Bridge.'

In the back Byzantia yawns.

Jocelyn disapproves of Scarlet leaving Edwin.

'You undertook something when you married him,' she says. 'Marriage is a serious matter.'

Jocelyn is having a civilized afternoon affair with a young man. It is known in her circles as 'having tea at the Ritz', and though it hardly counts as infidelity, it has both increased Jocelyn's reverence for the institution of marriage, and her irritation with her husband. She is made angry and anxious at the thought that marriages can and do break up.

She suspects that Philip may be having an affair with his secretary; her only evidence is her consciousness of her own bad behaviour.

Philip, she feels, has failed her. Philip does not take her out to lunch, admire her, hold her hand, tell her she is beautiful, take her to his hotel room and cover her with love bites, reduce her to all orgasm and then politely take her to tea at the Ritz, where she can satiate eccentric desires with cucumber sandwiches and lemon tea; then put her in a taxi and send her home in time to take the dog for a walk and have a bath before supper. This young man does, and has been doing so twice-weekly for months. They are dream afternoons. She can hardly remember the young man's name. His face is oddly like Philip's, but his body is singular, leaner, harder, wirier, and shocking through its unfamiliarity. She will wake up in the night and recall its feel so vividly he might almost be there beside her, with Philip lying sleeping, quiet, remote, and polite three feet away. Philip is a peaceful sleeper. You would hardly know he was there. She wonders if he has dream visions of her conduct. There is something mysterious about Philip asleep.

Jocelyn's mind, brain and intentions seem to have nothing to do with her twice-weekly afternoon behaviour. It is only her body which does the desiring, walks her towards her lover, makes her stand quiet and compliant beside him in the lift, allows her to receive him without argument or doubt. It is nothing to do with *her*. Her body, moreover, is quite without taste or judgement. Jocelyn suspects that any man would do.

Jocelyn is really shocked.

She is, moreover, three months pregnant. It is, amazingly, her husband's baby. She has not told her lover. She knows he will think it gentlemanly to conclude the affair. She does not want the affair concluded. She does not want Philip to find out about it. Supposing he doubted the parenthood of his own child?

'Marriage is a serious matter,' she says to Scarlet now. 'And what about Byzantia? She needs a father. If he's keeping you now he is a good, kind man. And that, after all, is what we all want. There is something very rich and rewarding in just seeing a marriage through its bad patches. He hasn't done anything bad, has he? He hasn't been unfaithful, he hasn't hit you, he supports you. And Byzantia too, don't forget that. What possible reason have you for leaving him? It's irresponsible.'

Jocelyn listens to herself talking and is aghast. She hears her mother in every word.

'Excuse me,' she says, and goes to her pink and orange bathroom and is violently sick.

'What's the matter with you?' asks Scarlet. 'You never used to be quite as bad as this.'

'I just don't know,' says Jocelyn. 'Except I'm pregnant, and bloody trapped, and miserable as hell.'

'That's better,' says Scarlet.

Jocelyn regrets her indiscretion, and is thereafter cold and formal with Scarlet. She parts with her lover. Every morning she is sick. Every afternoon she is lonely, and sees her life as something finished, over. She has withered and perished like a leaf on the tree. Oh, Miss Bonny! That was the fate Jocelyn mapped out for you and grieved for you over, as you sang lustily in morning assembly. Yet she never dreamt of it for herself.

The very fertility of Jocelyn's body now seems something macabre and unwholesome. How can someone so dead as she produce anything that is alive and good?

Jocelyn miscarries, sure enough. She resumes her former life, but without her lover, who has found a new married lady to take to tea at the Ritz. She sees them both one day, walking down Piccadilly. The woman looks like her; it is as if she sees herself approaching, another young woman who dresses, walks, talks like Jocelyn. The man looks like Philip, dresses, walks, talks like Philip. Jocelyn has forgotten the saving graces; the importunate nature of his body; the flurry of orgasm; the communion, not just with another body, but with the whole common pulsing universe of experience. Now she feels only the humiliation, the waste, the passing of good things.

She runs home, crying. 'We are all alike,' she says to Philip, who comes home early, for once, and is concerned because her gloss seems to be cracking. 'We are all just the same people. I can't bear it. I want to die.'

'Poor Jocelyn,' he says. 'You need a baby. You need something to occupy yourself with,' and he makes a real effort to provide her with another. She has trouble conceiving. She takes her temperature first thing every morning, and on the nights following the two mornings in the month on which her temperature rises, he attempts to impregnate her. Jocelyn doesn't really want a baby, though she says she does. She thinks it might look like Philip, or like her lover, or both. Poor lost Jocelyn.

She takes the dog for a walk one day, and throws a stick out into the Round Pond, which is frozen over. The dog, unusually for him, sees fit to chase out after it. He skitters and skates over the ice, which cracks. The dog falls through and is drowned.

Philip buys her a tropical aquarium and asks her to make sure she doesn't electrocute both the fish and everyone else in the house. She sulks for days after this remark, and refuses him that night, even though it is Ovulation Day. She has never refused him before; never really, of course, having had much opportunity.

('Frigid I may be,' she said to him once, lightly, lying still, stoical and unmoved, 'but I'm not mean. I can't stand mean women who use sex as a weapon.')

Philip, angry at this uncalled for rejection, goes to visit that same original stripper, whom he has called on occasionally through the years. She doesn't laugh at him now. On the contrary, she seems to admire him, and look forward to his visits. He drives her out to a lay-by outside London in his large shiny car and there in the sinful dark of the back seat he conquers her; and punishes her for that female depravity which he both loves and despises. They could stay peacefully and more comfortably together in her bed, but the very thought of such domesticity causes Philip to become as nervous, limp, and ineffectual as he is with his wife.

Sometimes Philip enquires of Jocelyn after Sylvia; she remains in his mind as a vague, pale, drifting figure. Jocelyn by comparison is strong and vivid, as clearly defined and precise as her table arrangements. He does not regret marrying her – she is all he could want as a wife – but he wonders sometimes what life would have been like had he not called on Sylvia that day and found Jocelyn washing her hair instead.

Philip is having trouble with his vision. Sometimes, as he stares at letters, research papers, memos, marketing documents, folios of this and folders of that, his eyes blur and he can make no sense of what he sees. At other times, sitting in meetings, elbows on the highly polished board table, flanked by shrewd, talkative men in expensive grey suits, his ears simply seem to stop hearing.

Otherwise, he has no trouble with his work. He does what he has to efficiently and quickly. He makes decisions with no trouble. He does what he can, and does not get ulcers. He is liked and trusted. Sometimes he wonders if it is because he lacks imagination that he survives so well in office life. For he has no fear of what might happen next. He simply deals, with an eye to both past and future, with the exigencies of the present.

Belcher and Watson now have two adjacent ex-town houses

in Mayfair. Their receptionists are beautiful. Their accounts include instant coffee, dandruff shampoo, a new soft toilet tissue, and a detergent washing powder. Times are good. There seems no end to progress.

Y's paintings have become fashionable. Fans from all over the world come tapping at the studio door, and if X answers it, they do not know who he is. X finds it bitter.

X has trouble selling his paintings. He is thirty-three. New young men have arisen, to wield brushes and sprays with a flashy expertise which outdates his, caking paint on paint with meretricious abandon and taking away, with the shallow energy of youth, the acclaim which is rightly his.

'You mustn't worry,' says Y. 'It is fashion. Acceptance should make no difference to what you do. In fact it's a very bad sign to be popular, look at me.' And she laughs nervously.

But she knows, and he knows, that she is working better than ever before, and that he is getting nowhere, nowhere, except older. And that when he shouts at the children they ignore him. And that flesh is gathering around his waist; and that when he and she are in bed together, her success, his failure (for so far as he is concerned, the one implies the other) folds itself like some monstrous filmy french letter between them, and interferes with the very act of love.

Y is unwilling to sell her paintings. 'Look what happened last time I had any money,' she says. 'You couldn't stand it.'

'Helen was a witch-woman,' X says, 'it had nothing to do with you. She laid a spell on me. She thought she could lure me to some kind of doom; but you saved me.'

Y smiles and feels safe.

Helen encounters X at a Private View. Her connoisseur lover, Carl, escorts her. He likes to show her off, and indeed she is magnificent. On this particular evening she wears a white brocade dress and solid African necklace. Her eyes glitter. She is strong, bold and vivid; though there may be perhaps something slightly bovine about her these days, a heaviness, a resignation, an idleness.

Carl is a small, wiry man – he darts round her, here and there, tugging her this way and that, adjusting her hair, straightening a seam, ever careful of his possessions, like a tug servicing a steamer. Helen regards him with a kind of disdainful surprise.

X and Y make their entrance. They are accustomed to making entrances; though the pattern has changed. Now it is Y who walks first, and he like a handsome shadow behind. Y looks better now than she ever has or ever will. She wears a limp green dress which clings to her limp body and makes the limpness seem blessed. Her movements are as weary as ever, but now as if the ecstasies of vision have tired her, and not just the housework. Her fine silky pale hair curls up at the ends, and she has mascaraed her pale lashes. She is gracious.

Carl darts, tug, terrier, gnat, all at once, to Y's side. He buys her paintings, not X's.

Helen follows, shaking off her admirers like a wet animal, getting rid of rain. She approaches X and Y.

'See,' she seems to be saying to them, 'I am handsome and happy. I don't need you. I never really did.'

All the same she does not quite meet X's eye, as if she feared what she might see in them, or worse, fail to see.

'Why, Helen,' says Y, kindly. She is holding X's hand, and feels proud and powerful. She speaks to everyone around. 'Helen used to be our model.'

'I'm afraid I wriggled,' says Helen. Her voice is pitched lower than ever. It has a husky note, now, which she has taken pains to develop. It involves the listener, willy-nilly, with the night she spent before – was it full of sex or tears, or both? What dreadful, fearful, marvellous things might that voice not speak of next?

X goes off to fetch drinks.

Helen is left alone with Y.

'I'm sorry,' says Helen, eyes downcast. 'I have been so wretched, thinking how I betrayed you.'

'It wasn't a betrayal,' says Y. 'It was all just rather silly. Don't build things up into dramas.'

'Will you forgive me?' asks Helen.

'Of course,' says Y, and even smiles.

'I'm happy now with Carl. But I miss your friendship. It was so important to me and I threw it away.'

'Forget it,' says Y. 'It's all over now.'

'Well anyway,' says Helen, 'you're doing so well now. Perhaps you could use the experience in your work? I wish I was creative. I just have horrid experiences, you see, and that's that. I can't turn them into anything. I can't transmit them.'

Y looks a little blank, but still benign. She strokes Helen's hair, lightly, as if blessing her with a touch, and Helen seems

189

to bloom, and the heaviness falls away as if some miracle had taken place.

Y asks Helen round to a meal. She feels invulnerable. She offers blessings. She bestows kindnesses. She indulges X. She paints.

That evening she feels a little less sure of herself.

'How did you think Helen was looking?' she asks X.

'Like one of Carl's ladies,' replies X.

'And what are they like?'

'He has a crude taste,' says X, and she is satisfied.

When X finds out that Y has asked Helen round to a meal he is perplexed. He rings Helen to explain why he thinks she should not come. They meet for lunch. They talk about Y, which sanctifies the feeling they both have, which is that if they cannot sleep together they will surely wither up and die.

They talk about Y all the way back to Carl's flat in the taxi, not touching, not looking; they admire Y's works, her looks, her talent, her sensitivities; they agree how she must be protected from too violent memories of the past. By the time they reach home they are in a full-scale conspiracy against Y.

Carl is out, as both have known.

'And what about you?' X asks Helen. 'What about you?' Y's pictures hang where once his used to.

'I hate it here,' says Helen. 'I feel like a meringue full of whipped cream. I am not alive. I have not been alive since I was close to you and Y, I need you both.'

She spreads her hands, stares at them. They are broad, powerful, freckled hands. Y's are thin, tapering, delicate. They are done unto, they do not do. Helen's hands move, take command, control. X loves them. He always has. It is her hands which now he places round his waist.

She wears a white open-necked shirt and full pink skirt. The carpet is red, her skin opalescent. He pauses to admire the colours and the textures, but only briefly.

At four o'clock she says, 'At five Carl comes home.'

At ten minues to five X leaves, with a last look round Y's overseeing paintings –

'She's the best painter,' he says, 'the best woman painter the world has known for a long time.'

'It was as if she was here with us,' says Helen, 'and forgave us.'

At dinner that night she sits quiet and smiling.

'A penny for your thoughts,' says Carl, who is mid-European and careful to use colloquial English expressions, which he utters in precise and cultured tones.

'How good a painter is Y?' she asks.

'She will fetch a pretty penny now,' he says. 'She will fetch an even prettier penny in a year or two.'

'That is not what I meant,' says Helen.

Carl does not bother to reply. He leans under the table as far as he can go, and pinches sharply between her legs.

'That made you squeal,' he says, and laughs merrily. Helen picks up her glass of wine and sips. The glass is real Venetian and the wine real Beaujolais.

She goes, on the appointed day, to supper with X and Y. They eat haricot beans and bacon, and elderberry wine. (The children are with Y's sister, who is married to a farmer, and lives in Wales.) It is like old times.

When the children are away, Y thrives. Her cheeks grow pink: she laughs. She does not care about anything, anything. If her husband and Helen were to make love on the floor in front of her, she would watch with interest, and not with terror and despair.

For it is the children, when they sleep upstairs in their bunk beds, in a litter of dust and toys and old sweet papers, who make her turn to X with such angry and possessive desperation. 'Look,' she says in her heart, 'you have altered me for ever; you have given me children and I can never be myself again, I must be part of them. Look how they cry, and whine, and sap my strength; I have to feed them, fill them up. I have to fight them for my being. And you, look at you. You stay the same. You implant your seed in me and walk away and leave me to it.' And she binds him to her with chains of guilt and penance, and won't let pleasure in.

But when the children are away, when she is free, can sleep and wake when she wants, can sit, and sit, at breakfast-time, and tea-time, and supper-time, how young and gracious she can be. 'Run off,' she almost says. 'Run away, do what you want. Come back to me with a smiling face, that's all I need.'

She lets X take Helen home. What largesse! And when they are gone she washes up the dishes and sings, so great is her confidence and her cheerfulness; and X and Helen have a quick and furtive engagement in the alley that runs beside Carl's house; she standing, he awkward but imperative; and then Helen goes in to Carl, and he goes back to Y; and she takes more pleasure in Carl than she ever has before, as X does with his wife.

11

Crucifixions

Rose comes to me with stories. Rose lives in a tower-block where sub-culture myths abound – they spread across the country like the german measles, in and out of Council estates, up and down the tower blocks.

I shall repeat two of them. They are nasty stories, but they are not true. Myths are not true. Myths simply answer a need.

But what kind of need can it be, down here among the women?

MYTH NO. 1

A detective told us, so it must be true. It's not in the papers, it's too horrible. It happened in Clapham High Street. A young woman took her five-year-old boy shopping. He wanted to go to the toilet. She took him to the Ladies but the woman there said he was too big, so he had to go to the Gents by himself. His mother sent him down and waited on top of the steps for him to come out. She waited and waited. A gang of young boys went down and when they came up she thought they were acting a bit strange. But still no child. Finally, she asked a passer-by to go down and fetch him. There was her child, dead. They'd cut off his willy and he'd bled to death.

MYTH NO. 2

A young mother has three children, a daughter of four, a boy of two, and a new baby. The little boy wets his pants. The mother is in the habit of saying, 'If you do that again, you naughty boy, I'll cut your willy off!' One day she's bathing the baby when there's a shriek and then silence. The little girl calls out, 'It's all right, Mummy. He was a naughty boy again, but I cut it off.' She drops the baby and rushes to see. The boy dies; when she gets back the baby has drowned.

What about that poor little girl then? Down here among the women. Would you like *your* little boy to sit next to her at school?

My children come up to me. They are cold, and sit on either side of me. I wrap the edges of my cloak around them and we all three sit and stare out into the world.

So we all protect our children, or try to, but they too must come to it, and be part of the past like us. Where is little Alice now, Helen's child? She used to play with my children. Mine are still here, mine can still feel hungry, cold and frightened; mine still play. Alice is a pile of little bones. I would like to feel her spirit has entered some other body, and was not wasted, so terribly, but can one believe such things?

Well. Fortunately, there is more to life than death. There is for one thing, fiction. A thousand thousand characters to be sent marching out into the world to divert time from its forward gallop to the terrible horizon. It seems as if, bewildered, he has to pause to scoop them up as well. Give yourself over entirely to fiction, and you could have eternal life. That's what Jesus said – though look how that story ended.

Certainly not down here among the women. Who ever heard of a crucified woman? Who would bother?

'Socks,' says Emma-Audrey to Jocelyn. 'Socks. Two male children, and one man. Six socks a day seven days a week. Forty-two socks a week. Why? Why do they wear them, and worse, why do I feel obliged to wash them? Millions starve all over the world, other millions go barefoot – I wash socks. Jocelyn, I am so bored.'

They eat lunch in a Kardomah Café. Cottage-cheese salad, and good coffee. Emma-Audrey is discontented. She looks at her hand-knitted sweater with contempt. She raises her wash-sodden hands to her hair – home-washed in rainwater which Paul tests with a Geiger counter for radioactivity – and longs for the feel of lacquer and artifice, carcinogenic though such frivolities tend to be.

'Can't you take more interest in the hens?' suggests Jocelyn.

'Hens are boring birds at the best of times,' says Emma-Audrey, 'and battery-reared hens are worst of all. They have no character. They have no one to talk to. They are reared in isolation.'

'It is strange the way Paul has gone over to the other side,' says Jocelyn, who never liked Paul, which is presumably why Emma-Audrey has now sought her out. 'He used to be all for healthy living. Quite the nut-cutlet man.'

'He's an Egg Marketing Man now,' says Emma-Audrey. 'He puts penicillin in the mash, and hormones, and do you know what, every year he looks more and more like a hen.'

Jocelyn is shocked. Jocelyn never speaks of her husband in disparaging terms. Even to her lover, Jocelyn spoke well of Philip.

'I would love to live in the country,' she says vaguely.

'Why?' asks Emma-Audrey, sourly.

'To be in touch with the seasons.'

'All one is in touch with is mud. You can't think how much there is. On the floors, and the walls, and all over clothes, and in one's hair. Mud. Smelly mud, too. You can't think how filthy battery farms are. On mucking out days I take the children to friends. I can't go to my mother's, of course, because Paul won't let me.'

Jocelyn does not pursue this.

'It must be profitable,' she says.

'Oh, it is,' says Audrey-Emma, plucking at her knobbly skirt. 'But he's so mean. Look at the rags I have to wear.'

'I thought you liked weaving,' says Jocelyn.

'No,' says Audrey-Emma, firmly. 'He told me I liked weaving, and I believed him, more fool me. Now look at me. Stuck away in the country, with only hen farmers to talk to, mud up to my ears. I can't go on like this.'

'You have the children to consider,' says Jocelyn, who still has none.

'Oh, yes,' says Audrey-Emma vaguely, 'the children. Paul doesn't like the children. He has no time for them. If only they were chickens he'd feel differently.'

'Where are they today?' asks Jocelyn.

'He's looking after them. They'll be nervous wrecks by the time I get back. He's an anal obsessive, I think. He makes them scrub their nails and examines between their toes. Well of course there's mud there. There's mud everywhere.'

Jocelyn wonders if Audrey-Emma is not having some kind of nervous breakdown.

'If I stay,' pleads Audrey-Emma, 'I will go mad.' There are tears in her eyes. 'But I can't leave,' she goes on, 'because if I do he will follow me and kill me. I know he will. He believes in marriage. It looks,' says Audrey-Emma, 'as if I have to choose between madness or death.'

'I'm sorry,' murmurs Jocelyn, inadequately. This is not the kind of conversation she is accustomed to having in the Kardomah.

'If only some man would come along and rescue me. But who would look at me? That's another thing Paul has done – he has aged me prematurely. He nags me, long into the night.'

'About what?'

'Everything. Anything. He believes I personally carry fowl pest with me, I think. I slave away in that house, and all he ever says is how he could do it better. If that's the way he feels, why doesn't he? But oh no, that's woman's work, he won't demean himself. If he'd let me take over the business side of the batteries we'd be rich in no time, but will he? No. He's terrified I might do it better than him. What am I going to do? Why does he always find fault with me?'

'Perhaps you find fault with him,' Jocelyn ventures, but

Audrey-Emma doesn't hear.

Audrey-Emma's face has lost its girlish roundness. She looks peaky, as well as dowdy, and there are lines of resentment deepening round her eyes. Jocelyn smooths hers away nightly with beauty creams. Audrey-Emma smears honey on her face from time to time.

'You have let yourself go a little,' murmurs Jocelyn.

'I have, haven't I,' says Audrey-Emma, not without satisfaction. 'Why should I be pretty just for him? He wants me to be a dowdy housewife, so that's what he's going to get.'

'I think you should make the best of it,' says Jocelyn. 'You have three children, after all. Once you have children you can't just think of yourself, you have to think of them too.'

'What kind of future will it be for them?' Audrey-Emma laments, 'with a father like Paul.' She consults the menu. 'Do you think I could have a cream pastry? Paul says cream's all right so long as it isn't sweetened.'

She eats her pastry. Presently a worldly man with greying hair and a journalistic air comes in for coffee. Audrey-Emma, hampered only slightly by the bulk of her tweed skirt, darts over to join him, deserting Jocelyn instantly. It is her old Editor. The lines on her face smooth out as if by magic; she grows prettier and more animated minute by minute. She clasps the Editor's hand. How white her skin is; how female and nonsensical her whole being. He laughs at her but is entranced. She practically lays herself down, there and then, legs apart, offering herself as a sacrificial victim. How can he fail to deliver the ritual blow?

They leave together.

Audrey-Emma whispers a farewell to Jocelyn. 'You don't mind do you, darling? He's such an old fool, but he might do a thing on chicken farming. I'm not deserting you, am I? It's for poor Paul's sake: I have to chat him up a little.'

And they're gone, the Editor holding Audrey-Emma's little elbow closely, as if afraid she might wander off by accident.

Jocelyn, pale, elegant Jocelyn, so longing for love, so afflicted by discrimination, is left to pay the bill.

Scarlet has discovered the C.N.D. She works in its headquarters. Byzantia addresses envelopes in her childish hand. Edwin is furious.

'Long-haired lefties!' he mutters. 'Do what you want, if you insist on being associated with cranks and perverts, but leave Edwina out of it.'

'Do you want the world to be blown up?' enquires Scarlet. They are touring through Boreham Wood. Byzantia dozes on the back seat. ('She stays up too late watching television,' as Edwin has already observed. 'She's not getting enough discipline.')

'You over-simplify issues,' he complains. 'You are absurdly naïve, even for a woman. We must defend ourselves, or the reds will simply walk in.'

'You're mad,' observes Scarlet.

He drives rather fast and badly, when they are quarrelling, which they do frequently. It is a miracle they are all still alive. It is their ninety-eighth weekly outing.

'It's very depressing,' he says. 'What a flighty mind you have. All those Common Cause meetings and they taught you nothing.'

'I suppose you think better dead than red,' she sneers.

'Indeed I do,' he says. 'Without freedom life is not worth living. If this country went red I would kill Edwina with my own hands.'

'Do you hear that, Byzantia?' asks Scarlet of her daughter, who fortunately is too busy counting pubs to hear. Scarlet has weighed up the emotional disadvantages of their car rides with Edwin, and the financial advantages, and decided to continue them. What she cannot do, not even to save her daughter, is to behave decently during their jaunts. Is it so difficult to appear to agree, to appear to accept criticism? she asks herself, and the answer comes back, yes, difficult to the point of impossibility. She usually returns home with her nails bitten to the quick, one or two outbursts of grief and rage the worse. ('You are a hysterical woman,' he complains. 'I can argue rationally, why can't you? It is a fact that I am older than you. If you would just agree that my experience of the world is greater than yours, we could be perfectly happy.' His back pains are much better, these days, now there is no likelihood of him finding himself back in bed with Scarlet.)

'I wish you would stop calling her by that ridiculous name,' he says now.

'It's her real name,' says Scarlet.

'I have been consulting my solicitor about it,' he says. 'An individual's real name is the one he is called by. All the same I would like to have her Christian name changed by Deed Poll.'

Scarlet does not reply at first. He has a certain tone of voice which he uses when he makes final ultimatums; he does not add, 'Or I will stop the money.' He does not have to.

'Isn't that rather expensive?' she asks, finally, with what she feels is cunning. 'Wouldn't it be a good idea just to let one person call her one thing and another another?'

'Not if one of those names is Byzantia.'

'What's so awful about Byzantia anyway? I've never known.' Scarlet sounds quite cheeky. There is going to be real trouble.

'It's foreign,' he says. 'Not that I have anything against foreigners, but why call an English child by a foreign name? Her father wasn't foreign, was he? Black, or anything?'

'Does it look as if her father was black?'

'That kind of thing can skip a generation.'

'Please,' requests Scarlet, 'do we have to have this conversation in front of Byzantia?'

'In front of whom?'

'Byzantia.'

'Oh, Edwina, you mean. Edwina is too young to understand what we are talking about.'

'Your fantasy child Edwina may be. My Byzantia is not.'

'I support, feed, clothe, care for and love that child. I suggest that makes her as much mine as yours.'

'Oh no,' says Scarlet. 'Oh no.'

'What is more,' he says, 'I think the time for this nonsense is over. If you are mentally disturbed that is a pity, but it has been going on for too long. It is time you returned home. People are beginning to talk.'

'What? After two years? How impetuous people are in Lee

Green!'

He stares at her, wondering if she is being sarcastic, and nearly crashes the car into a bollard.

'Would you mind driving more carefully?' She is polite.

'I am a very good driver. I am taking my Advanced Motorists' Test presently. Please do not change the subject.'

'You changed it yourself by trying to kill us. You are so full of hostility and anger it has to come out somehow. You are the most violent person I know.'

'And I certainly have no intention of paying another bill for this trick-cyclist of yours if that's the kind of nonsense he feeds you.' (Scarlet has been seeing an analyst weekly. She charges 50/- a session.)

'I am a very mild and civilized person. Anyone else would have beaten you to death by now. I demand a straight answer, Scarlet. You can't play silly-buggers with me. When are you coming home?'

Scarlet does not reply.

'I have supported you and Edwina for two years, out of the kindness of my heart. Anyone else would have divorced you. I think it is time I received my reward.'

'You want me back in your bed, do you?' Scarlet is smiling. It is a bad sign. Byzantia begins counting lamp-posts, feverishly.

'I want you back in my home, where you belong.'

'But not in your bed?'

'You know my state of health,' he says. He is pale, 'I love you and need you, Scarlet. I miss you. My most earnest desire is to have you and little Edwina back. I think I am more conscious of the higher states of love than you, Scarlet.'

'But not back in your bed? Not that I was ever in it, more than once.'

'I am an ill man.'

'Ill? You are a stupid, impotent, elderly old dribbler,' Scarlet shrieks. 'All you've ever been good for is to pay the bills. Skinny Winny!'

Edwin slams on the brakes. Scarlet allows herself to fall forward and bangs her head badly. Byzantia starts to cry.

'Now we know,' says Edwin, above the noise. 'Now we know your true motives. I always suspected it. Well, now we know. Prostitute!'

'Prostitute –' she laughs, holding her head, where a lump is already beginning.

'Whore,' he hisses. 'Slut. Sex-mad animal. Thank God my mother never lived to see me tied to a foul creature like you.'

Scarlet decides it is madness to be sitting in a stalled car with other cars hooting all around, with an insane elderly school inspector. She tries to get out. He tries to stop her.

'If you go,' he says, 'not another penny, not another penny.'

'Mum –' says Byzantia from the back.

Scarlet heaves herself over into the back seat and clasps Byzantia.

'I'm sorry,' she says to her daughter, 'sorry. Really it's all right. It's going to be all right. It will never happen again –'

The car jerks forward.

'Quieter now, are you?' asks Edwin.

'Yes,' says Scarlet, with apparent docility.

'That man should give you shock treatment,' says Edwin.

'It's what you need.'

At the next red traffic light Scarlet opens the door and shuffles herself and Byzantia out of the car. Edwin shakes his fist and holds up Scarlet's handbag, which she has left behind, and drives off in triumph.

They are twenty miles from home. Scarlet smiles. She has a ten-shilling note in her pocket; otherwise she would not have abandoned her handbag.

A car pulls up beside them. It is a dirty Jaguar.

'Can I help you?' asks the driver. He is quite young, and has good white teeth, which he is now showing, for he is smiling broadly. Scarlet feels she is unused to seeing men smile.

'No, thank you,' says Scarlet, with a feeling of discovery. 'I can look after myself perfectly well.'

It is a useful discovery, because the following day she receives a letter from Edwin's solicitors saying she will receive no more maintenance. He rings in the evening to see if she is prepared to be reasonable about Edwina's name, but Scarlet is not.

'In that case,' says Edwin, 'that is that. You are a wicked woman. You have ruined my life, and you mean to ruin your child's. What will you do, go out cleaning again?'

'No.'

'No, perhaps not. You are not very good at it, are you? The house is much cleaner now you have left. There are vacancies for porters on London Underground. You should consider it. It might suit you. You can put Edwina in a home, I suppose, amongst strangers. I am starting divorce proceedings, for your information.'

'So am I.'

'What?'

'I am proceeding against you for mental cruelty.'

He puts the telephone down abruptly, and comes straight round. His eyes are red from weeping.

'I was never cruel to you,' he says, 'never. I was always kind. I loved you and Byzantia. If I have offended you please forgive me. I will try and do better. I would cut off my right arm to please you.'

'No,' says Scarlet, who is tired. 'You were never cruel to me. I was only joking.'

'Not a very funny joke,' he says, recovering quickly enough at the slightest sign of weakness from Scarlet. He has brought her handbag back.

'How did you get home?' he enquires.

'A man in a dirty Jaguar picked me up,' says Scarlet. 'He is a rather eccentric solicitor, and a very kind man.'

'He put you up to divorcing me for cruelty, didn't he? After all I did for you and Byzantia. Rescuing you both from the gutter. Admit it.'

'No.'

'Yes, he did.' Edwin begins to cry. 'Everyone's ganging up on me. All I ever do is try to be kind.'

Scarlet picks up the poker.

'If you don't go away I'll kill you,' she says.

He goes, passing the solicitor who is on the way in. The solicitor's name is Alec. Scarlet has heard the gate click, and knows Alec is on his way. Now she has, as it were, the law on her side, she is prepared to murder Edwin.

She certainly wants to. She can bear depending on Edwin, hating Edwin, despising Edwin, but she cannot endure being sorry for him.

Edwin never returns. Scarlet receives divorce papers from him through the post, and does not argue; a private detective comes to examine the double bed she shares with Alec, but she never actually sees Edwin again.

Sometimes he moves through her dreams, grey, thin and fidgety, making her feel bad.

There is a sale of Y's paintings. They fetch a record price. Y is dead. There will be no more paintings. The art columns of the Sunday papers tremble with loss and grief. The greatest painter of a generation. Perhaps the only real female painter who ever was, hounded to death, destroyed by her own hand. Helen takes the blame. X is exonerated. His own pictures go up in value. He is popular again within six months.

Picture the scene one evening, when Carl and Helen still lived together, when Y still lived. Carl arrives home early, champagne under each arm, to celebrate a successful sale.

As he turns on the light in the living-room, there is a scuffling on the floor. It is Helen, his mistress, and X, once his most promising young painter. He turns off the light and goes away.

'He must have seen,' says Helen, appalled.

'Do him good,' says X.

'He'll murder me,' says Helen.

'You're a big girl,' says X. 'Murder him back. I'll look after you.'

'Supposing he tells Y?'

'He won't dare. Y does as I tell her. If there's trouble he'll get no more of her paintings.'

Helen struggles to get to her feet, but X pins her down and forces her legs apart. She giggles, pleased by thoughts of rape, relieved of guilt by the knowledge that she is helpless.

An hour later they are both still there on the floor, entwined, when Carl comes in with Y.

('Sex drives you mad,' says Helen to Jocelyn, months later. 'We must have known what would happen. If he'd gone when Carl first came back Y might be alive now. Perhaps we just wanted to hurt her. Perhaps all X has ever done is want to hurt Y. Even now she's dead he gets at her, through me.'

'What do you mean?' Jocelyn is puzzled. They are both pregnant. Jocelyn eight months, Helen six. But all Helen can say is – 'By loving me.')

Y is silent, and stands like a pale doll in the doorway, limbs limp, staring. Carl flies at Helen and strips her remaining clothes from her. She stands naked.

'That's how you came to me,' he says. 'That's how you can go.'

X laughs. 'What a foreigner you are, Carl,' he says.

'What do you mean?' asks Carl, alarmed even in this extremity of situation by the suggestion that he is not behaving like a true Englishman.

'You take sex so seriously,' says X, adjusting his clothing. He turns to Y. 'What's the matter? Cat got your tongue? I am sorry this malicious pig has seen fit to bring you here.'

'He is not a pig,' says Y. 'He is a friend. I think he is the only friend I have ever had.'

'I am your friend,' whispers poor naked Helen, but Y does not seem to hear.

'Get out,' says Carl to Helen. 'Leave me alone. You are a dispensable and interchangeable woman. You are not even ornamental. Look at you, with your great orange nipples. You are coarse. I like a woman with little pink nipples.'

'Yes. Get out,' says Y. 'I do not want you in the same room as my paintings. You defile them.'

This remark irritates X. It is as if she rated her paintings higher than she did him.

'If she goes,' he says, surprisingly, 'I go with her, nipples and all.'

Carl and Y are taken aback. Y begins, at last, to cry; a gentle subdued painful sound. X steps forward and takes Y's coat off. She lets her arms be moved, never helping or hindering, but does not stop sobbing. X puts the coat on Helen, who is more positively co-operative, and then puts his arm round her to offer yet more protection, and they leave.

'I've had enough,' X says, 'of all this hysteria. I just want to live in some kind of peace.' He adds, speaking to Carl, 'I blame you for this. It need not have happened. You ridiculous foreigner, your taste is lousy. You are the con-man of the art world and I'll see that everyone knows it.'

Helen and X go and live in the country. Helen gives out that she is pregnant: she sends flowers to Y one day, asking for forgiveness and a renewal of friendship, and offering to look after her children so Y can get on with her painting.

Since X left Y has felt paralysed. If she tries to paint she falls asleep. She has been sleeping with Carl but it does no good. Y plaits Helen's flowers into a wreath and pins the letter above the gas-stove, and turns it on, and dies, as she has always known she would. She is thirty-five, and feels that life has been going on for a long, long time.

Helen receives anonymous and non-anonymous letters, blaming her for Y's death. X is distraught. 'You came into our lives,' he says to Helen, 'and destroyed them. Now you have killed my wife.' For weeks he is silent, but he does not leave Helen. Nor does he ask her to marry him. 'Y is my wife,' he says. 'You are my destiny. I was born under a fearful star.' Art-conscious local people ask him round to dinners and parties. Helen is not asked. X goes. Helen, swelling and helpless, stays at home and waits, as Y once did.

Helen embroiders white linen cloths. She thinks, in her fantasies, she should have been some diplomat's wife. She could have lived elegantly, in some European capital, and been gracious to important people. She thinks that would suit her. But she knows in her heart that nothing she ever does now will make any difference. Wherever she goes, Y will pad softly along behind, dressed in a white suit, pale and slightly stooping. X writes a monograph about Y's work.

Helen rings Jocelyn once, but Jocelyn pretends to be out. Since Y died, Jocelyn thinks Helen is too wicked to be endured. She is grateful yet again for the enduring boredom of her own marriage.

Helen rings Sylvia, but Sylvia has left home. Butch now lives in their little house with a girl called Rachel. It was Sylvia who first met Rachel in the ante-natal clinic, where the latter was doing research, and brought her home, a plain, stark girl with up-swept horn-rimmed spectacles, a plump figure, hair unfashionably back-combed into a beehive, and a braying laugh. It does not occur to Sylvia that Butch will find Rachel attractive: that her own pale languor now bores, rather than appeals. During this last but successful pregnancy both her hearing and her eyesight have become worse, and she sometimes peers at Butch as if she could not remember who he was.

Rachel has no such handicap. She looks at hearty, healthy Butch with bright brown alert eyes and challenges his interest, and laughs uproariously when he makes dirty jokes. Sylvia, at such times, just looks bewildered and ladylike, and asks him to say it again. He can't stand it.

On the day Butch's divorce finally comes through he confides in Sylvia that he has been having an affair with Rachel for some months and that he wants to marry her. Sylvia asks Butch to repeat what he said. He hits her hard on the side of the head – the left side, the side of her best ear. Her ear whistles for days, and when it stops, it is because she can hear nothing.

Sylvia, after a lonely day or two, goes to stay with Jocelyn. When she is gone, Rachel – who has been keeping an eye on the house – moves into it with Butch. So far as Rachel is concerned, Sylvia has been making Butch unhappy, and so deserves whatever she gets.

Butch and Rachel live happily ever afterwards.

As for Helen, she types X's monograph on Y, and waits for her child to be born. X says it is Carl's child. She knows that it is not.

12

Nice People

Down among the women.

Miss Rogers is a nice person. She helps at the Old People's Home. She is forty-five and has never married. She walks home across the park, and sometimes joins me on my bench.

'It's not men's fault,' she says to me, quite out of the blue one day.

'What isn't?' I ask.

'Women,' she says. 'I used to blame men for women's condition, not now. In the end men are irrelevant. Women are happy or unhappy, fulfilled or unfulfilled, and it has nothing to do with men.' She sighs. She is a handsome, large woman: she wears a bold red coat. I wonder why she has never married. 'A forty-year-old man has no trouble going off with a twenty-year-old girl,' she says, as if I had spoken aloud, 'but who is going to go off with me?'

'You never know,' I say.

'No,' she says. 'It's too late for me. And don't think I don't regret it, because I do.'

And instead of throwing a pellet of bread in front of a pigeon, she throws it at the unfortunate bird, so it rises into the air with fright.

'I would have liked to have made some man happy,' she says.

'What?' I ask, trying to cheer her up. 'Cook and clean for someone just as able-bodied as you?' She is such a bold dark clever-looking woman her softness surprises me.

'Yes,' she says. 'That's the whole trouble. One likes to serve.'

And off she goes, carrying her basket of goodies to her old people, an aged Red Riding Hood with no wolf pursuing.

Susan goes to visit Wanda. She wears a little hat. She must be the only young woman left in London to do so. Wanda is packing. She is moving yet again. Her new flat will cost ten shillings a week more but there are fewer stairs to climb. Wanda's legs are beginning to feel their age.

Susan is surprisingly practical about the green and yellow lino. She levers it up, ignoring the dirt and grime beneath it, and stacks it in piles.

'Scarlet used to do that for me,' says Wanda. 'But of course she's too busy now.'

'What at?' asks Susan.

'Being kept,' says Wanda sourly. 'That girl has the soul of a prostitute.'

'I'm kept too,' says Susan. 'I don't work or anything.'

'Yes, but you pay for it,' says Wanda, who is almost fond of

Susan. 'You're married.' If Wanda has had too much to drink she will lurch over to Susan and embrace her. And too much drink, for Wanda these days, is anything to drink at all.

Susan laughs nervously. She is at a loss to explain her liking for Wanda. She does not tell Kim she visits his former wife – but then she cannot tell Kim much at all, for he is seldom at home.

Watson and Belcher grow more powerful each year. Kim works hard and late, goes off on location whenever he possibly can, and occasionally dresses Susan up and propels her forward as hostess at some grand party he fancies throwing. He hires an outside caterer, for Susan's cooking remains New Zealand provincial.

Kim has a large house now in Windsor, with a staff of five, and a studio specially built for Kim to paint in. There is, indeed, one half-finished painting on the easel. Susan has described it to Wanda, who says it was a painting he started in 1939, and never finished. Certainly, he spends no time there, in his beautiful half-timbered studio, with the cool north light. He never goes to the Oxford Street pub either. He lunches at the Savoy on consommé, grilled steak and salad, and black coffee, or occasionally melon, grilled sole and tomatoes, and black coffee. He watches his waist, and keeps his blood pressure down. He means to live to a hundred, and see his paintings resurrected at the Tate, as a fortune-teller lately implied would happen.

Susan sees Jocelyn on occasion. Their worlds are similar, and although Susan, as wife of a director, has the social advantage of the wife of a senior executive, Jocelyn does have a university degree, and does design her own home. Kim sees to Susan's, with the help of the Art Department. Susan feels inadequate.

'Do you remember Sylvia?' Susan asks Wanda. 'She is staying with Jocelyn. She is pregnant and deaf, and her boyfriend wouldn't marry her.'

'You sound quite jealous,' says Wanda, and it is true. Susan would be glad of anything that actually happened. Her life is empty of events.

'Philip used to fancy Sylvia,' says Susan. 'In fact Jocelyn took her away from him. I think it's risky, don't you, having her in the house now?'

(Philip, actually, can hardly bear to look at Sylvia. He scarcely recognizes this swollen, distressed woman as the vague and lissom Sylvia he still, from time to time, has dreams about, and in which his mother always interferes.)

'I wish you could have more normal friends,' he complains to Jocelyn. 'It doesn't reflect well on you.'

'At least,' says Jocelyn, 'I have friends.' It is a sharp and unkind remark. She makes them quite often, these days. It is true, too. Philip finds himself friendless. He has colleagues, with whom he is on good enough terms, but he suspects they regard him as square and dull. He has outgrown his former Rugby friends, who work in insurance or in the seedier branches of industry. It is not that he feels he is too smart and sophisticated for them; but that they feel inadequate. The more he buys the drinks, the less at ease they are.

Jocelyn makes him more uneasy than ever. She has become astringent of tongue, and she is pregnant. He regards her bulky body with fear, as something unknowable.

'What a guilty thing you are,' says Wanda to Susan. 'Always expecting punishment. Only the good get punished and I shouldn't think Philip was a good person. Dull, yes. Good, no.'

'I don't know how Jocelyn stands it,' says Susan. 'Philip kisses my hand at parties, and he has such a limp, clammy hand. And at the same time he manages to leer. I get leered at quite a lot, of course, being married to someone so much older, but Philip does it more than most.'

'You talk as if marriage was something that happened to you. Not something you'd done.'

'That's what it feels like,' complains Susan. 'I was too young. They should have stopped me.'

'They!' sneers Wanda. 'They! Where is this mysterious They? The closest I ever got to They was Scarlet's Edwin and look what happened there.'

'Poor Scarlet,' says Susan. 'I wish she liked me more. I went all the way down to Lee Green to rescue her and still she doesn't like me. I've only ever wished her well.'

'You've kept her away from Kim,' says Wanda.

'Oh no,' says Susan, shocked. 'Never. I am his daughter.'

'What did you say?' asks Wanda.

'I said she is his daughter,' says Susan.

Wanda sighs and does not pursue the matter. Susan, however, does.

'I think it's unfair to say I kept Scarlet away. She's been welcome to come at any time. Good God, she even had her child in my bed. Was that keeping her away?'

215

Wanda says nothing.

'It wouldn't have helped her to have given her money,' says Susan. 'People must learn to stand on their own feet.'

'Do shut up, you silly little bitch,' says Wanda, 'and help me pack. It's all you're fit for.'

'Don't speak to me like that,' says Susan, with dignity, but she does as she is told. She even asks Scarlet round to dinner.

Scarlet telephones her mother in panic.

'I've nothing to wear,' she says. 'Can you give me some money?'

'Ask your boyfriend,' says Wanda.

'He has his wife to support, he can't. And I can't wear cheap clothes any more. I'm such a funny shape, cheap clothes always look strange on me.'

'Then go naked.'

'How very unhelpful you are,' says Scarlet, all hoity-toity. 'I look worse naked. Deformed. It's your fault. You should have put me in a plaster cast when I was a baby.'

'I did,' says Wanda. 'You were born with a dislocated hip. You were in a cast until you were nine months.'

'I never knew that.'

'It was something I did not wish to remember. What would you have felt like if Byzantia had been born deformed?'

'A dislocated hip isn't deformed.'

'No? That's not what your father said. He could paint nudes with toe-nails growing out of their ears but one baby with a dislocated hip and he went to pieces. He hardly ever came home for six months, he'd never touch you or pick you up, and I never trusted him after that. That's why I left.'

'I thought you left because you disapproved of his paintings.'

'That as well. But the initial disappointment started with you.' And Wanda laughs. It is quite like old times.

'I don't think it's a laughing matter,' says Scarlet.

'Neither do I,' says Wanda, trying to take the top out of the gin bottle with her teeth, because she has the telephone receiver in one hand.

But she only succeeds in hurting her teeth, so she replaces the receiver and concentrates on the gin.

Susan has dinner laid for three in the morning-room, which is chintzy and informal.

'We should eat in the dining-room,' says Kim. 'Or do you want to palm her off with second-best?'

Susan is taken aback by such aggression. Kim is normally polite to the point of indifference.

'Of course I don't,' she says. 'I just thought it would be more homey in the morning-room.'

'I think she would see it as an insult,' says Kim, staring at her with hard, bright, elderly eyes.

'What's the matter with you?' she asks, bewildered. 'What have I done?'

'Deprived me of a family,' he says. She cries, from the surprise, the injustice, of such a sudden accusation. He comforts her, automatically, but without interest. She wonders if he is ill; the thought that he might be makes her angry. It is his function to look after her. For what other reason has she endured all these years? She shuts her eyes.

And lo, her kauri forest springs up around her: wraps her once again in its dark protective silence. It has not been lost: it has been hiding: too dark and powerful ever to dissolve. She takes her time amongst the massive trunks; she brushes the creeper ropes aside; she listens to the silence; she is a child again. She opens her eyes. She smiles remotely at Kim, and rings for the maid, and has dinner re-set in the dining-room, on the vast mahogany table beneath the chandelier.

'Are you better now?' he asks.

'Oh yes,' she says. But she does not care. He is nothing to do with her. He never has been. He is Scarlet's father, Byzantia's grandfather, Wanda's husband. He has acknowledged it, and so can she. She has her inner life back again.

Scarlet arrives. She is dressed in orange silk; she is charming, almost soignée; she is slim and entertaining. Her shoes are not cleaned and her stockings are laddered, as if she had lost interest in herself at knee-level, but – so long as she is sitting – she reflects credit on her father. He is impressed. They talk, laugh, confide.

Susan feels dull, stodgy, and isolated. She sits in the highly-polished, glittering world she has created. Each pendant of the chandelier above has been washed and polished. Upstairs in cedar chests are folded snowy sheets and pillowcases, thick towels and blankets. In the kitchen all is order and cleanliness. In the garden not a weed shows more than half-an-inch high. Simeon sleeps dutifully, with clean face and fingernails in pyjamas fresh as today. None of it comforts her.

She can see her face in the mirror. Her eyes are beginning to pop slightly, as her mother's did. She hopes and believes that Kim has not noticed.

'Perhaps I should go and live with Wanda,' she says, 'and

Scarlet could come and live here,' but she must have spoken very softly, for no one hears. She is relieved, on reflection, that they do not.

'I have given up complaining and reproaching,' says Scarlet, after several glasses of good red wine. 'It takes up too much energy. I have a lot to be getting on with and life is short.'

'It has taken you a long time to get round to it,' says Kim, who has had not only wine but nearly half a bottle of whisky, as well as a prawn cocktail in a brandy glass, roast chicken, with stuffing and bread sauce, roast potatoes and green peas, and a peach melba. Sometimes he thinks he will offer Susan cookery lessons at the Cordon Bleu, but fears her eyes will pop even more than they do already.

'You can't accuse me of making a nuisance of myself,' says Scarlet. 'For a daughter, I keep myself very much to myself.'

'Your entire life so far,' he complains, 'has been a not very subtle reproach to me.'

'Or to Wanda,' says Susan, but they ignore her. Is it, she begins to wonder, that she speaks softly, or is it that they have blotted her out of their minds?

'I came to you once,' says Scarlet, 'to ask you what was to become of me.'

'What did I say?'

'I had Byzantia, and never got round to it. Perhaps that was answer enough.'

'In my bed,' says Susan.

'Our bed,' says Kim, hearing her, but not looking at her. 'These days, being the gentry, we have separate rooms, with adjoining bath.'

'You've never supported me,' says Scarlet. 'Why not?'

'I have had Susan to support,' says Kim. 'And of course Simeon.' Though he has difficulty in remembering that he has a son.

'But if you like,' says Kim, 'I will make you an allowance now.'

'I don't need it now,' says Scarlet. 'I live in sin with a solicitor. In any case, I am sure Susan would object. I have very few needs; Alec pays the rent, and the State pays for my analysis.'

'I don't see how you can stand it,' says Susan. 'People messing about in your mind. All this turning inwards! It just makes people self-absorbed and selfish. What good has it done you?'

'I am sitting here at this table,' says Scarlet, 'behaving really quite well, and even believing that you're both human.'

'Charming!' says Susan.

Kim drives Scarlet home in his new Bentley. He feels, for all the gleaming metal around him, that he is a shadow of what he might have been.

'When your mother left me,' he says, 'she took something away from me. I wasn't sorry to see it go at the time, but I think it was a pity.'

'Shall I tell her so?' asks Scarlet. 'She'd be pleased.'

'No,' he says. 'It is too late. We are both too old. The future, for both of us, has become a thing of the past.'

He drives silently for a while. He feels himself to be a ridiculous elderly man, wearing too-tight purple trousers and a lambswool sweater. He does not understand how it has happened. He is accustomed to being young. And is this his daughter? Scarlet, his baby, lying in her awkward plaster cast, limbs akimbo! Did she really grow into this? In his mind, time becomes confused.

'You should have gone into hospital to have the baby,' he mumbles, mistaking Scarlet for Wanda. 'You're very obstinate. You didn't really know better than the doctors, you see. You're not as tough as you think you are. Now see what you've done to her.'

'What did you say?' asks Scarlet, puzzled, and he shakes his head like a seal out of water and regains his sense of the present.

'I'm working too hard,' he says. 'It's all these dependants.'

'What are you working hard on?' asks Scarlet. 'Toilet paper?'

'That's right,' he says.

'What an asset you are to the community,' she says. 'All those nice clean bums, all thanks to you.'

'You are like your mother,' he says. 'It's not surprising I get confused.'

It is impossible, he thinks, when he returns to Susan, to make everyone happy. All the same he tries. Susan sulks for twenty-four hours, and then, surprisingly, allows him to make love to her. Kim dies suddenly and painlessly, in mid-intercourse. It has always been his fear – the pounding of the heart, the soaring of the senses, the high spasm of nothingness – supposing the spirit goes so far it does not return?

Well. It does not return on this particular evening. He dies as he has lived, unburdened, and perhaps more appropriately in Susan's arms than in Alison's.

The day after she dines with her father, Scarlet fills in an application form for a place in the London School of Economics. She even posts it.

'You might almost say,' she says to Alec, 'that I have grown up. And that's another thing – out!!'

'Who?' he asks, looking round.

'You,' she says.

'Why?' He is surprised, if not really upset.

'Your wife is a nice woman,' says Scarlet.

'So are you,' said Alec. 'Anyway how do you know what my wife is like? You have never met her. You and I are doing no one any harm. All we do is add to the sum of human happiness.'

'We are doing me harm,' says Scarlet. 'I want a proper husband of my own age, and some more children; I'm fed up with other women's left-overs.'

'Oh, charming,' he says. 'Charming. I don't think you have the temperament for marriage. I am sorry for your ex-husband. You have no sense of humour.'

'Get out,' says Scarlet, made more furious by this than any other insult he has ever offered her. 'Get out.'

'Very well,' he says, lingering. 'Ring me at the office when you change your mind.'

'Supposing I rang you at your home?' she enquires.

'You wouldn't do that,' he says. 'In any case you don't know the number. You are being very rash. Supposing you don't find anyone to marry you? The world is full of unmarried women. I might just be a fluke, a flash in the pan.'

'I am a divorced woman,' says Scarlet, 'and statistically that is a good sign. We tend to remarry.'

'I shall miss you,' says Alec. 'When I first saw you in that car I thought you were some dismal daughter out with her father. Then I saw you snarling and knew no daughter ever snarled at a father like that. That was marriage, that was. Then you heaved over into the back seat showing a lot of suspender and nice white thighs, and I fancied it, married or not. Nice unused thigh, Scarlet. I made good use of it.'

'Oh, get out,' says Scarlet, sadly enough. 'It won't work any more. I'm not a naughty little girl. I'm a grown woman. Good-day.'

The next day Wanda phones Scarlet, in tears, to tell her that Kim has died. Scarlet rings Alec, at the office, and cries. He comes round at once and comforts her, and admits he has been making up his wife, and asks her to marry him.

'It is like a happy ending,' Scarlet complains to Jocelyn, later. 'Kim dies and everything comes right. Was he really such a villain?

I had stopped hating him; now I am forced to wonder again. He had seemed, lately, so little worth hating. Just an elderly, ordinary man, with a rather simple nature; a rather vain person, wearing trousers too young for him. A little boy, showing off his smart house and his shiny car. What a lot of my life I have wasted spiting him; and when I wasn't spiting him, worshipping him like the graven image he always was in my mind, with a painting done in 1939 in one sculptured hand, and the other pinching Susan's bottom. Sculpted flat, not three-dimensional, I may say, like the Elgin marbles. All the same, I am glad we parted on good terms.'

Kim's house, of course, is not paid for. Neither is the Rolls. He has not paid a household bill for, it appears, five years. He has only one insurance policy, the rewards of which he had transferred, only the day before he died, from Susan his wife to Scarlet his daughter. A cheque for £8,532 is brought round to Scarlet within an hour of news of his death. Susan does not quibble. She has not the energy.

Official auditors and executors move in. The house is sold to meet bills. Susan takes the flat below Wanda's. Simeon is taken from his prep school and goes to the local school; he is bullied for a time, but only until his accent loses its eccentricity and he becomes like the others. He is happier for it. His dull eyes become quite bright. So do Susan's, being daughter, wife and mother to Wanda. She gets a job as a shorthand typist. Her life begins. Her eyes stop popping.

Some six months after Kim's death Susan has a nervous telephone call from a woman called Alison. She says she is Kim's ex-secretary. She has in her possession some fifty paintings done by Kim over the past eight years. What should she do with them? Wanda goes, on Susan's behalf, to inspect the paintings.

Alison is fifty; a grey-haired, plain, peaceful, stoical woman. Kim has been visiting her daily for years: to paint, to talk, to make love. She has asked for nothing better. She has never wished to marry. But she had thought perhaps Susan was entitled to the paintings.

'You mean,' says Wanda, 'you wanted to make your presence

felt.'

But she knows it is not true. Alison is not like that. Alison is a pleasant woman and simply wishes to be obliging. Wanda has never felt more at a disadvantage. The paintings, she suspects, are very good indeed. She leaves them with Alison, who has no idea, one way or the other, of their quality, and who in the end puts them in the Methodist Jumble Sale.

13

Solutions

Down among the women.

Let us now praise fallen women – those of them at any rate who did not choose to fall, but were pushed and never rose again.

Let us praise, for example, truckloads of young Cairo girls, ferried in for the use of the troops, crammed into catacombs beneath the desert floor. More crowded even than Paul's battery hens, as plucked of fine feathers and as raw of breast, and even more diseased.

Where is their Ministry of Agriculture official, where their vet, where their Marketing Board? Where are their post-war treats; their grants, their demob suits, their cheering crowds? Come reunion day, where have they gone? Lost to syphilis, death or drudgery.

Those girls, other girls, scooped up from all the great cities of East and West, Cairo, Saigon, Berlin, Rome. Where are their memorials? Where are they remembered, prayed for, honoured? Didn't they do their bit?

Let us now raise a monument in the heart of the London

Stock Exchange. Let us call it the Tomb of the Unknown Whore. Let the Queen pay homage once a year. Whose side is she on, anyway? The men have taken the top-of-the-milk, and left us with whey for our cornflakes.

So at any rate says Helen, when Scarlet calls to visit her, to show off her wedding ring and photographs of beautiful Byzantia.

X is having an affair with the wife of a neighbour. Her name is Barbara. He does not trouble to hide it from Helen. He paints Barbara naked, and takes Barbara, not Helen, to Private Views.

When Helen protests all he can say is 'Now you know what Y felt like. Stay quiet and put up with it, as you expected her to do.'

'Do you want me to die too?' asks Helen.

'That's up to you,' he says. 'You carry death with you, in any case. I knew that, from the moment I first saw you.'

Helen, looking at herself in the mirror, sees that he is right. When X is away at night, and the blackness of the country closes round the cottage, and the silence mounts, it is death she hears creaking the floorboards and the beams, and death who rustles the leaves against the windows. She is frightened now of the supernatural, as she has never been frightened of anything alive. She will pick the baby Alice out of its crib and sit rocking it against her breast hour after hour, and then become frightened to even pull back the shawl and look at her child, in case it stares back with Y's eyes, suckles with Y's mouth.

'Do you want me to go?' she asks X.

'No,' he replies, and falls silent again.

'I can't live like this,' she tells him.

'You must live as you wish,' he replies. 'It is nothing to do with me. We are bound together by Y's death. It is not up to me to break those ties.'

'It is your fault as much as mine,' she says, and he laughs, loudly and shockingly, at the absurdity of such a notion. They both accept that it is not true. Y's death is established as Helen's fault.

X thinks that Helen is turning from a domestic into a wild animal. She has become gaunt: her lips stretch back over teeth that seem too large: the whites of her eyes show unnaturally. She seems to him to lurk in dark corners, embodiment of all reproach. She is his punishment. He will not turn her away for fear of something worse.

He is fearful of Alice, who mews and suckles like a little animal. She too is monstrous, he thinks, with her tiny, blind searching head. He has relief only when he is with his Barbara, whom he sees as a calm, pleasant, stupid woman. She has no imagination. To her a table is a table, a death is a death. Barbara disapproves of Helen, and believes in saying what she thinks.

'She is a femme fatale, that's all,' says Barbara. 'One day you will grow out of her, and you will stop feeling so depressed. In the meantime, of course, you are painting beautifully. Perhaps the strain is good for you?'

Barbara does not really want the situation altered. Why should she? She has such status now as she has never dreamt of. A successful farmer for a husband, and a famous artist for a lover, and the black beast Helen, snarling in her corner, defeated.

'You can't stay,' says Scarlet to Helen, for tales of Barbara have drifted back to London. Helen is still seen as the witch-woman, but Scarlet is now on Helen's side. 'You must leave. There are more men in the world.'

'Things may get better,' says Helen. She is wearing what seems like many chiffon scarves. When she moves, she drifts in a waft of fabrics. They flutter round her strong, bony, tough-skinned face. She has become very thin.

'You are fixated on that man,' says Scarlet, 'and what is he? Just another man.'

'He has become my life,' says Helen. 'I have invested everything of me in him. I have nothing left but him.'

'Well,' says Scarlet briskly, 'I am not in love with him, and see him quite clearly. He is self-indulgent, conceited, sadistic, and as neurotic as all get out. None of it's *real*.'

'Y dying was real,' says Helen. 'I saw the certificate. In fact, do you know, I registered the death. No one else could bring themselves to do a sordid thing like that. I always have to do the dirty work, the same as I have to deal with Y's ghost. While he's off having a good time somewhere else.'

'You've got to get out of here,' says Scarlet.

'I can't leave him,' Helen repeats. 'He is my existence. Anyway, I can't until he asks me to go. He may need me. I inspire him, I always have. His work is more important than my feelings.'

X comes home and ignores Scarlet, except to nod curtly to

her as he passes through the living-room to his bedroom. He shuts the door firmly.

'He is not inspired,' says Scarlet, 'he is mad. I've been mad in my time, so I can tell. You've been a bit odd, but never mad. You owe him nothing. For Alice's sake, get out. You are a mother now, not a woman. What kind of a father is he to her?'

There was a time when Scarlet never used to interfere in other people's lives. As she gets older she realizes more and more that she knows best.

'Where would I go?' asks Helen. 'How would I live? I have never been without a man. I have always been someone's mistress. It will not suit me to be an unmarried mother.'

'I was one of those too,' says Scarlet, 'and every year it gets easier.'

'You don't understand,' says Helen, helplessly. 'I have never been responsible for anyone except myself. I can't start now. I can't do anything new. Only the same as I did yesterday.'

Scarlet is shocked by the change in Helen.

'You're like someone in prison,' she says. 'You'll die if you stay.'

'All my family died in prison,' is all Helen will say. 'Mother, father, aunts, uncles. My sister. Why should I be different? I don't mind dying, or prison. Better late than never. Off to the great kibbutz in the sky.'

Scarlet wants to slap her.

'I was joking,' says Helen feebly.

'Give me Alice,' says Scarlet. 'Go on being as wicked as you like, but let me save Alice.'

'There is no saving her,' says Helen smartly. 'She is doomed, she is female … What's more,' Helen adds dismally, 'she is mine.'

And she sinks again into lethargy, sitting slumped in her chair. She raises her hand and points.

'Here she is,' says Helen. 'Here comes Y.'

And Scarlet goes quite cold, because it is true that a pale stooping figure is coming up the drive. It is only the girl who delivers the milk, as Helen must surely know, for the milk is delivered at the same time every evening.

Scarlet takes it upon herself to knock upon X's door, go in, and tell him that Helen needs a doctor as she is having a nervous breakdown.

'A doctor?' enquires X, apparently bemused. Then he laughs and says, 'We don't need doctors. We need priests. We will exorcise her.'

And as if on cue he leaves the bed on which he lies and broods, and strides off to the local library, where he is a celebrity, in search of a book on exorcism.

'Look here,' says Scarlet to Helen, 'he is going too far. Are you just going to sit here and be exorcised?'

'Not in such a cut-price fashion,' says Helen, with what seems like returning spirit. 'Not by him. Am I not even worth a priest? Who does he think he is?'

'Come to London with me,' says Scarlet.

'No one will talk to me in London,' says Helen. 'They blame me.'

'It may surprise you,' says Scarlet, 'but there are at least fifty million people in the country who have not heard of X, Y or you.'

'I am so old,' says Helen. 'Old as death. No one will want me.'

231

Scarlet takes Helen's bony hands in hers.

'Y once stroked my hair and brought me back to life,' says Helen. 'I do not think that you can do the same for me.'

All the same she allows her hand to remain in Scarlet's, and gazes at it fixedly. And Scarlet, conscious of her own years in the darkness, tries to transmit, by simple touch, some of her own harshly-acquired strength. Scarlet is generous. She wishes to share. She is prepared to give at least a portion of her own happiness away. And it is, indeed, as if the dark tide begins to recede from Helen's brain as she holds Scarlet's hand. Her mouth, which has been so tautly held, relaxes into what is almost a smile.

('I made death leave her,' says Scarlet to Jocelyn later, 'just for a little.' And Jocelyn nods politely, rather embarrassed, and thinks, but does not say, what many other people also think, that if only Scarlet had left Helen alone, matters might have been a good deal better.)

'All right,' says Helen, unexpectedly. 'I shall come to London. Quick, quick. We must be gone before he comes back. He will kill us.'

And she runs up the narrow staircase to her room, and starts gathering her things together, quickly, quickly. Scarlet helps. How white the linen, how fragile the underwear; how Helen's fingers caress and care for them, automatically, even in this extremity of fright. For now Helen has decided to go, her fear of X is sudden and extreme. For their very lives, it seems, they must be gone before he returns.

Scarlet wonders for a disconcerting moment whether Helen intends to leave the baby, but Scarlet has misjudged her friend. Helen stops to scoop up Alice as she leaves; wraps her in a snowy-white, beautifully washed shawl. Now they half-walk, half-run, over ploughed fields towards the station. Their shoes are clogged with mud.

Scarlet does not dare look back, for fear of seeing X looming on the skyline; she has invested him, in the space of just ten minutes, with supernatural powers. Threading through her fear is a vein of excitement. She is running away again. She has always run away, and always found it exhilarating. There has always been, with Wanda, a new school, a new father, a new flat to run to; later a new man, a new baby, a new life. Every new event ensures a host of old ones thrown out, run away from, left undone. She remembers what it felt like to be a naughty little girl; excited by disaster and her own wilfulness.

And here she is, a grown woman, stumbling through muddy fields, still at it.

'Nothing changes much in life,' Scarlet observes, panting.

'Don't say that,' says Helen. 'It is too depressing a thought.' The station is in sight. Sanity returns. They walk demurely now. Helen nods graciously to the villagers, who stare back, either in non-comprehension, or in unabashed hostility.

'I very much hope that change is possible,' says Helen. 'I have spent my life so far amongst enemies. As a child I was hated and feared as an enemy alien. Later I grew beautiful and was disliked for that. Then I loved too fixedly – and people don't like such constancy, it frightens them. It indicates there is a purpose and a doom, a plan beneath the chaos. It is too strong a concept for ordinary people, who can only love for a minute at a time.'

'Like me,' says Scarlet.

'There are excuses for you,' says Helen, charitably. 'You have difficulty surviving.'

On the train she chatters about the fate of women, plans a tomb to the Unknown Whore, and says she will set herself up as a painter of portraits.

She stays for a while with Scarlet and Alec in their comfortable house, and is much attached to Byzantia.

'She is a lovely girl,' says Helen. 'You see what good things can come out of so much trouble? Do you remember when we all promised to pay you ten shillings a week? We never did. There was no time. Life caught up with us too fast.'

And she rocks her own baby and changes its clothes unceasingly, and curls its wispy hair with her finger, and waits for X to come and take her home. He does not come.

One day she says to Scarlet, 'I saw Y in the street the other day; I have to leave here. X won't come, so she has come instead. I know I am talking nonsense, but I also know I have to leave.'

Scarlet thinks that Helen is being kind and making excuses; that the desire to go is on Scarlet's account. For Helen has been eyeing Alec with automatic lust. It is not that she really likes or desires him; just that she is unused to being without a man. Scarlet is confident enough that Alec will not return Helen's interest, for Alec is made nervous by intensities of feeling. All the same, Scarlet catches herself opening doors as if fearful what she might find, and she has a pale, watchful, stooping feel, as if Y's mantle was falling across her shoulders. So she does not resist.

'Yes,' she says to Helen. 'In that case you had better go.'

Alec finds Helen a flat in Wembley Park. It will not be ready for a month, so in the meantime Helen stays with Audrey in her love-nest.

Audrey's love-nest is a pretty Georgian house in St John's Wood, which Audrey has deigned to allow her magazine Editor to buy, decorate and furnish for her. She is very unkind to him. She has, she maintains, had her fill of men, domesticity, sex and children. The more elusive Audrey is, the more admiring of her he becomes. She insists on having other lovers – and condescends to allow the Editor to visit her for the night, perhaps once a week – or once a fortnight if he has displeased her.

'You are such a bad lover,' she says, 'it is really an ordeal for me. Paul was very, very good in bed. It was just he was so impossible out of it. You're fine out of bed, but not really much good in it. So don't get above yourself. Because you choose to pay out money on my behalf doesn't mean you own me. I can look after myself. I once ran a chicken-farm single-handed. I am afraid of nothing. Not poverty, not loneliness, not your wife.'

He gazes at her in admiration, and buys her another dress, another holiday, organizes a still better job for her to play with.

It is not true to say that Audrey is afraid of nothing. She is afraid of Paul. Paul assails her and the Editor through the post and in person. He paints obscenities on her walls and his car: he throws stones with rude limericks engraved upon them through the windows: he makes phone calls to her employers and the Editor's Board of Directors. He threatens murder, and mutilation. He prophesies madness and suicide. He is not angry (he says) because she has deserted him; in fact, he maintains, he has done really well since she left, and even the hens, relieved of her baleful presence, have been laying splendidly – but at the outrage to principle, the despoiling of his vision of womanhood, inherent in her abandonment of the children.

Audrey is both flattered and frightened by these attentions.

'I never knew he loved me so much,' she says. And to the Editor – 'You could never love anyone as deeply as that.'

The Editor protests when Helen comes to stay, disturbing the grossly flimsy structure of his idyll.

'It is none of your business,' says Audrey. 'I have who I want here, and what's more Helen and me will share a room. I like talking in bed, and you're always too tired or too drunk or too randy for proper conversation. You'll just have to stay out.'

Forced into his wife's company, evening after evening he finds it the more boring.

'I wish he would go back to her,' says Audrey to Helen. 'I don't want him. I just want to be myself, like you. I don't want to be married, or do housework. I just want to have a good time, and earn money, and have lovers until I'm too old. Then I'll take to drink like Scarlet's mother.'

The Editor calls one evening when Audrey is out to dinner with a television producer. He sits and talks to Helen. Audrey, returning, finds them sitting peacefully and at a distance discussing Russian icons, and has a fit of hysterics. She

236

screams at her Editor, belabouring him with her fists, accusing him of infidelity, and drives him physically from the house. Afterwards she sobs and weeps for hours.

'I don't know what's the matter with me,' she says to Helen. 'Do you think I'm going mad? I tried all these years to be something I wasn't; now I'm trying to be the opposite, and it's just as upsetting.'

'You don't have to be anything,' says Helen, piously, 'except yourself.'

'I haven't got a self to be,' complains Audrey. 'I change every five minutes. It was much easier when we were all younger. Ever since I've had the children, I've been confused. I always thought I was the one who was supposed to be the child. And it was all my own doing, that's what I can't get over. All the same, the children were the only real thing that ever happened to me. But of course Paul won't let me have them. It's not that he loves them, he just wants to punish me.'

Presently, when Helen has gone, and she has forgiven the Editor, and he has been re-instated as a once-weekly visitor, she asks him if she could not have a manservant.

'I would like to have your children,' she says. 'To do that I have to have space, money and time. These are the three things children need most. I can give them space and money; but time? I can't give up my work, it wouldn't be fair, and all the rest of my life and energy is spent in either meeting your sexual demands or cleaning this house of yours.'

'But *you* live here, not me –'

'– at your insistence. I would be just as happy living on a park bench, if not happier. However, you've landed me with

237

this bourgeois monstrosity. I think the least you can do is not burden me with the task of cleaning it. I need a daily man – not a woman, they lie and steal and nag – to do it for me.'

The Editor hires a manservant-cum-chauffeur – an out-of-work actor with a beard, who flirts with Audrey, and lives with his wife and children in the basement flat.

Soon she is pregnant. She spends days in Harrods, in the baby-clothes departments. She sends the bills to the Editor's home, where his wife comes across them.

'You should have been more careful,' Audrey accuses him. 'You probably meant her to find them, in your neurotic way. You know what it means, don't you? I can't possibly have the baby. I shall have to have an abortion.'

He pleads with her, but it is no use. He makes the arrangements, gives her the cash, and the manservant, who likes to be called the chauffeur, takes her off to the clinic.

The Editor has a painful vision of his future vanishing down the plughole with swirling pink finality; but it only makes him more conscious of the present and he insists on visiting Audrey twice a week. Sometimes she won't let him into her bed – 'Since you made me have the operation, I have become sexually anaesthetized. It is not just a matter of indifference to me now – more like revulsion –' but she does let him stay in the house. He finds that when he insists, she complies. This is, for him, a great and useful discovery. Although if he presses too hard, he discovers, her personality disintegrates altogether, like a blob of mercury flying into bits, and when gathered together again, has incorporated flecks of dust and foreign matter which take yet more getting used to.

Once, when she complains about the cost of the food he eats when he stays overnight, and refuses to give him an egg for breakfast, he points out that as he pays the food bills, the mortgage, the electricity, laundry and servant bills, he is entitled to as many eggs as he pleases. What's more, he suggests, if she wants him to go on doing these things, she had better cook his breakfast graciously. Audrey gets as far as cracking a large brown egg into the pan before dissolving into tears, accusing him of blackmail, and becoming too hysterical to continue the cooking process. Still, she did crack the egg, and he considers this an advance.

At his wife's home he sits down to a properly laid, three-course, punctual breakfast every morning, the eggs peppered and served with vinegared butter; and every morning boredom makes his very mouth muscles limp, so that coffee trickles down his chin, and his wife can watch with fastidious delight and disgust, pleased to be able to tell herself that if he finally goes for good, she has lost very little.

And here he is – he knows it – trying to make Audrey behave like a proper woman; like his wife.

Audrey is upset by his insistence on a cooked breakfast.

'All my life,' she complains to Jocelyn, 'people have been taking advantage of me. This terrible man! He treats me as if I was a menial, but I have a brain like a man's – everyone tells me so at work. What a terrible fate it is, to pass from life with Paul to life with this bully.'

'It didn't just happen,' says Jocelyn. 'You did it. You chose it.' It is Jocelyn's refrain nowadays, spoken faintly from depths of unfathomable boredom. She likes to listen to the tales told

239

her by her friends: it is as if they stretch their hands down towards her, trying to raise her to the light again. Her little boy is sleepless and bad-tempered. She tries to love him but she can't. He has Philip's face, and watches her with Philip's eyes – or is it with the eyes of that other man, long ago?

Jocelyn wrote to Miss Bonny when Edward was born. She had a letter by return. Miss Bonny now breeds dogs in the Lake District. Miss Bonny told her – why? as a cautionary tale? – about a wilful spaniel bitch who managed to mate with a collie, and then fortunately aborted. Later, properly mated with a spaniel, one of the pups was unmistakably collie. 'Female fidelity,' writes Miss Bonny, 'is the cornerstone on which the family, the heredity principle, and the whole of capitalism rests.' Virginity, thinks Jocelyn has gone to Miss Bonny's head, and she throws the letter away. But she's upset.

Jocelyn leaves the electric blanket on in Philip's bed during one of his weekend absences, and it bursts into flames. The fire brigade has to be called. One of the attendant policemen, kindly staying behind to help clear up, propositions her. Jocelyn, these days, is beautiful enough in her chilly fashion. Made distraught and dirty by flames, smoke, and fear, she must appear, to the policeman, a likely lay. Jocelyn declines his offer with a haughty disdain which does not disconcert him at all.

For months afterwards, lying sleepless, waiting for Edward to stop crying and sleep, or wake and start crying, the policeman enters her fantasies, fully-clothed, brandishing his truncheon like a phallus, bullying, humiliating. The more extreme her sexual fantasies, the more in her head she moans and squirms in masochistic frenzy, while lying still and motionless in her bed – the more remote and frozen does she become by day.

Jocelyn handles Edward as if he was a rather strange, noisy doll. She does what is necessary for his survival, and little more. She can hardly bear to be touched by Philip.

Philip drinks later and later at the Watson and Belcher club. Drinks are free. The rumour goes the firm are trying to save paying out on their pension scheme by killing off the staff with drink at an early age. Philip begins to look quite old, and has a puzzled air.

Jocelyn is glad that Philip is so seldom at home. She likes to sit by herself in the evenings; or with her women friends. Her snobbish fit has passed. She goes round the corner to C. & A. for her clothes. She has given up Harrods. She makes no move to have the bedroom re-decorated, liking to lie in the smoky ruins and dream of rape and destruction.

Eventually Philip complains. So Jocelyn hires a fashionable firm of decorators to re-do the whole house, and not just the bedroom, in pop-art style. The bill, in the end, is £2,500, which Philip does not have, and nor does she. Philip is angry. He hates the look of the house. He had thought, when he first saw it, that such crudity would at least be cheap. Jocelyn has never seen him angry, and it pleases her, and she spends a whole night actually sleeping in his bed, and wakes feeling like a whore. The feeling frightens her, and she retreats again into chilly respectability.

In the meantime, the bill remains a reality. It overshadows their lives. Philip, in punishing mood, takes to washing his own shirts to save the laundry bills.

When Jocelyn says she is perfectly prepared to wash his shirts herself, if that is what he wants, he says, 'No. You are too much of a lady for that.'

Jocelyn shrugs. She doesn't care what he thinks, or what he does.

Sylvia lives in a bed-sitting room, with her little daughter, and is supported by the National Assistance Board. She goes to the Ear, Nose and Throat Hospital once a week for treatment to her ears, and once a week to Moorfields Hospital where they are investigating her sight. Her ability to see fluctuates, experts consider, in an unreasonable, even bizarre fashion. 'When I'm cheerful,' she assures them, 'I can see perfectly well. When I'm miserable I'm blind as a bat. I will never be able to kill myself; I won't be able to see to do it. Isn't that something? You might almost say I did it on purpose.'

They refer her to a psychiatric clinic, and continue their investigations.

Sylvia's vision improves. The sense that things are as bad as they can be reassures her. The National Assistance money comes regularly – so do the inspectors to ensure that she doesn't have a gentleman caller. If she does, the money will be stopped. Thus protected, Sylvia begins to bloom. A woman neighbour looks after little Claire when Sylvia is visiting her clinics or the Welfare Offices.

Sylvia has a successful operation upon her right ear. Now she can hear when Claire cries, which is seldom, for Claire gave up crying as a bad job some time ago. Not that Claire bears a grudge against her mother, not at all. She loves her, puts her tiny arms around Sylvia's legs and worships her.

'They shouldn't have made me have that abortion all those years ago,' says Sylvia to her psychiatrist. 'All I wanted was something to love. Everything went wrong because of that.'

'It is not enough to give love,' says the psychiatrist, 'one must be able to receive it as well.'

It is surprising the things Sylvia hears, these days, even with one good ear.

Moorfields give up and provide her with contact lenses. Her eyes look large, misty and beautiful. She feels, as she clasps Claire to her, this gift of God, like a virgin again, untouched and full of hope.

'The State,' she says to Jocelyn, 'must have spent at least £5,000 so far rehabilitating me. Why? What have I ever done to deserve it, besides merely exist? The State has done far more for me than my father ever did. I feel grateful, and that is something I have never felt in all my life before. Never gratitude, only resentment.'

('She has a new life now,' says Jocelyn to Philip. 'The State is her father and mother.' But Philip does not want to discuss Sylvia. He likes talking about advertising matters, which Jocelyn feels too superior to discuss.)

Presently Sylvia takes a job in the Civil Service. She works patiently and methodically in the Department of Child Welfare. She moves into a Council flat. Claire goes to a State nursery by day, and seems happy. Sylvia's ears and eyes are functioning; the psychiatrist says she need come to see him no longer. Sylvia sends a Christmas card home at Christmas, and receives one in return, and a doll for Claire. Her child is at last acknowledged.

'It is perfectly possible to live happily without a man,' says Sylvia to Jocelyn in gratified astonishment, but in the New Year she meets a quiet, gentle, kind, unmarried Probation Officer, and within three months is married to him.

They are married at St Pancras Registry Office. Sylvia and her Peter hold hands. Scarlet is there with Alec; and Jocelyn (Philip is at a conference); and Wanda, stumbling slightly for she has been celebrating, with Susan; and Audrey in a cartwheel hat and very short skirt; and Helen, at her most dramatic and beautiful in white velvet – Sylvia wears dove grey – escorted by a handsome, dark young man who clearly loves her. Sylvia's parents send a telegram of good wishes.

Scarlet throws them a party in her Hampstead house. Alec has inherited a good deal of money. Scarlet has her sociology degree. She is hoping for a lectureship at the London School of Economics. Byzantia plays Beatles records very loudly in the basement, combs loose her flowing black hair, and tells her mother she means to change her name to Joan. She asks her uncle Simeon down into the basement, and there, hour after hour, attempts to seduce the bewildered lad. 'Although his hair is long his heart is square,' she complains to her mother. (Byzantia has a poetical sense, and writes long narrative poems in her Physics lessons at school.) 'He keeps claiming incest, but that's just an excuse. An uncle is as distant as a cousin, and cousins are allowed. Well, anyone's allowed, now there's the pill. Either he won't, or he can't. The whole incest taboo thing is on genetic grounds, after all, and since no one has to get pregnant these days, as a taboo it's *très* outmoded. Personally I

244

think incest is a very exciting thought. I don't fancy Alec, I don't know why. You should never have deprived me of my natural father, Mother.'

Jocelyn, Wanda, Audrey and Susan think Byzantia should be put on the pill, but Scarlet, Alec and Sylvia agree that she should not.

'I am not filling up any daughter of mine with artificial oestrogen,' says Scarlet. 'I did not bring her into the world to drug her, neuter her, fatten her, and render her passive. Her own mother to turn her into a sexual object? And for what? What profound pleasure? A safe fuck with her own uncle?'

'Half-uncle,' says Wanda. 'And what alternative do you suggest? If you think I'm going to look after a great-grand-child-cum-step-grandchild, you've got another think coming.'

'Abstinence,' snarls Scarlet, repairing to the many and varied pleasures of her own marital bed. 'That filthy word! That's what I suggest.'

Fortunately Byzantia loses interest in Simeon the moment he actually manages to achieve an erection, and falls in love with the dancer Nureyev, who at least is unattainable. She talks at length, as she follows her mother round the house, about her feelings, her actions and her reactions. She has a melodious voice, but it seldom stops: nothing is hidden, nothing is feared. Every subject, every relationship, every event, must be aired, discussed, categorized, rendered harmless, and then not even shelved for future reference, but simply forgotten.

'Did I bring her up like this?' Scarlet asks her mother, 'or is it the world in which she lives?'

'I see nothing wrong with her,' says Wanda. 'She lives in the present, that's all. She means to be free and happy now, not some time in the future. You and I lived by saying "one day I am going to". Byzantia says "Now! Let's go!" It's much healthier.'

Helen is entranced by Byzantia, and Byzantia likes Helen, and will go over to Helen's Wembley Park flat on Saturdays to visit; they will take Alice for walks in the park, and feed her ice-creams, or bring her over to tea with Scarlet, or with Jocelyn. But mostly Byzantia likes the ritual of having tea with Helen – the white embroidered tablecloth, the flowered porcelain cups and saucers, tiny cucumber sandwiches, the iced cake, the afghans – little chocolate biscuits with a half-walnut on top of each – and Alice finely dressed and curled. Alice is a rather nervous, chattering little girl, who breaks into dance when she thinks no one is looking, bowing and swaying like a very young sapling swept by a gale.

Helen has tried. She has done what she can do to build a new life. She goes to parties, makes friends; allows herself to be taken out, wooed, even bedded. But there is a dusty film over all experience. She sees with dead eyes, hears with dead ears. She moves herself through the world like a puppet. She pulls strings to make herself dance, go to fortune-tellers, play with her child.

Presently X seeks her out. He says, 'Let us be friends,' and stays the night from time to time. Helen's nightie is yellow scattered with white stars. She pretends she is a girl again. She pulls the strings that make her love. She loves. If anyone asks her, she says she loves.

He says, 'Perhaps one day we will get married.'

246

'When?' she asks.

'When we have grown new skins,' he says, 'renewed ourselves like the snakes we are. It takes seven years, I believe.'

They go on holiday to the Isle of Skye. Helen climbs a mountain, stands on the edge of a precipice and teeters.

'Not here,' she says, presently.

'Not here,' he says. He hasn't moved. 'Besides, look at the sky. It is beautiful.'

Helen looks at the dusty sky.

'Besides,' he says, 'who would look after Alice? I have no gift for children. I do not like them.'

'Yes,' she says. 'Who would look after little dusty Alice?' and he thinks he has won. His other children live with a sister of Y's, whose husband is an ex-R.A.F. man. They run a paper shop in Essex.

After the holiday he goes back to the village and his Barbara, who never has visions of self-destruction, or urges to suicide. She is shocked at the very thought. When she is depressed she makes jam or a batch of cakes. 'I have my own ways of being creative,' she says, and he finds such presumption amusing and even touching.

'One day,' he says to Helen – he visits her once a month or so, when he has business in London, 'we will live together. We might even marry, with the full rites of the Church.'

'When?' she asks.

'One day,' he says. He no longer talks about Y. Helen thinks it might be true. One day he will marry her. Days slip into days. Now when she looks in a mirror, she sees herself as dusty, too, not just the world around her. She has been in mourning for too long. She complains to Scarlet.

'It's no good,' says Scarlet. 'You must break with him, never see him again. The world is full of men. You have so much to offer. You are still young; you are handsome, Alice is an asset, not a liability.'

'No,' says Helen. 'I am thirty-six. I am going off.'

'Your life is only half-way through.'

'I am not interested in the second half.'

'You need to meet a proper man.'

'There is only one man for me, and that is X. I cannot get interested in the others. God knows I try. I went out to dinner with a young man; and there was a woman at the next table who looked familiar. I realized it was Y. It wasn't really, of course. How many tall pale women there are in the world; I'd never realized. After that I had nothing to say to him, and he lost interest. When there is something so enormous to be said, you see, which can't be said, then silence is the only possibility.'

'Stay to dinner tonight,' says Scarlet. 'Meet some more people.'

'I must go back to Alice,' says Helen. 'I like to be there at her bedtime.' She is growing closer to Alice. When they go walking, they hold hands. Helen is more and more reluctant to be separated from her.

'I wish Alice had been born a boy,' she says. 'What kind of life is it for a girl? I am thirty-six. Being young lasts so short a time. Do you really see me as an old lady?'

'So am I thirty-six.' says Scarlet, 'or nearly. But I don't feel it as you do. Life goes on. It gets better, even.'

'You were – forgive me – very plain when you were a girl.

Life has got better for you as you went on. Mine has been a falling away. You are accustomed to living unadmired, but loved. I have only ever had admiration, and envy. Now even that will be taken away from me. I am to be left with nothing. I have achieved nothing in my life. I should never have survived. I should have died with the others.'

'I hope,' says Scarlet, 'You won't do anything silly.'

'Kill myself? Why not?'

'Because of Alice.'

'Ah yes,' says Helen. 'That's what everyone says. Does one want life for one's children? Can one?'

'Of course,' says Scarlet, shocked.

'The pain so outweighs the pleasure,' says Helen.

'Not for everyone,' says Scarlet. 'You feel like that now. You probably won't tomorrow. Anyway you have no business to feel it for Alice.'

But Helen does not look convinced.

'If only he would marry me ...' she says.

'It would make no difference,' says Scarlet. 'Your happiness must come from yourself. It will never come from others.'

Helen smiles politely: it is a beautiful smile, as always, although disbelieving. These days Scarlet almost loves her.

X has an exhibition of paintings in a London gallery. It opens on a Saturday. He spends the Friday night with Helen; he asks her, not Barbara, to be with him at the opening. She meets him at the gallery.

No one speaks to her. All these years after Y's death, she is still shunned, abhorred and witch-hunted. She doesn't mind much. Their hatred too has a dusty flavour. X is surrounded by admirers, swooped on by ageing vulture ladies with large sad eyes. He ignores Helen: he behaves as if she was a stranger, as if he had brought her with him to prove how much of a stranger she is. She is an episode in his past, no more. His life goes on from strength to strength. Helen goes home alone. X does not visit her the next day.

Instead Y walks beside her, holding her hand, explaining how Helen can stop crying. Byzantia is supposed to be coming to tea. Helen half hopes she will arrive, half hopes she won't, so that Y will fade again into the wallpaper. Byzantia does not arrive.

Helen puts Alice to bed. Alice, hot and restless, grizzles and cries, and disturbs her conversation with Y. Y is being very kind.

'It should have been you and me,' Y says. 'Not you and X. You would have been my daughter. Well, it can still be like that. The world is an imperfect place. The only perfection is death, silence, and completeness. One fights it too much, too hard, and too long. Will you join me?'

In the next room Alice cries.

'What about Alice?' asks Helen.

'Alice? Alice should never have been. Listen, how unhappy she sounds. She has no lawful place in the world.'

Helen goes into Alice's room, and gives her half a sleeping pill. Alice drifts happily into sleep.

'Millions of people are born every day,' says Helen. 'Other millions die. What does it mean?'

Y smiles as if she knew.

'What do I mean when I say "I"?' asks Helen. 'I wondered that when I was six. I still don't know. All I know is that I is the bit that suffers, and without the I there would be peace.'

Y says nothing. Really, there is no more need.

'I cannot bear to wake up another morning, knowing that the day will hold no pleasure, only pain,' says Helen, 'and that the next day when I wake it will be just the same, except I will be a little older, a little further down the path I am now obliged to travel. I can look back over my shoulder, but that is all. I cannot turn, and go back the way I came, which was through green grass and flowers, bright days, and black nights with brilliant stars. I want to finish now, sit down and fall asleep, while these good things can still at least be seen when I look back. Soon I will have travelled so far they will have faded altogether.'

Y nods. Helen thinks her friend is getting impatient.

'Wait,' she says. 'I will be with you soon.'

She goes into Alice's room, shuts the windows and turns on the gas; she does not ask Y in, but sits there patiently by herself, not unhappily. She feels she has been half-dead for so long that the difference in state will not be very great.

14

Down Among The Women

Down among the women.

> *'A million housewives every day –*
>   *Pick up the goods, forget to pay –'*

And then presently stand in the dock, respectable, brazen, tearful, villainous or confused as the case may be. It was a mistake, it was my nerves, it's the pills the doctor gives me, I'd had a row with my husband. I wanted it. Well, if not that, I wanted something, I don't know what. All I know is I haven't got it.

You can clean and tidy a Council flat in half an hour. You can shop down the Supermarket in another half hour. What kind of achievement is that? Where are the wolves to be kept from the door? Where are the lice to be picked from the clothes? What pleasure is there in the sliced plastic bread, compared to the loaf you've made from the flour you had to sleep with the miller to get?

So says Jocelyn. Jocelyn now lives in a Council flat with a printer. He is a card-carrying communist, which is an old-fashioned thing to be, but then he is a romantic man; not a

Trotskyite, a Marxist, not even a Maoist, but a Stalinist. He knows it is folly; so does she: there is splendour in such misplaced loyalty. They are happy. She is entranced by the crudeness of his language, the violence of his passions. She watches him scrub his dirty nails as he cleans up after work. He gazes in admiration as she reads, and listens when she talks. They spend a long time in bed together. He despises advertising, and laughs at Philip. She met him in a café, and within six weeks had joined him in his flat. She took Edward with her, who was not pleased by the move.

Almost, she left the child with Philip; but then her courage failed her. She hopes Edward will grow to look more like her Ben and less like Philip, but he shows little sign of doing so. She has a daughter now, Ben's child, with Ben's dark eyes and strong features. She loves her daughter, and calls her Sylvia.

She once gave to Scarlet the following account of her parting with Philip:

'It was the day Helen died. I'd had a phone call from the police. They'd found my number in her address book. I shouted and swore at them over the telephone; I think they were shocked. Or perhaps they're used to it, I don't know. Then I abused Helen to them, a good deal. I was angry about Alice. I would have looked after her; well, any of us would. Afterwards, I calmed down, and cried for Helen, and then I wanted to talk about it all, very badly, but the only person I wanted to talk about it to was Helen herself. We would have had such a rich female conversation, and dissected everyone's emotions, and tried to decide what it all meant. And now she had deprived us both of this pleasure. Perhaps they were right,

253

and she was always just a mean, wicked woman? But no, she was my Helen, and as I grew older I grew fonder and fonder of her; as you did, Scarlet. And now, quite suddenly, she is just someone who lived and died in the past. As for Alice, well, I can hardly bear to think about that. Sometimes I think how wicked, how terrible, how monstrous of Helen. She was of course insane. She must have been insane if there is to be any forgiveness. But at other times I think no, that wasn't madness, that was sanity. She did the right thing. For what kind of life would Alice have had? And if, as I think happened, death became to Helen not the absence of life, but a real and positive state, she would want to take Alice with her. She became a better and better mother as time went on.

'Philip came home that evening troubled and anxious, and waiting to be asked why. But I wouldn't ask, at first. I was angry with him because when I rang him up at the office to tell him the news of Helen's death, all he would say was "Oh yes? Oh dear. Well, I'm rather busy, I can't talk now." He was beginning to believe, you see, that advertising campaigns were the only real things in the world. Or perhaps he was just too angry, with me, and himself, to take anything real in. We had been having money troubles. He was making five thousand a year but I was making us live at the rate of at least eight.'

'You sound quite pleased about it,' says Scarlet.

'I was. While I was living with Philip I was a very disagreeable person. Now I live with Ben I am quite nice and reasonable. It was sex, of course, the whole thing, although I would have been horrified by the suggestion at the time. If I couldn't get what I needed in bed – while denying the need for it, of course – I'd bloody get what I could out of him in other ways. Poor Philip.

'Anyway, I finally gave in that evening and asked Philip what the matter was. He had an important New York client in town, it transpired. He had arranged for a call-girl to spend the night with the client, but the girl had developed 'flu and called off. All his other normal sources were useless, he claimed; not only was there a 'flu epidemic, but London was bursting with conferences and randy big businessmen, and the city's high-class sexual resources were strained to their uttermost. You can't give a big-businessman just anybody, you know. The girls have to be well-spoken, mannerly, and of course, free from disease – or the whole thing becomes sordid.

' "Why Philip," I said. "I had no idea you were a pimp."

'Now of course I knew he was. Executives are expected to see that clients have a good time, and having a good time includes girls. I did not myself believe, at the time, that Philip shared in these good times. I thought not only that I, in some mysterious way, was responsible for his impotence, but that the harm I did him would pursue him wherever he went.

'When I made my joke about the pimping, Philip became quite violent. Perhaps he was more upset by Helen's death than I thought. At any rate that evening we both behaved out of character. Or perhaps, indeed, for once, in character.

' "You don't care if I go bankrupt, do you?" he said. "People lose accounts for this kind of thing. And if I lose accounts I lose my job, and you lose everything. Because all you care about is bloody money. You don't care about people."

' "Yes, I do," I said. "You're talking about yourself. I just wish I was married to a successful pimp, not a failed pimp."

'(You must remember how mild, polite and decent we normally were to each other, to appreciate the full trauma of this conversation.)

' "You are a frigid, anti-sex, English bitch," he said. "And a liar. You make my life a misery. You are against pleasure in every form."

' "I have not much chance to be anything else," I said, "being married to you."

' "Bloody nonsense," he said. "You'd be the same, with anyone."

' "You are wrong," I said. "I know for a fact how wrong you are."

' "Whore," he said. "Slut."

' "All right," I said, "if that's what you want to believe, that's what I am. You are quite right; I only care about money. I would sell myself for money. Come to that, I would be perfectly happy to give myself away."

' "Prove it," he said. "You go along. You spend the night with him."

'That silenced me. I left the room.

'One of things which made me continue to see sex as a kind of life force, and not – as I am sometimes tempted to believe in these days of pornographic advertisements and see-through dresses – a feeble human activity which needs all the artificial fostering it can get, is the way the nearness of death compels one to make love. And I say make love, that old-fashioned word, not fuck, on purpose. But who had I to

256

make love to? If it can't be the former, the latter will do. Or so I thought in my rage.

'I drank a quarter bottle of Scotch in the kitchen, and went back to Philip.

' "Very well," I said, speaking the jovial language he best understood, "for the sake of Britain and the export drive. Lead me to him."

'I did not believe that Philip, my husband, with whom I had shared, albeit without satisfaction, so many beds, breakfasts, holidays, mortgages, bills, cars and wallpapers, would actually undertake anything so extreme or definite. But he just smiled, this pale, limp, weary ad-man, and with a confidence I had never known in him before, led me upstairs to the bedroom. I think it was that he had, on that instant, ceased to see me as a wife and now saw me as a whore, and he was quite at ease with whores.

'He went through my drawers as if he knew them well, and I wondered if examining them had perhaps been one of his secret pleasures. He selected black underwear for me, and dressed me in it, and made me look at myself in the mirror, turning my head so that I was obliged to see.

' "You would pass for twenty-five," he said. He would not let me wear a dress; he made me wear a raincoat over the underwear. As for me, I felt alternately foolish, excited, and embarrassed. I could not imagine now what our future together would be. I saw, and rightly, that our marriage was ended.

'We went by taxi to a large hotel. In the lift he said, "I was lying about the girl having 'flu. She's still waiting for the telephone call. I wanted you to do it. I've been thinking about it for weeks."

'I would not have gone back then for all the world. I remember you, Scarlet, telling me about the man you sold yourself to for a pair of stockings; it had entered into my fantasies. Is it because we are English that we are all so masochistic? Do the French, the Italians, the Americans, yearn for degradation? I wanted to know what it was like to make the fantasy real; to discover whether – in the same way that fiction is so much more satisfactory than real life, having a beginning, a middle, an end, and a point – the fantasy is not more fulfilling than the fact.

'He had to push me along the corridor, just the same. He knocked on the door of Room 541, and opened it. His client was lying on the bed; he was about forty-five, I suppose, with a city pallor, a flat face, square jaw, rimless glasses, close-cropped hair; I felt I had seen ten thousand men just like him before.

' "Hi," he said. He was very amiable. "Philip, glad to see you. What a lonely city this is. But all large cities are the same, aren't they? All I ever want to do is stay at home, and sit in the garden with the wife and kids, and grow beans. But no, life isn't like that."

' "This is Una," said Philip.

' "Hi, Una," said Mr Rigby, and after that ignored me. "Like a drink, Philip?"

'Philip, to my alarm, accepted. I had thought he would leave at once. Mr Rigby poured himself and Philip a drink and did not offer me one. I sat on a hard chair in the corner.

'You know what it's like in hospital, when you're ill, or having a baby, and you become de-personalized, and just a body, to be directed here and there, and ministered to, and hurt or healed as luck and the institution will have it. All sense of personal identity goes. That's what I felt like, sitting in my corner, waiting.

'They talked about marketing. After about a quarter of an hour, Mr Rigby directed a gracious word to me.

' "Take your raincoat off, Una," he said. "You look a bit hot. These hotels are always stuffy."

'Philip crossed and took off my raincoat. I sat down again, knees together.

'Mr Rigby smiled, and asked me to take off bra and pants.

' "Una a friend of yours?" he asked Philip, when I had done so, and had sat down again, as one does in the cubicle of out-patients, only without the towelling gown, of course.

' "Yes," said Philip. "On and off." I wished he would go. I did not like waiting. I was having trouble breathing. They continued to talk about market research and the tragedy of the research-orientated society, in which nothing new can happen, but only what is known repeated.

' "Mankind is on a pollution binge," said Mr Rigby. "He pollutes his outer world with chemicals, and his inner world with research."

' "I tell you what," said Mr Rigby, eventually. "I've got a feeling I'm getting 'flu, like everyone else. Supposing you stay and make the most of Una here. It would be a pity to waste her."

'I cannot be so disagreeable as I sometimes think, because my first concern was for Philip. I thought, he will acquit himself badly. He will be impotent, he will be despised, he will lose the account. We will be bankrupt. I need not have worried.

259

Under Mr Rigby's observing eye, according to Mr Rigby's specification, Philip behaved like a sexual athlete in a schoolboy's dream, taking me – and I say taking, because that is what it felt like – this way and that, using hands, mouth, penis in a complex pattern worked out beforehand, I imagine, by Mr Rigby's research-conscious brain, until indeed I was transposed, for the first time, into that other black, tumultuous parallel universe, where I had never been before. Mr Rigby's smiling and observing face loomed through it, however, and he seemed the familiar one, and Philip was the stranger.

'After they had finished and I was replaced upon my chair, and the waiter had brought coffee, which – allowed for this purpose at least to be something more than animal – I was asked to pour, and Philip and Mr Rigby were going through a folder of research statistics, it came to me that of course this was the normal pattern of events in an evening with Philip and Mr Rigby. But why had Philip wanted it to be me, when so often it had been other women? To reduce me to the level of the others, to vilify me, to demonstrate to me my proper function in the world? Did he really need so badly to humiliate me? Was his revenge so important? Or was it just to prove to me that given the right circumstances he could be as potent as the next man? Or perhaps, Scarlet, he just fancied me? Perhaps men are as simple as that?'

'Why, come to that,' says Scarlet, 'did you go along with him in the first place? What kind of revenge was that?'

'I don't know,' says Jocelyn. 'I just don't know. It was the end of our marriage. We limped along together, returned to our separate beds, for a month or so. I could not forgive him, yet I did not know what I had to forgive him for. It was my doing as much as his. Yet, because he was my husband, I had expected him to save me from myself. But why should he? I reminded myself of Edward in a rage, hitting another three-year-old on the head and shrieking "Be my friend!"

'Edward. That was the other thing. The accident I'd been working up to. All those accidents, like one's life, becoming less funny and more bitter as time goes on. I was bathing him, and forgot to put the cold water in, and lowered him into scalding water. There is, of course, no such thing as an accident. I did it on purpose to my child, because he looked like Philip.'

'He doesn't look in the least like Philip,' says Scarlet. 'Or not much, anyway.'

'I stayed with him in hospital. I would have died myself to save him the pain. Yet it wasn't love. It was the maternal instinct. There is no credit in that. It's just another kind of animal thing.'

'Is there credit in love?' asks Scarlet.

'Well, more,' says Jocelyn, 'if not much. Anyway, sitting beside his bed I envied Helen for the first and last time in my life. He was going to have those scars for ever, and I was going to have to live with him, and there was to be no more escape.'

'The scars hardly show,' says Scarlet. 'You don't notice them at all.'

'I do,' says Jocelyn. 'All other feelings are luxuries, you know. Love, hate, lust, despair, hope – once one is a mother one has no business feeling any of them. They are inappropriate to one's state. All the same, within a couple of weeks of Edward leaving hospital, I met and was in bed with Ben. I knew by then, thanks to Mr Rigby, that there are other universes to inhabit, and that I was really just like any other woman, and deserved as much and as little; and once I knew that, all kinds of reasonable, sensible things became possible.'

Down Among the Women

My name is Jocelyn. I sit in the park and consider the past, and what became of us all, and how little the present accords with our expectations of it. Hockey One, Hockey Two, Hockey Three and away! Oh, Miss Bonny, you and I, running for the bus and laughing, crackling over the winter ground. You and I, caught up for ever and ever in our moment of time, like flies trapped in amber.

Edward is over at the swings now, with little Sylvia, who is my favourite child. I can pick him out – he wears a red woollen cap which Audrey knitted for him in her domestic days – it was far too big then; it fits now, five years later. Perhaps Scarlet is right, and it is only to me that his scars seem so disfiguring? Perhaps he could stay at home, not go away to school, and I could abandon my last pretensions to gentility? I could hand Philip back the school fees and stop trying to get all I can out of him.

Perhaps the next time Edward comes homing in to me and stares at me in his absent way and smoothes my hair away from my face as he talks, I will not have to push him away, or tell him he's a big boy now. Perhaps I will just be able to sit, and accept.

There, I did it. I put my arm round him and smiled, and he smiled back. Every day he looks less and less like Philip – except of course when he's in a bad temper. And that isn't really so often.

One can learn, at least. One can go on learning until the day one is cut off.

I sit like a Roman matron, my cloak around my Edward and my Sylvia, and stare out into the dissolving universe. It's getting dark. Soon it will be time to go home, and I will cook dinner, like all the other women in the world – at least to date.

For let me report a conversation I overheard between Scarlet and her Byzantia. I do not see Byzantia cooking dinner.

Byzantia, kind Byzantia, throws a party for her mother's friends, for whom she has a weakness. She does not offer them marijuana, explaining to Scarlet that she considers them too unstable.

'They would have bad trips,' she says. 'All lows, no highs.'

'Perhaps so will you, at our age,' says her mother.

'I don't think so,' says Byzantia.

'We haven't done too badly,' pleads Scarlet. 'There's me with Alec, Jocelyn here with her Ben, Sylvia with her Peter, and I daresay Audrey will bring her Editor, if she thinks he'll have a bad enough time. And even your step-grandmother Susan will be able to bring your uncle Simeon.'

'You amaze me,' says Byzantia. 'Fancy seeing success in terms of men. How trivial, with the world in the state it's in.'

'Merely as a symbol of success,' pleads Scarlet, 'I don't mean to offer it as the cause.'

'A symptom more like,' says Byzantia, 'of a fearful disease from which you all suffered. One of you even died on the way. I think the mortality rate is too high.'

When asked to define the disease, Byzantia cannot. Definitions, she says, are in any case no part of her business. It is enough to tear the old order down.

Byzantia, like her grandmother Wanda, is a destroyer, not a builder. But where Wanda struggled against the tide and gave up, exhausted, Byzantia has it behind her, full and strong.

Down among the women.

We are the last of the women.